ALSO BY SHARI LAPENA

The Couple Next Door

A Stranger in the House

An Unwanted Guest

Someone We Know

The End of Her

Not a Happy Family

Everyone

Here

Is Lying

Everyone Here Is Lying

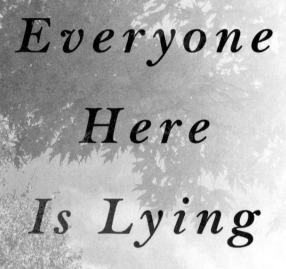

SHARI LAPENA

DOUBLEDAY CANADA

Doubleday Canada and colophon are registered trademarks
of Penguin Random House Canada Limited

Library and Archives Canada Cataloguing in Publication
Title: Everyone here is lying / Shari Lapena.
Names: Lapena, Shari, 1960- author.
Identifiers: Canadiana (print) 20220475075 | Canadiana (ebook) 20220475105 |
ISBN 9780385698900 (softcover) | ISBN 9780385698924 (EPUB)
Subjects: LCGFT: Novels.
Classification: LCC PS8623.A724 E94 2023 | DDC C813/.6—dc23—dc23

This book is a work of fiction. Names, characters, places and incidents are products
of the author's imagination or are used fictitiously. Any resemblance to actual events
or locales or persons, living or dead, is entirely coincidental.

Cover design: Ervin Serrano
Cover images: (top to bottom) (tree canopy, detail) Liam Grant/
Stocksy; (treehouse) Francisco Solipa/Getty Images; (rope ladder)
Muenchbach/Shutterstock; (field and trees) Tony Myshlyaev/Stocksy

Printed in the United States of America

Published in Canada by Doubleday Canada, a division
of Penguin Random House Canada Limited

www.penguinrandomhouse.ca

1st Printing

To Julia

Acknowledgments

It's so nice when a book is finally finished and I get to thank all the people—and they are legion—who believe in an idea, who help shape the book into its final form, outfit it in dazzling covers, and get it to market so that it's noticed and sitting proudly on shelves everywhere. It takes a lot of talented and dedicated people, in different geographic areas, and as I've said before, I'm extremely fortunate to work with the best people in publishing. Now we are at book seven, and once again I give my heartfelt thanks to all the people who believe in me and make my books the best they can be, every single time. Thank you to Brian Tart, Pamela Dorman, Jeramie Orton, Ben Petrone, and the rest of the team at Viking Penguin in the U.S.; to Larry Finlay, Bill Scott-Kerr, Sarah Adams, Tom Hill, and the rest of the team at Transworld in the U.K.; and to Kristin Cochrane, Amy Black, Bhavna Chauhan, Emma Ingram, and the team at Doubleday in Canada. Thank you each and every one.

Editing is hard work, and I owe huge thanks to Sarah Adams and

Jeramie Orton for their insight and expertise in editing *Everyone Here Is Lying*. And kudos to Sarah for coming up with such a great title!

Thanks, again, to Jane Cavolina, my favorite copy editor. It's a pleasure to have you work on my books.

Thanks once again to my faithful agent, Helen Heller—you celebrate my successes and lift my spirits when I need a boost. Thanks also to Camilla and Jemma and everyone at the Marsh Agency for representing me worldwide and selling my books into so many foreign territories.

As always, any mistakes are all mine.

Thanks, always, to my readers. I appreciate you more than I can say. I have you in mind every time I sit down to write—I want you to have that wonderful feeling of being totally caught up in a book!

And finally, thanks to my family, even Poppy the cat, who seems to have retired and doesn't join me in the office anymore. Julia especially deserves a mention for some brilliant ideas. And Manuel—thank you, as ever, for all the technical and other support. I'd be lost without you.

Everyone
Here
Is Lying

One

They don't speak as William walks her to her car parked behind the motel; they never leave their cars out front, where they might be recognized. No one will ever know they were here. At least, this is what they tell themselves, what they have told themselves every time over the last few months as their affair kindled, burned brightly. But now it has been abruptly snuffed out. By her. He didn't see it coming.

They'd met at their usual motel on the outskirts of town, where no one knows them. It's on the main highway. They had to be discreet. They couldn't meet in their own homes because they're both married, and she, apparently, wants to stay that way. Until half an hour ago, he hadn't really had to think about it. He feels like he's had a rug pulled out from beneath his feet, and he still hasn't regained his balance.

They stop at her vehicle, and he leans in to kiss her. She averts her face. Despair and desperation take hold, the realization that she really means it. He turns quickly and walks away, leaving her standing there, keys in her hand. When he gets to his car, he looks across to her, but she is already starting the engine and driving away in a burst of speed, as if making a point.

He stands there, bereft, watching her go. Something had seemed different about her today. He always arrived at the motel first, checked in, paid in cash, got the key, and texted her the unit number. Today, when she knocked and stepped inside, she'd pulled him close and kissed him more hungrily than usual. There were no words. They tore off each other's clothes the same as always, made love the same as always. Afterward, she usually lay with her head on his chest, *listening to his heart*, she'd say. But today she sat up against the headboard and stared straight ahead, looking at the two of them in the bureau mirror. She'd pulled the white sheets up to cover her breasts. Also unlike her.

She wasn't listening to his heart anymore.

"We have to end this," she said.

"What?" He looked up at her, startled, then pulled himself up to sit beside her. "What are you talking about?" He studied her—such a beautiful woman. The bone structure, smooth blond hair, and natural glamour reminiscent of an old-fashioned film star. He felt a surge of alarm.

She turned her head and looked at him then. "William, I can't do this anymore. I have a family, kids to think of."

"I have kids too."

"You're not a mother. It's not the same."

"It didn't stop you before," he pointed out. "It didn't stop you today."

She looked angry then. "You don't have to throw it in my face," she answered.

He softened, reached for her, but she shrugged him away. "Nora, you know I love you." He added, "And I know you love me."

"It doesn't matter." There were tears in her lovely blue eyes.

"Of course it matters!" He was panicking. "It's all that matters! I'll divorce Erin. You can leave Al. We'll get married. The kids will adjust. It will be fine. People do it all the time."

She looked at him for a moment, as if surprised he suggested it. They'd never spoken about the future; they'd been living in the moment. In their pleasure and unexpected happiness. Finally, she shook her head and brushed the tears from her face. "No, I can't. I can't be that selfish. It would destroy Al, and I can't do that to my kids. They'd hate me. I'm sorry."

Then she'd risen from the bed and quickly started putting her clothes back on, while he watched her in disbelief. That things could change so quickly, so fundamentally, without warning—it was disorienting. She was reaching for the door when he cried, "Wait," and hurriedly began to dress. "I'll walk you to your car."

And that was it.

Now he gets into his car to drive down the highway back to Stanhope. It's 3:45 in the afternoon. He's too upset to go back to his medical practice offices or to the hospital. He has no patients scheduled. It's Tuesday; he always reserves the afternoon for her. At loose ends, he decides to go home for a bit instead. The house will be empty. Michael will be at basketball practice, and Avery has choir after school. His wife will be at work. He'll have the house to himself, pour a much-needed drink. Then he'll leave again before anyone gets home.

Their house is at the top of Connaught, a long, pleasant residential street that ends in a cul-de-sac. He's still thinking about Nora as he uses the button on the car's visor to open the garage door. He drives in and presses another button to close the door behind him. She'll be home by now, in her own house farther down the same street, maybe already regretting her decision. But she hadn't looked as if she would change her mind. He wonders now if she has had other affairs. He'd never asked. He'd assumed he was the only one. He realizes he doesn't really know her at all, even though he thought he did—even though he loves her—because he'd been taken completely off guard.

He puts the key in the lock of the side door leading from the garage into the kitchen. He thinks he hears a sound and pauses. There's someone in the kitchen. He opens the door and finds himself looking at his nine-year-old daughter, Avery, who is supposed to be at choir practice.

She turns and stares at him; she'd been reaching for the cookies on the counter.

For fuck's sake, he thinks, *can he never get a moment to himself?* He doesn't want to deal with his difficult daughter right now.

"What are you doing here?" he asks, trying to keep the annoyance out of his voice, but it's hard. It's been a shitty day. He's just lost the woman he loves, and it feels like he's lost everything.

"I live here," she says sarcastically. And she turns away from him and reaches for the cookies, opening the package with a crinkly sound and plunging her hand in.

"I mean, aren't you supposed to be at choir practice?" he asks, reminding himself to breathe. To not get upset. She's not being deliberately obnoxious, he tells himself, she can't help it. That's just the way she is. She's not wired like other people.

"They sent me home," she says.

She's not allowed to walk home from school alone. She's supposed to be picked up by her older brother; basketball practice and choir end at the same time, at 4:30. He sees the time on the stove clock—4:08.

"Why didn't you wait for your brother?"

She's stuffing Oreos into her mouth. "Didn't want to."

"It's not always about what *you* want," he tells her crossly. She eyes him warily, as if sensing his darkening mood. "How did you get in the house?"

"I know about the key under the front mat."

She says it as if she thinks he's stupid. He tries to control his growing temper. "Why did they send you home? Was choir canceled?" She shakes her head. "So what happened?" He finds himself wishing that Erin were here, so that she could handle this. She's much better at it than he is. He feels a familiar pain starting between his eyes, and he pinches the bridge of his nose and begins moving restlessly around the kitchen, tidying, putting things away. He doesn't want to look at her because the disrespect in her expression infuriates him. He thinks of his own father: *I'll wipe that smirk off your face.*

"I got in trouble."

Not today, he thinks. *I can't deal with this shit right now.* "For what?" he asks, looking at her now. She just stares at him, stuffing her face. And he can't help it, he feels that familiar spurt of anger at his daughter. She's always getting into trouble, and he's had enough. When he was a kid, his father smacked him when he misbehaved, and he turned out fine. But it's different nowadays. They have coddled her. Because the experts say she needs patience and support. What they've done, he thinks, is enabled her to become a spoiled brat who doesn't understand limits.

"Tell me what happened," he says, a warning in his voice now.

"No." And it's that defiance in her voice, as if she holds all the cards, as if he's nothing and has no authority over her at all, that sets him off. In three long strides he's across the kitchen, in a blind rage. Something inside him has snapped. It happens so fast, faster than conscious thought. He strikes her across the side of the head, harder than he meant to. She goes down like a stone, the expression of defiance wiped from her face, replaced by shock and then vacancy, and for a fraction of a second, he feels satisfaction.

But it's short-lived. He stands over her, horrified at what he's just done. He's shocked, too, that he could do this. His hand is stinging with pain. He'd only meant to slap her, he tells himself now, to slap some sense into her. He hadn't meant to *strike* her. He bends down over his daughter, where she is slumped across the floor; she cringes away from him. He quickly but gently pulls her up to a sitting position, with her legs out in front of her and her back against the kitchen cupboards. "I'm sorry, honey! Avery, I didn't mean it! I'm so sorry." The words come in a rush. He's blinking back tears.

She looks back at him blankly, not mouthy now. He's sickened by what he's done. He's a decent man. A doctor, not a brute. He's not his father. And he loves his daughter, he does. How could he have lost it like that? "I'm so sorry. I'll make it up to you, Avery, I promise. I shouldn't have done that. It's just, I lost my temper— I've had a very bad day. I know that's no excuse. You know I love you, sweetie. I love you more than anything."

Her eyes are a bit glassy, but otherwise she seems fine. She looks away from him then, won't meet his eyes.

His voice is pleading, and he hates the sound of it. "Look, I'm sorry. I know it's unforgivable, but let's not tell your mother. She has a lot on her plate right now." Avery doesn't answer; she won't speak to him. He pauses and says, "And we won't tell her you came home by yourself, because that will get her upset, and you know she will have to give you consequences. You can say you walked home with a friend."

She ignores him, staring sullenly straight ahead. He thinks she'll tell, and it's what he deserves. There's going to be a bruise. He supposes he could try to deny it; there's no predicting who Erin will believe. His daughter has a history of telling lies. He does, too, but his wife doesn't know that.

He stands up and backs away from Avery. He has to get out of here, away from the sight of what he's just done. He's filled with self-loathing. He can feel his little girl's reproach, imagines her calculating. She has something to use against him now. One more nail in the coffin of his marriage. He turns around and heads back out to the garage.

But when he gets to the car and reaches for his keys, he hesitates.

Two

Nora arrives home about a quarter to five. She'd run a few errands after leaving William at the motel, so that she'd have something to show for her absence. Faith is at soccer practice and should be home soon. Ryan must have gone out; his car is gone from the driveway. Her husband, Al, won't be home till around six. She doesn't have time for a shower, to lather away the smell of William. The smell of what they did together. How would she explain a shower in the afternoon if Ryan suddenly arrives home? Instead, she washes herself with a cloth at the bathroom sink.

She lets herself cry. It had to be done. Her own feelings don't matter, she tells herself. She must live with the choices she's made. She's strong and she must get over him. But it won't be easy—she's in love with William. She knows now that she'd never been in love with her husband, even in the beginning. She and Al had loved each other once, but there had never been true passion there. Not like there is with William. Was.

She's only forty-two. She still has her figure, her good looks. She's not as stunning as she was twenty years ago, but she still turns heads when she enters a room. She can't help it that she's fallen for William, a handsome and charming doctor, that she still wants to be desired. But she can change her actions. She can stop seeing him. It's too risky. She's been selfish. Too many people will be hurt if they are found out: Her husband and children. His wife and their children. She doesn't want to cause all that damage. She will have to stop volunteering at the hospital. She won't be able to bear it, seeing him there, after this.

William's impulsive suggestion that they leave their respective spouses and marry each other had come as a shock. Did he mean it? It had never occurred to her as even a possibility, but even if he did, it's out of the question. Her kids, Faith and Ryan, would never forgive her, and they mean the world to her. No, she can't risk losing them.

It's right that she ended it. It's a wonder they weren't caught. No one must ever know. She's been so worried that it shows—that she's been feeling younger, prettier, happier, more alive these last few months. She has tried to hide it. She had to end things now, before someone noticed. Before Al noticed—if he hasn't already. He's been quieter than usual lately, more detached. But maybe something is going on at work. How could he know about her and William? They've been so careful.

MICHAEL IS SWEATING after basketball practice. The coach is clearly pleased with him today, and it makes him glow. He wants to tell his mom and dad what the coach said about his play today.

In the locker room, he wipes himself down with the towel from his gym bag. He slips off his basketball shorts and pulls on the sweat-pants and sweatshirt in his bag. It's almost mid-October, and it's cool outside. He says a reluctant goodbye to his friends, who head out of the school in a pack, wishing he could go with them and enjoy being part of the team a little longer. Instead, he turns away and follows the halls to the music room at the other end of the school to pick up his little sister. He resents having to do this every Tuesday. Why can't his mother get off work early one day a week and pick up Avery herself? She's such a little pain in the ass, he thinks. He's twelve now, in sixth grade, and he wants to hang out with his friends. There's nothing cool about walking home with your little sister. He wonders what his friends are saying, what he's missing.

He rounds the last corner to the hall with the music room. His sister isn't sitting in her usual spot on the bench along the wall, with her backpack on her shoulder and impatiently scuffing her feet against the floor, waiting for him. He pokes his head inside the room and then enters. The music teacher, Ms. Burke, looks up and smiles at him. She remembers him—he was in choir, too, until he got to quit for sports instead. He glances around the room, but Avery's not there.

"Are you looking for your sister?" Ms. Burke asks.

He nods. "Yeah."

"I'm afraid I had to send her home. She was being disruptive."

Michael's heart sinks. Not again. When Avery gets in trouble, his parents usually argue. Avery sucks up all their energy; they seem to barely notice him. Lately, Michael has to do something spectacular to get their attention. All Avery has to do is misbehave, which she does all the time—while he quietly gets good grades and makes the basketball team and mows the lawn without argument. It's not fair. "She's not supposed to walk home by herself," he tells the music teacher.

Concern flickers across Ms. Burke's face. "She should have waited for you," she says, "if that is your arrangement."

Michael leaves the music room and retraces his steps through the empty school corridors. His mood drops further; the glow from the coach's praise has disappeared. Now Avery's really going to be in trouble. His parents won't like it that she went home on her own. What was he supposed to do? He was at basketball practice. He didn't know. Now he's angry at her too.

He walks home alone, hurrying, head down, knowing that everyone is going to be in a bad mood tonight. No one will care that the coach thought he was playing great. It's usually a twenty-minute walk with Avery, but he does it in fifteen. When he gets home, the front door is locked, which is unexpected. He uses his key and throws open the door. His mother will be home soon, at about 5:30. It occurs to him then that he and Avery can say they came home together. Or just say nothing at all. His mom doesn't have to know that Avery got in trouble and that she walked home without him. It's tempting. But what if Ms. Burke calls his mother? Should he risk it? They'd be furious if they found out and he hadn't told them. He's never lied to them before.

Michael automatically heads to the kitchen, calling for his sister. "Avery! Where are you?" He stops inside the kitchen, but there's no sign of her. If Avery was home, her backpack would be on the floor. Worried now, he walks through the first floor of the house, looking for her. "Shit," he mutters. Then, raising his voice, "Avery, where are you?" He mounts the stairs to the second floor two at a time and looks in her bedroom. She's not there. He looks in his own room—she's been known to snoop through his things—but she's not there either. He's really starting to worry. She's not in his parents' bedroom, the office, or either of the bathrooms, or in the empty garage either. She's not in the basement. Now his heart is pounding from rushing around the house and from fear. He's responsible for her, and he doesn't know where she is. He opens the back sliding doors off the dining room onto the patio and calls her name in the backyard. But no one answers. He goes farther into the backyard toward the back fence and turns around and looks up at the roof. She's climbed onto the roof before. But he doesn't see her. He's scared now. She didn't come home. Where the hell is she? She could be playing in the woods behind the house. She could be anywhere.

He pulls his cell phone out of the pocket of his sweats. Avery is only nine, she doesn't have a cell phone. He calls his mother.

"Yes, honey, what is it?" His mother sounds like she's busy. When isn't she?

He swallows. "Um, Avery's not here."

"What do you mean she's not there?" His mother's voice is sharp. "Where are you?"

He has to tell her the truth now.

ERIN WOOLER CLOSES her eyes as she listens to her son. A moment later, she's making her way as fast as she can toward the office's exit. She'd mouthed *family emergency* to her boss and got the nod that it was okay to leave. "Let's not panic," she says to her twelve-year-old. "She's probably gone to Jenna's. I'm on my way home. Can you go to Jenna's house and see if she's there? Call me as soon as you find her. I'll be home in fifteen minutes."

She makes her way to the parking lot, gets into her car, and puts the phone down on the console where she can reach for it quickly. She's worried, naturally, but she's not afraid, not yet. She loves her daughter, but Avery is a challenge. Always pushing the boundaries. *Why can't she just do what she's told?* Erin thinks, in frustration more than fear. When they find her, they will have to decide how to handle it. How can they get Avery to learn from this rather than becoming more oppositional? That's what usually happens when they try to rein her in.

Erin thinks of her son, Michael, and the quiver in his voice just now. He's such a good kid. He's going to feel responsible; she will have to reassure him that this is Avery, not him—that he is not to blame for his sister's behavior. He's so sensitive, so worried about displeasing anyone, especially his parents. She drives a little faster. No one ever tells you how complicated it is being a parent. How much energy it sucks out of you. The toll it takes on a marriage. Somehow simply growing up in a family isn't such great preparation for having your own.

As Erin drives, it begins to rain. She keeps glancing at her cell phone, expecting a call any minute, that he's found her. She's at her friend Jenna's, across the street, she must be. But then she remembers that Jenna is in choir, too, and she didn't get sent home. The woods then. Avery likes to play in the woods behind their house, in that tree house. She's pulling into the driveway when her cell rings. She picks it up quickly.

"No one answered the door at Jenna's. I'm at the tree house, and she's not here either," Michael says.

He's obviously thinking along the same lines that she is. Her son is breathing heavily, and she can hear the alarm in his voice. It immediately infects her with panic too. But she's the adult, she must remain calm. "Okay, Michael, come home. Wherever she is, she'll probably show up now that it's raining. If not, we'll search for her. I'll call your father." She disconnects and gets out of the car.

The front door has been left unlocked, and she hurries into the house. She kicks off her pumps by the door and quickly searches, calling Avery's name; maybe she came home while Michael was out looking for her. She runs up and down stairs, fans out around the house. Maybe Avery's hiding, playing a trick on them. She searches under beds and behind clothes in the closets, everywhere she can think of. Avery isn't here. She shouts her name again and again. No answer.

As she returns to the kitchen, Michael comes down the hall from the front door and meets her. He's drenched, and he looks shaken, his face pale even though he's obviously been running.

"I'm going to call your father," she says. "And then I'm going to call the police."

Three

William arrives home at 5:40, after the call from Erin. He'd heard the distress in her voice, although it was clear that she was trying to keep a lid on it in front of Michael. *Avery is missing,* she'd told him. *I'm going to call the police.* There is a police cruiser parked on the street outside their house. He feels his stomach lurch at the sight of it.

He parks his car in the garage and takes a deep breath. He must keep it together. He must be the rock in a crisis that everyone expects him to be. He's the man of the family, a doctor. He must call on his training—he can't let himself fall apart. His wife's strained voice echoes in his mind. *Avery is missing. I'm going to call the police.*

When he gets inside, he finds his wife and son sitting in the living room at the front of the house with two uniformed police officers. The female cop is older, and the male police officer—he seems impossibly young, barely out of his teens—is taking notes.

Erin looks up at him, her face drawn. And it hits him, what's happening. It hits him so hard he can't breathe. His wife doesn't get up and come to him for a hug. Nor does he go to her.

The female officer rises and says, "Mr. Wooler?"

"It's Dr. Wooler," he manages.

She nods. "I'm Officer Hollis, and this is Officer Rosales. Your wife reported your daughter missing a few minutes ago. We just got here. We'll take particulars and get a search started. The detectives will be here shortly."

He nods and sits down in another armchair. He watches the sudden rain hammering against the glass doors of the dining room that look out onto the backyard. It's been such a strange day.

"Do you have any recent photographs of Avery?" Hollis asks.

"They're all on my phone," Erin says. She reaches for it and thumbs through and shows her photos of Avery. Her hand is shaking.

Hollis says, "May I?" and tags and sends several of them to her own cell. "Blond, blue eyes," Hollis says, studying the photos. "Height? Weight?"

Erin answers. "She's four foot two, maybe sixty pounds."

"What was she wearing today?"

It's as if William isn't there. Erin seems to think for a moment. "Jeans—dark blue, they were fairly new. Pink running shoes. A white T-shirt with daisies on the front. She was wearing her jean jacket and her backpack is navy blue."

"Any distinguishing marks? Scars?"

Erin shakes her head, then looks at him. William shakes his head too.

"You say no one has seen Avery since she left choir practice," Hollis says, speaking to Erin. "What time was that?"

William can't find his voice; it's as if he's paralyzed. The opportunity passes.

Erin turns to Michael. "I don't know," Michael says nervously. "She was kicked out of practice. I don't know when, exactly." He adds, "It starts after school, at three thirty and goes until four thirty."

Hollis glances at the young cop beside her. "We need to talk to the teacher."

"It's Ms. Burke," Michael tells them.

Hollis nods. "So she left school, and we don't know where she went. She never made it home?"

Erin shakes her head. "Her backpack isn't here. She doesn't have her own key either, because she's not supposed to walk home by herself."

William swallows and still says nothing. He feels dizzy, as if he's standing at the top of a tall building and leaning over, looking below. He knows that Avery was home today after school. She used the key under the front doormat to get in. He talked to her. He hit her. He's a monster and a liar. He feels sicker by the minute; he's afraid he might throw up. But he must not. He swallows down the bile, clears his throat, and suggests, "Maybe she ran away."

His wife turns to him. "Why would she do that?"

He averts his eyes. "Maybe she was angry for being punished at choir practice; you know how she gets." He immediately wishes he could take that back.

Hollis says gently, "How does she get? What's Avery like?"

Erin sighs heavily and says, "She's complicated. She's a lovely nine-year-old girl. Very bright—gifted, actually. But she's challenging. She has a learning disability and ADHD. She also has behavioral problems."

Hollis looks at the two of them. "What do you mean, exactly?"

William lets his wife speak for them.

"She's smart but she struggles in school. She's easily frustrated. She's impulsive. She often acts without thinking. She's willful, defiant of authority. She does what she wants, basically. We're doing our best."

Erin doesn't seem to mind telling them this, but William knows that when a child goes missing, the parents are regarded with suspicion. Now they will think they've done something to her. He wishes she hadn't told them.

But Hollis just nods. "Okay. Has she ever run away before?" She looks at him now.

William can feel himself coloring slightly and says, "No."

Hollis studies him more closely and asks, "Everything all right at home? Any problems we should know about?"

William meets her eyes and says, "Of course not. Everything's fine." Erin says nothing. Michael is staring down at his lap.

"All right." She turns to Erin. "Thank you for the photos." She stands up and says, "If you don't mind, we'd like to look around the house. Could be she's hiding somewhere. You'd be surprised how often that happens; they hide and then fall asleep."

"We've already looked everywhere," Erin says impatiently.

But William knows what they're thinking. They're suspects, of course they are. Maybe there's something to find in the house. "Sure, go ahead," William says. "But please hurry," he urges, his voice breaking. "You have to find her."

ERIN FRETS WHILE a search gets underway for Avery. Her photo and a description of her and what she is wearing are being circulated to all police and media. Patrol cars are looking for her, police officers are already knocking on doors, talking to people who live between Ellesmere Elementary School and the Wooler residence, and going up and down Connaught Street, where they live. Maybe someone has seen her. Erin knows something is terribly wrong—Avery would have come home in time for supper if she was able.

It has just made the local evening news at seven o'clock. *Breaking News . . . A nine-year-old girl has gone missing while walking home alone after school in the town of Stanhope, New York . . .* Her photograph appeared on the screen. It's all unbelievable. Erin feels as if she's living inside a ghastly dream, the kind brought on by a fever.

A local ground search is being hastily organized, led by police officers and using volunteers, despite the increasingly heavy rain. It's October, it will soon be dark, and it's getting cold; time is of the essence. But Erin is trapped in the house, like a fly in amber, unable to go anywhere, unable to look for her daughter. She must stay inside and speak to the detectives, answer their questions. William is here, too, sitting by her side on the living-room couch, sometimes getting up restlessly and looking out the large picture window as if he might see Avery coming up the driveway, as if she had somehow avoided all those out there looking for her and made it home, oblivious. They haven't let Michael join the search either. They are keeping him in the kitchen, with a female officer, so they can speak to the parents alone.

The two detectives arrived just as the first police officers, having found nothing in their search of the house, were on their way to track down the music teacher. Detective Bledsoe is Caucasian, in his midforties, an average-looking man wearing a serviceable gray suit. You wouldn't notice him in a crowd. Erin hopes he's sharper than he looks. Stanhope is a fairly small town, and how much experience can they have had with this kind of thing? She can't remember a child ever going missing here. Bledsoe's partner, Detective Gully, a Black woman maybe ten years younger than Bledsoe, with close-cropped hair and a smart trouser suit, is the one that Erin connects with. Perhaps because she is a woman. Perhaps because her eyes are more lively and her expression more sympathetic than her partner's.

Bledsoe's cell vibrates against the coffee table, making Erin jump. Her heart freezes, terrified of bad news. He has a short conversation and disconnects. He puts his cell back down on the table between them and leans forward in the armchair that he has pulled closer to the coffee table. "That was Hollis," he says. "They spoke to Ms. Burke. She says that Avery began acting up as soon as choir began. She reprimanded her, but she says she had to dismiss her at about three forty-five."

"Is she allowed to do that?" Erin asks, her voice shrill. "Can a teacher send a child in third grade home by herself like that?" For the first time it occurs to her that someone is to blame.

"Let's not focus on that right now," Bledsoe says. "But we now know that she left the school at approximately three forty-five."

"Unless she didn't," Gully says.

Erin turns to Gully. She's stated what should have been perfectly obvious. Bledsoe had assumed that something happened to Avery on the way home from school. They had all assumed.

Bledsoe bites his lip, looks at Gully almost as if he's annoyed at her for speaking out, but maybe he's annoyed at himself. He takes a deep breath, pushes it out. Then he nods. "We have to search the school," he acknowledges. He picks his cell up off the coffee table and walks to the dining room, where he can have a bit of privacy, but they can all hear him giving instructions for the school to be searched from top to bottom.

Erin closes her eyes, thinking of all the places you could hide a little girl in that sprawling school. The storage cupboards, the lockers, the basement, the roof. She could have been dragged into an empty classroom at that time of day, with no one to see it, and anything might have happened to her. At the thought, Erin feels off balance. She grips the edge of the sofa until the feeling passes. When she recovers, she opens her eyes and leans toward Detective Gully, who she thinks is smarter than Bledsoe. She says, "Promise me you'll find her."

"I'll do everything in my power, I promise you that," Gully says.

Four

Nora Blanchard is glued to the evening news, the shock of it displacing her own puny concerns. They are all seated around the television in the living room—her, Al, Ryan, and Faith. William's daughter is missing. It's too awful to contemplate.

She thinks about earlier that afternoon, how she'd ended her relationship with William, and regrets the timing of it. How rudderless he must feel. She tries to imagine what he must be going through. Her heart breaks for him, and she wishes she could comfort him. His wife can't comfort him. There is no love left between them—he's told her that—and she must be hurting even more than he is. She's the mother, after all. Nora can't begin to imagine the anxiety William's wife must be feeling. Nora's own daughter, Faith, is only two years older than Avery, two grades higher, at school. *What if it was Faith who had gone missing?* Faith, at eleven, is very athletic, wears her hair short, and can still be mistaken for a boy. But not for much longer.

But Nora can't go to William and comfort and support him. Their relationship is a secret. His family will be under a microscope, and she can't reach out to him. The only way she can contact him is by phone. Her dirty little secret—her second phone, which she uses sometimes to communicate with him. He has one, too, just for her.

It occurs to her now, with sudden dismay, that if Avery isn't found quickly, the police might find out about his second phone, the one his wife doesn't know about, and her heart seems to stop. *They will be found out. He will have to tell them what it's for. He will have to tell them the truth.* She can feel the blood drain from her face.

"Hey," her daughter says, reaching out to pat her shoulder, "they'll find her."

She jumps when Faith touches her. She turns away from the television to look at her family. All three of them are watching her in concern. She realizes that she's been crying and wipes the tears away with her fingers.

"Sorry," she says, trying to smile. "You know how emotional I get. That poor family."

Al shakes his head. "I can't believe anything could have happened to her on the way home from school. Faith walks home from school every day. We live on the same street. This is a safe community. I'm sure they'll find her."

That's just like her husband, Nora thinks, looking at him. He has no imagination. Head in the sand. Everything is fine. Even when it isn't; even when it's right under your nose.

"She'll turn up, Mom," Faith says. "She's probably doing it on purpose. Everybody knows what she's like."

"What do you mean?" Nora asks her daughter. William has never said anything about Avery to her; they speak very little about their families when they're together.

"She's always getting in trouble. She does whatever she wants. The teachers always send her to the office because they can't deal with her."

Her son, Ryan, announces abruptly, "They want volunteers. I'm going to help look for her."

"That's a good idea," Nora says. She's glad that her son wants to help, though she'd looked forward to having him around tonight; his evening shift at the plant had been canceled. He's not usually home for supper. He stands up, a tall, well-built, good-looking boy of eighteen. So much potential, and yet he has caused her so much anxiety this past year.

"I'll join you," Al says, surprising her. Maybe he's not so sanguine about the neighborhood after all.

"Can I come?" Faith asks.

Nora shakes her head. "No. You're too young. You stay home with me."

Al and Ryan put on their hiking boots and jackets and rain gear, scramble for flashlights, while Nora and her daughter return to the kitchen and start clearing the dishes. Nora stops to watch them go, and soon dismisses Faith to go do her homework. She wants to be alone with her thoughts. She imagines her husband and her son out there in the deepening dark, in the pouring rain, searching the woods between the town and the river, looking for

William's daughter. She hopes they find her soon, safe and sound. They have to.

TIME TICKS BY, all too quickly. Detective Gully knows that when a child goes missing, every minute counts. There's a team now inside the school conducting a thorough search. So far, no results from the door-to-door; it seems no one saw Avery walking home. But that doesn't mean she didn't leave the school—she might simply have gone unnoticed. If she isn't found soon, they will start looking into all the staff and volunteers in the school that day. They're already going through all the registered sex offenders in the area. They have a large group of volunteer searchers fanning out in the empty, undeveloped fields to the north of the Woolers' house and the woods behind the Woolers' street, toward the river. They have flashlights, but it will be completely dark by eight o'clock and visibility will be poor. If the girl isn't found, they will have to cover the same ground again in the morning. They will look in the river, too, drag it if they have to. They will do a television appeal and set up a tip line. They will leave no stone unturned. It could be Avery hopped on a bus and they'll find her in Manhattan. Stranger things have happened. But Gully doesn't like the feel of this one. There's an uneasiness in the pit of her stomach. She loves her job. What she does is important, necessary. But it takes a toll.

She has worked missing child cases before, in Chicago, before relocating to Stanhope. She doesn't think Bledsoe has ever run an investigation like this. Not here. He's a bit defensive, and she's younger, and a woman. He'll take her suggestions, at least; he doesn't shut her down. He's not that bad. She's seen worse.

She studies the two parents sitting across from her. They've answered all the questions put to them, about Avery, about her routines, who she knows, who the family knows, where they think she might have gone. They know that she likes to play in the woods and that there's a tree house there that she often goes to. Her brother has already been there to look for her, but even so, they have sent a team to take a closer look.

Avery's parents have been frank about her behavioral issues, describing a girl who is hard to manage and quite oppositional. For example, Avery is not on any medication for her ADHD because she refuses to take it. They're on the edge of a precipice, waiting for news. The mother has been distraught but stoic, making an obvious effort to keep it together. The father interests her more. There's something about him, something off. She doesn't like to think it, but she does. It's not her first rodeo. He seems to be hiding something. She senses that his frequent trips to look out the window for Avery are a show put on for their benefit. The mother doesn't do anything like that. She simply looks terrified.

The uniformed policewoman who's been in the kitchen with the son pops into the living room to say, "Michael's just helped me put on a pot of coffee. Anybody want some?"

The two parents shake their heads in unison.

"Yes, please," Gully says gratefully; it's going to be a long night.

"Yes, great, thanks," Bledsoe says.

Bledsoe turns back to the parents and asks, "Do you know of anyone who might have a grudge against you? Is there anyone you can think of who might want to harm Avery?"

Erin and William look at him in surprise. "Of course not," Erin says.

William answers. "No. We're just normal people. There's no reason for anyone to harm our daughter."

An uncomfortable silence falls because they all know the most likely reason someone might take a little girl.

"You're a doctor?" Bledsoe says to William.

"Yes. I'm a GP with hospital privileges at Stanhope General. I have a practice downtown."

"And you, Mrs. Wooler?"

"I'm a legal secretary. With a firm in town—Levitt and Levitt."

He nods his head slowly. "Anyone angry at you?"

She pauses to think. "No. I'm just a secretary. Our firm doesn't have any nasty cases. And anyway, it's the lawyers they'd get mad at, not me."

"Anyone angry at you, Dr. Wooler?" Bledsoe asks. "Have you lost a patient recently? A child perhaps?"

William shakes his head. "I'd remember that. No. Nothing out of the ordinary. Some sad cases, but natural illnesses. No one is angry at me that I know of."

"So, no professional complaints against you?" Bledsoe persists.

"None," William answers crisply.

Gully can smell the coffee coming from the kitchen. She stands up. "I'll get the coffee." She steps out of the living room. To her right is the front door and down the hall to her left is the kitchen. In the hall, closer to the front door, is a double line of coat hooks along the wall. The hall isn't well lit, but she sees various jackets and coats hung up in two rows. The house has been searched already by the first officers on the scene. But Gully notices something that no one has mentioned. She sees a child-size jean jacket hanging on one of the hooks. She peers closer. It's too small for Michael. This must be the jacket that they think Avery was wearing that day. What's it doing here?

"Bledsoe?" she calls from the hall. "Can you come here a minute?"

Five

Gully feels her pulse quicken as Bledsoe joins her in the hall. She finds a light switch and flicks it on, filling the hall with light. The officer in the kitchen comes closer to see what they're doing.

"Look at that," Gully says, pointing with her chin. "A little girl's jean jacket."

Bledsoe takes in a deep breath beside her. "Fuck," he mutters.

Erin and William now come into the hall. "What is it?" Erin asks.

"Is that your daughter's jean jacket?" Bledsoe asks.

She looks at it, as if confused. "Yes."

"You said she was wearing it when she left for school today," Bledsoe says.

"I thought she was. Maybe she wasn't. I'm not sure."

"What's your morning routine like?" Gully asks. "Who gets her ready for school, sends her out the door in the morning?"

"We both do," Erin explains. "It's a bit chaotic in the morning. Michael and Avery leave for school together. I saw them leaving this morning and I'm pretty sure she was wearing that jacket." Her face looks sallow beneath the harsh overhead light.

Gully looks at William. He's frowning. He looks ill. "Dr. Wooler, do you remember?"

"I don't know. I saw them leave, said goodbye, but"—he turns to his wife and shakes his head—"I don't think she was wearing it this morning." He adds, "But I don't know, I'm not very observant, I'm afraid." He avoids Gully's eye, and she wonders why.

She glances toward the kitchen, sees Michael standing behind the police officer, silently watching. "Michael, come here a sec."

He walks slowly into the hall, glancing nervously at his parents and the detectives.

Gully points at the jacket on the hook and asks him gently, "Was Avery wearing this jacket this morning when she went to school with you?"

He looks confused, wary. She waits for his response.

"I don't know. I'm not sure," he says.

He overheard his parents disagreeing about the jacket, she thinks. Is that why he's afraid to give a proper answer? What is the subtext here in this family?

Erin turns to her son and says, "Think, Michael. Try to remember. It's important. Was she wearing the jean jacket, or something else?"

Michael swallows and says, "She was wearing the jean jacket this morning."

Gully glances at Bledsoe and understanding passes between them. Gully says, "Avery must have been back here, in the house, today."

Bledsoe turns to the parents. "You've said they don't come home for lunch. Does she have her own key?"

"No," Erin says.

Into the strained silence, Michael speaks up, his voice reluctant, tremulous. "She knows about the key under the mat at the front door. She's used it before."

WILLIAM CAN FEEL the sweat forming in his armpits, and his hands are clammy. He stares at his son. They all realize, now, that Avery was home, in the house, after school today. He should have admitted it before, when he first had the chance. He should have told them he was here earlier, that he saw her. But he hadn't spoken up when he had the opportunity because he was afraid. Afraid of what they might think, the conclusions they might leap to. He's lied to the police. He must have been in shock; he hadn't been thinking clearly. He hadn't been able to think at all. What if someone saw him, coming or going? He resists the urge to wipe his palms on his trousers. He should have told them he was here, and now it's too late.

Gully says, "Thank you, Michael."

Erin asks Michael, anxiety in her voice, "Has she done this before, come home without you?"

Michael looks down at the floor, his face pale, his lower lip quivering. "Just once. I wanted to stay at school with my friends and . . . I told her about the key." He starts to cry. "It was just once, I swear."

William is stricken anew at the sight of his son's tears. He realizes that Michael might carry this with him for the rest of his life.

The knowledge that if he hadn't sent his sister home alone that one time and told her about the key, she probably wouldn't have walked home by herself today, and none of this would have happened. Michael's only twelve years old. William feels sick; he can't move. But his wife bends down and folds their distraught son into her arms, shushing him, telling him that it's going to be all right, that it's not his fault.

William steals a glance at the detectives. Gully is looking thoughtful. She meets his eye, and he quickly averts his gaze. He feels like he's under a microscope. He moves closer to Michael and puts a hand on his shoulder. "It's okay, champ," he says, his eyes suddenly filling up. This is unbearable. How will any of them survive it? It's his fault. He should never have come home today.

The officer slips back into the kitchen and starts searching for coffee mugs. It breaks the tension, and they all move into the kitchen except for Bledsoe, who disappears into the living room, his cell phone already out to make the necessary calls. Gully follows him, but although William strains to hear what they say to each other, he can't make it out.

Gully soon returns to the kitchen while William prepares coffee for the two detectives and the uniformed officer. He speaks up while his back is turned to the others. "If she came home after school, she must have gone out again," he says.

Bledsoe appears at the door to the kitchen and announces, "They found her backpack in her locker at school."

Erin says, her voice breaking, "She sometimes forgets to bring her backpack home."

Bledsoe returns to the living room, his cell phone at his ear. Gully says, "It's possible she might have come home at lunchtime and gone back to school in the afternoon without her jacket. We have officers trying to verify that she was at school all day. We have to be certain that she only came home after she was dismissed from choir."

WILLIAM SWALLOWS. His hands are shaking as he places the coffee mugs on the counter for Gully and Bledsoe. He wishes he had handled this differently. He wants to tell the detective he was here and saw Avery after school. That he left again. *My God, what if someone saw him?* But his nerve fails him. He never knew till now what a coward he is. He glances at his wife, who still has her arms around Michael. She looks wrecked, and Michael seems almost catatonic. The detectives are going to want to question them all further, of course they are. He wonders what his wife and son will say about him.

GULLY CARRIES the coffee through to Bledsoe in the living room as he ends a call. She hands him the mug. She takes her time; this has to sound unthreatening. "I'm wondering," she says, taking a sip of her coffee. Her voice is low so that the parents in the kitchen can't hear her. "Maybe she wasn't alone in the house."

Bledsoe gives her a sharp look. "You think someone was inside the house with her? Why?"

"I don't know. I'm trying to keep an open mind. But that jacket."

"What about it?"

"It's on one of the upper hooks," Gully says. Bledsoe continues to look at her, but a flush creeps up his neck as he realizes what she's getting at.

"A child of four foot two couldn't reach that hook," Bledsoe says.

Gully nods. "There are empty hooks below. Avery didn't hang up that jacket. Someone was in this house with her."

Six

Ryan Blanchard pulls his jacket up higher around his neck under the rain poncho and pulls the hood of the poncho farther forward. It's dark, it's raining steadily, and the temperature is dropping. He's already soaked, and he can hardly see anything. He glances at his watch: 8:06. The volunteers fan out in a ragged line, about six feet apart, slow-moving shapes wielding flashlights pointed at the ground. They started at the beginning of the woods behind the houses on Connaught Street and are working their way to the river.

Ryan moves forward in step with the others, eyes trained on the uneven ground in front of him, sweeping his flashlight back and forth. It feels ominous in the woods. As they progress, he has to push back wet ferns and brambles, weave around trees. He can hear branches snapping, and the footsteps of the searchers on either side of him, smell the damp, fecund earth. A bird flushes out of a tree ahead, startling him.

He should be working at the plant right now. He'd be halfway through his shift, getting tired, looking forward to his day off tomorrow. But his shift had been canceled—production has been cut back—and now he is out here in the pouring rain helping to look for a missing girl. They've been told that she may have gone into the woods and gotten lost or fallen and hurt herself. But he knows what everybody here is thinking—that she was snatched on her way home from school and what they're looking for is her body. Still, the leaders shout out regularly, calling her name across the night.

He doesn't want to think about Avery Wooler. He tries to distract himself with thoughts of the future. Next year for sure he will get out of this place, go away to college. The itch to get out of Stanhope grows stronger every day.

His father is moving alongside him, to his right, his bulk familiar, comforting. Ryan wonders what his father is thinking as he sweeps his flashlight back and forth, intent on his task. He seems grimmer out here than he was at home, with his glib assurances. But everyone here is grim. It's more real now, out here in the cold rain, not just something on the television.

He and his father are not as close as they once were. They've grown apart. They have nothing in common since he learned to ride a bike, to camp, to play baseball. They don't spend any time together. This, searching for Avery Wooler, is the first thing they've done together in ages, Ryan realizes, as he plays his flashlight over the sodden ground. His mother is the heart of their family—they all know it. His father is on the periphery, there but not there. His dad is . . . detached. But Ryan isn't as close to his mother these days either. There's a chasm between Ryan and both his parents, and Ryan knows it's his own doing. He hasn't turned out to be the son they thought he was.

NORA HAS THE TELEVISION on in the living room and waits anxiously as the night wears on. There is no new information online or on the television, and with every passing hour her dread increases. She desperately wants Avery to turn up safe and sound. She imagines her husband and son out there scouring the woods in the cold rain. Will they find anything? Will they stay out there all night? Perhaps Avery is being held captive somewhere or is already dead. Her head swirls. She worries about William. She wishes now she had not told him it was over. Where had she found that strength? It's left her now.

She doesn't dare text him. She thinks of her second, secret phone, so carefully hidden behind the air vent in the bedroom she shares with Al. She must not contact him, not now. The police are in his house. They will find his phone.

There is going to be fallout from his daughter going missing, and she's going to be part of it. She must brace herself, think of what to do. They will be found out. She grows wilder in her thoughts.

Nora does something she almost never does. She gets down on her knees and prays, for all of them. She wonders if what has happened to Avery is punishment sent by God for what she and William have been doing. Maybe she has that little girl's blood on her hands.

THE WAITING IS UNBEARABLE, the tension inside the house palpable. Erin Wooler moves restlessly between the living room and the kitchen, her body tensing whenever one of the detectives takes a phone call. But so far, nothing. It's as if Avery has vanished off the face of the earth. The school has been thoroughly searched, but they haven't found her. The team sent to the tree house has reported that there are no obvious signs of Avery having been there or of foul play, and they are not treating it as a crime scene.

Michael is distraught. She has done her best to comfort him, to reassure him. But inwardly she is deeply distressed that her son sent Avery home by herself once before and told her about the key. Her heart had almost stopped when he'd told them. She'd had to assure him that it's not his fault. She doesn't blame him—he couldn't have known what would happen—but still, it's hard. She wouldn't be human if she didn't think of the what-if—what if he hadn't done that? Avery probably would have been waiting for him on the bench outside of choir practice. She'd be here with them right now, instead of these detectives. But she mustn't think this way. She feels William could have been more demonstratively supportive of their son. But he seems to be in shock.

She sits on the sofa and watches her husband now, as he stares out the living-room window into the dark, all nerves. Beyond the raw, visceral terror they both feel about Avery—*Where is she? What is happening to her?*—there is another fear running alongside. What if she isn't found quickly—what will happen then? The detectives will look at them. They will tear away at all the careful layers they've constructed in their family and expose them for who they are. William won't come out of it particularly well.

Bledsoe disconnects from another call, glances meaningfully at Gully, and asks William to come back and sit down. Erin's heart falters; he has something to tell them. William complies and falls back against the sofa as if exhausted. He looks awful. She must look the same; she feels like she's aged years since her son phoned her at work that afternoon.

"We're treating the house as a possible crime scene," Bledsoe says carefully.

Erin looks back at him, trying to grasp what he means. She glances at Gully. "What?" she says.

Bledsoe explains. "We now have confirmation that Avery has been accounted for at school all day today—she was in detention over the lunch hour and present all day in class. She could not have returned to the house and left her jacket here at any time except after school, after she left choir at three forty-five. She would have arrived home at around five after four."

"We know this," William says impatiently. "She must have come home, used the key under the mat to get in, and gone back out again and forgotten her jacket. And someone took her." He's grown visibly agitated.

"Try to remain calm, Dr. Wooler," Bledsoe says.

Erin watches her husband, feeling frightened.

"The thing is," Bledsoe says carefully, "we don't think Avery was alone in the house today after school."

"What are you talking about?" Erin says, her stomach turning over.

Gully says, "We think someone was here, inside the house with her, after school today." She adds, "That's why we need to treat the house as a crime scene. We're going to have a forensics team come in and go through the house thoroughly, as soon as possible. We will need your cooperation on this."

Erin is dumbfounded. "Why do you think that?" she asks. Her husband, beside her, has gone completely still.

Bledsoe says, "Because someone else hung Avery's jacket up on that upper hook; she wouldn't have been able to reach it herself."

Erin feels the blood rush from her head; it makes her dizzy. They're right. How had she missed that? The jacket is on one of the upper hooks. Avery always uses the lower hooks, she has to. "But who could get into the house?" she asks. She feels hysteria approaching. This can't be happening. She looks at the two detectives. She turns to her husband; his face has gone ashen.

"The doormat isn't a very good place to hide a key," Gully points out. "If someone wanted to get in, it's probably the first place they'd look. And someone might have been watching Avery, and seen her come home alone, and use the key to enter a presumably empty house."

Bledsoe adds, "The key is still there. The forensics team will want to look at it."

William is now cracking his knuckles beside her, looking like he wants to jump out of his own skin.

"Oh my God," Erin whispers, fighting nausea, realizing how easy it is for someone to take a child. Even if you think you've done everything to keep them safe, it's never enough. Because the world is an awful place, full of evil. It's just hit home, and she can hardly breathe.

"Or—might she have let someone in?" Bledsoe asks.

"Like who?" William says, still agitated.

Gully answers, "A stranger? A family friend? The parent of a classmate? Anybody?"

Erin feels even more shaken than before. It was bad enough that Avery might have been snatched on the way home from school, but this—this is too much to bear.

"Would she?" Gully prods. "There's no sign of forced entry."

Erin swallows, tries to focus. "I don't know. Probably. If the doorbell rang, she would answer it. She wouldn't stop to think that she was home alone. She's not afraid of anything." And then she begins to sob. Because now, Avery must be absolutely terrified.

Bledsoe says, "It's unfortunate you don't have a porch cam."

While Erin sobs, she feels her husband put his arms around her.

Gully asks, "Is there anyone—anyone at all—who has shown an interest in Avery? Anyone hanging around your house lately? Offering to do odd jobs, that sort of thing?"

Erin stifles her sobs and tries to think. But her brain is stuttering, unable to function. She shakes her head helplessly. She glances at her husband beside her for help. But William seems as overwhelmed as she is.

"Does she take any lessons? Piano, anything like that? Any extracurricular activities you haven't mentioned?" Gully asks.

Erin says, "No, only choir. She couldn't settle to anything."

Bledsoe says, "We need to go through it all again—friends, family, acquaintances, anyone who knows you, even slightly. It's likely that she has been taken. And when a child is taken, quite often it's someone known to the family. You'd be surprised."

Seven

William excuses himself to go to the bathroom. There's a powder room on the main floor, but he goes upstairs instead. He can feel the eyes of the detectives on his back as he leaves. He makes his way along the upstairs hall and closes the bathroom door and locks it behind him. And then he leans over the toilet and heaves into the bowl. He remains there, sweating, thinking he wants to die. He pictures his little Avery, not as he last saw her, but smiling and happy, and he cries silently. Finally, he struggles to his feet and flushes the toilet, runs cold water over his face, and washes his hands. He can't bear to look at himself in the mirror; he hates himself.

He must decide what to do.

The damn jacket.

He'd hung up the jacket, which Avery had dropped on the floor, tidying up on autopilot while he was asking her why she was home by herself. He'd forgotten all about it until the detective found it.

And now the police know someone was in the house with her, and he's missed every opportunity to say it was him. If he now tells them he was here, and saw her, that he hung up the jacket, and tries to tell them that she was fine when he left, they will never believe him. So he must continue to claim that he was never here. But where will he say he was? He was gone for a long while that afternoon—he was with Nora and then he came home—and he can't admit to either of those things. He wasn't at his practice or at the hospital, and he has no one to confirm he was with them. He's fucked.

The police are going to search the house. They won't find strange fingerprints or anything else, because nobody else was in the house. And then they will focus on him and Erin. Isn't that what they do? Accuse the parents if they can't find anyone else? And he doesn't have an alibi.

Then it occurs to him that he has another problem, something they *will* find. His burner phone. For a moment he can't even breathe. Nora will be dragged into this, too, they will be found out, her worst fears realized. Oh, Christ. Nora had ended it—today, of all days. It's like she had some premonition of the shitstorm that was about to come. He wonders what she will think if it starts getting reported that the missing girl's father is the number one suspect.

They must be wondering what's taking him so long. He straightens up, takes a deep breath. As long as no one saw him—saw his car coming and going from the garage. He feels a disorienting surge of fear that he must deliberately tamp down. There's a good chance he wasn't seen, because someone would have mentioned it by now, surely? They've already had cops questioning neighbors up and down the street. It's a calculated risk, but one he must continue to take. Worst case, he can deny it, say they're mistaken.

Their house is at the top of Connaught Street, which runs north-south, parallel to the river, ending in a cul-de-sac. The only other street it connects to is Greenley Avenue, which leads east toward downtown. To the north of their house is undeveloped land, just scrub, that meets up with the forest as it curves down to the river. The houses are set some distance apart, and as far as he knows, nobody has cameras. There's no crime in Stanhope. It's a small place. Safe as houses. Until it isn't.

GULLY REMAINS at the Woolers' house as the difficult night wears on, yielding nothing about Avery's whereabouts. The family has been moved to a downtown hotel—the Excelsior—for the night, the female police officer accompanying them. Bledsoe has returned to the station to set up a command post. From there he will run the investigation, in constant contact with the search parties, the officers in the field, the ones in the station running down sex offenders.

Gully observes the technicians doing their meticulous work. They're looking for fingerprints, evidence of blood that has been cleaned up, fibers, hairs, anything. Of course, the scene has already been compromised. But maybe they'll get lucky. Gully feels that the area is too tidy if the little girl was home after school. Wouldn't she have had a snack? Perhaps she didn't have time. Or perhaps whoever was here with her tidied up so it would look like she was never here and simply screwed up about the jean jacket. Not everyone thinks clearly when they're committing a crime. Gully can't help thinking that hanging up a jacket is the sort of thing a parent would do.

Gully goes upstairs to Avery's room. Wearing a pair of gloves, she flicks on the overhead light and takes a long look. The room is painted off-white, the bed neatly made with a pretty pink-and-yellow quilt on it. There's a white nightstand next to the white bed, a small white desk and matching chair, some pictures on the walls—something undoubtedly chosen by her mother. It's hard to get a sense of Avery from looking at her room.

The dark and the rain press up against the bedroom window; the soft light makes the room feel cozy and safe. Gully feels a stab of anxiety for the missing girl—it's late at night, and she's out there somewhere, instead of here, tucked up in bed where she belongs. Gully moves farther into the room and opens the bedside-table drawer. She riffles carefully through its contents—pens and paper, a chocolate bar wrapper, some lip balm, and underneath all that, a diary. It's the kind that has its own little gold lock with a key attached, on a red string. She sets it down to read in a bit. She looks under the bed, beneath the mattress. She searches behind the pictures, through the desk and dresser drawers. She lifts up the small area rug on the floor. She's looking for anything that will help her understand what might have happened to the little girl. Even children of nine can have secrets.

She sits down on the bed and opens the diary. The first few pages have short entries, poorly written, about school and her struggles there. Avery doesn't seem to have any friends. She writes that no one likes her, except for one girl, Jenna, who lives across the street, but she can't always count on her. Gully allows herself for a moment to feel terribly sad for this lonely little girl. The entries stop suddenly, as if the novelty of having a diary had worn off. Gully fans the pages to see if there's anything trapped within it, but nothing falls out. No secrets here.

NORA HEARS AL and Ryan come in the front door, can hear them hanging up their jackets, kicking off their boots. She remains lying on her side on the sofa in the dimly lit living room for a moment, afraid of what they might tell her. She glances at her watch, sees that it's just after one in the morning. She sits up and turns on a lamp.

Al enters the living room, and she looks up at him, hoping to see good news written on his face. But if they had found her, they would have burst into the room with the news.

"Anything?" she asks, as Ryan comes into the room behind his father and stands beside him.

Al shakes his head. "No sign of her. They're going to have the volunteers start again in the morning."

"You're soaked. You must be frozen," she says. They both nod wearily, shivering, lips blue. "Will you go back in the morning?" she asks.

Al glances at their son. "I'll take the day off work. They'll understand."

Ryan nods. "I'll go back too."

"We both need hot showers," Al says. "You go ahead, Ryan."

"No, you go, Dad," Ryan says.

Al nods and turns to go upstairs. "I'll be quick," he says to his son.

For a moment, Ryan remains behind with her. It's as if he wants to say something. Or perhaps he just wants comfort, she thinks. He's only eighteen, just a kid. This must be disturbing for him; he has a sister not much older than the missing girl, at the same school, who takes the same route home every day. Nora moves toward him, but he turns away.

"Night, Mom," he says.

She watches him trudge up the stairs.

Eight

Early the next morning Erin wakes from a brief and restless sleep and is startled to find herself in a strange hotel room. Then she remembers, and the suffocating weight settles on her again. She wonders if it will always be like this, if she'll wake up every day and have to adjust to this new, terrible reality. William is not in the bed beside her. She raises herself up on one arm and sees him sitting in one of the hotel chairs, watching her.

"I didn't want to wake you," he says, his voice hollow. Then he stands up wearily and says, "I'm going to have a shower."

She watches him slip into the bathroom and falls back against the pillow. No one has come to tell them that Avery has been found, alive and well. Erin grabs her cell phone from the night table—it's barely six o'clock, her daughter has been missing for about fourteen hours—and starts scrolling. She's sickened by what she reads. The news stories say their house is being treated as a crime scene. There's a picture of it, with yellow crime-scene tape across the front porch. How damning. There's nothing about the jacket, about how it was hung up out of reach by a person unknown. The detectives told them last night that this information is being held back, in the interests of the investigation, and asked them not to share it with anyone. They also said they haven't changed the original description given out, which included Avery wearing the jean jacket. Often, keeping information from the general public can help police. She stares at the photograph of their house with the crime-scene tape and thinks that the detectives might just as well have told the media that the parents are the prime suspects. She feels her trust in the detectives eroding, a new fear sprouting.

"Have you seen this?" she asks William, holding up her phone when he comes out of the bathroom.

"Yes," he says, barely glancing at it.

"How dare they!" she says, shaken and furious.

He starts getting dressed. He breathes out heavily and looks at her. "I think we have to brace ourselves," he says carefully.

"But—putting crime-scene tape across the house—was that really necessary? It makes it look like they think we did something to her!"

"Maybe that is what they think," William says.

"No." She shakes her head back and forth. "No. They can't think that. If that's what they think, they'll stop looking for her. They can't stop looking for her!"

He grasps her firmly by both arms, looks her in the eye, and says, "We will not let them stop looking for her."

At that moment there's a tentative knock at the door. "Are you up?" It's the female officer's voice, the one who's been here all night, in a chair outside their rooms. Even so, she probably slept more than they did.

"Yes, we'll be out in a minute," William calls out.

Erin goes to Michael, asleep in an adjoining room. She shakes him awake, pulls him into her for a hug. "Come on. Put your clothes on, Michael. We have to get going." She returns to her own room and hurriedly gets dressed. As she opens the door to the hallway, William right behind her, she sees Detective Bledsoe and Detective Gully stepping out of the elevator and coming toward them. They are grim-faced, and for a moment she is stricken with fear, terrified of what they might tell her. They're both in fresh clothes, but as they approach, Erin can tell that they've barely slept either.

William steps past her into the hall, sees them, and blurts out, "Any news?"

Bledsoe shakes his head. "I'm afraid not." He looks at each of them and then at Michael, as he appears in the corridor beside them. "We'd like to ask you some more questions."

William glances quickly at her before turning back to the detectives. "We've already answered all your questions," he says impatiently.

Bledsoe adds reassuringly, "We're doing everything humanly possible to find Avery. We'd like you to come down to the station with us, if that's all right."

"What?" Erin says, her stomach curdling.

Bledsoe doesn't answer, just steps back so that they can follow Gully to the elevators. But Erin doesn't move.

"Why did you tell the press our house was a crime scene?" she asks.

"We didn't tell them anything," Bledsoe answers. "They draw their own conclusions."

WILLIAM GRABS a muffin and take-out coffee in the almost empty hotel dining room, and coaxes Erin to do the same. Michael gets a muffin and a carton of juice. None of them are enthusiastic about eating, though, and the muffins remain in the paper bag. The uniformed officer who spent the night outside their door has been sent home. Soon William finds himself with his wife and son in the police station downtown. He's never been inside the police station before, never been inside *any* police station, for anything. This one needs paint and smells of sweat and stale coffee.

Gully and Bledsoe lead the Woolers behind the reception area and down a hall to another, smaller waiting area. Here, William and Erin are told they will be taken into different interview rooms, while Michael waits. He will be interviewed later, with a parent present.

William starts to feel afraid. His heart begins to pound. He can see a similar fear in his wife's eyes, the anxiety and confusion in his son's. His wife is guilty of nothing. She could never harm their daughter—surely they will see that. William looks back over his shoulder at his son and sees his troubled face as his parents are led away.

The interview room is small and plain, with a metal table and four chairs. He sits down on one side, Bledsoe and Gully sit side by side on the other. William wonders if he should ask for a lawyer. But he's worried about how that will look.

"We won't be long," Bledsoe says. "This is purely voluntary, just to cover all the bases. You can leave at any time."

William isn't sure he believes him. "Sure, anything I can do to help. I just want you to find Avery."

Bledsoe nods. He sits back in his chair, relaxed. "We'd like to get some basic things out of the way. For instance, if you could tell us where you were yesterday afternoon, before you arrived at home at five forty. It seems you weren't at your medical practice, or at the hospital, from about two o'clock on."

So they've already checked. He tries to keep his voice steady. "No, I wasn't."

"So where were you?" Bledsoe asks.

He's already thought about this. He's been thinking about it all night. He knew they would ask. He could tell them about the affair and not give them Nora's name. He could. But he doesn't want to. He doesn't want Erin to know, not right now, not like this. But then he wonders if they've already found his other phone. He keeps it hidden in his car, an Infiniti G37 sedan. His car is in their garage. They must have searched it last night when they searched the house. But one of the reasons he recently bought that car is that it has a secret compartment in the rear-seat armrest. Do they know about that? Is it possible that they missed it? The room is too warm, and he feels himself beginning to sweat. They are looking at him, waiting for him to answer. He says, "I just needed to get out. I didn't have any appointments and I didn't feel like facing my paperwork."

"Where did you go?"

"I went for a drive. I drove north along the river, stopped at a viewing point for a while. I just wanted to think."

"What did you want to think about?"

Shit. "Nothing in particular." He adds, "You know, life."

"How's your marriage?" Bledsoe asks.

"It's fine."

"And if we ask your wife, she'll say the same thing?"

William doesn't know what his wife will say. "Look, what's this got to do with my daughter?"

Bledsoe ignores him. "Your daughter is difficult." He looks down at a file he has open on the table. "Attention deficit and hyperactivity disorder. Behavioral problems." He lifts his eyes. "That can't be fun."

William is getting angry now. "Yes, she can be challenging. We've been very up front about that. But it doesn't mean we don't love her. Of course we do." He adds urgently, "We just want her back."

"On this long drive," Bledsoe continues, "did you stop in anywhere? Get a coffee? Buy something? Get gas? Can you give us something that can verify where you were?"

Now William realizes something. The motel could verify where he was. He didn't use his own name, and he always paid cash. But the person on the front desk would certainly recognize him. She'll recognize him as soon as his picture makes the front page, probably today. He feels a spike of adrenaline shoot through his veins. He realizes, too, that the motel staff won't necessarily know what time he left, because he forgot, in the shock of Nora dumping him, to return the key on his way out. He'd thrown it away, after, into the river. He could say he left the motel when his wife called him. He and Nora always parked around back, so their cars weren't visible from the motel office. The motel staff probably won't know what time he left. Nora's not going to say anything. He swallows, balances on the edge of a decision. "No, I don't think so."

"So, no one can verify where you were between three forty-five when your daughter left school and when you arrived home at five forty. Good to know." Now he leans in. "Did you go home yesterday, Dr. Wooler? When your daughter was in the house?"

"No." He summons all his internal strength and meets the detective's eyes steadily. "I didn't go home till Erin called me, around five twenty. I got there at five forty. The police were already there when I arrived."

Bledsoe nods. "Okay. That's all we need for now. Thank you." He gets up. "If you don't mind, you can remain here while we talk to your wife."

Nine

Erin sits nervously in the interview room, waiting for Bledsoe and Gully. She doesn't know how long she'll be here. She's frantic about her missing daughter, thinks all this is a waste of time. She's worried about what the detectives think. She frets about Michael alone in the waiting room. He's only twelve years old. This will damage him. It will damage all of them.

Finally, the door opens, and Bledsoe makes his way in, followed by Gully. Erin's not so sure of Gully anymore.

"Let's get started," Bledsoe says, as he and Gully sit down across from her. He smiles at her. "This is purely voluntary. You can leave at any time."

This is a surprise to Erin. It doesn't feel that way. She wonders what they would do if she got up and left. Bledsoe has a file in his hand, which he places on the table. Erin wonders what's in it. She wishes she knew what her husband said in his interview.

Bledsoe begins. "You said that you were at work when your son called your cell yesterday at four fifty-five p.m."

So they are definitely suspects. She feels a mounting hysteria. Will they put their energies into finding Avery, or into trying to pin this on her and William? "Yes."

"Was there anyone else in the office?"

She nods. "Yes. There were several people there who can vouch for me being there all afternoon, until I left at about five." Maybe this is just a formality, she thinks, something they have to do, and then they will get back to looking for Avery.

"Okay," Bledsoe says. He pauses briefly, then says, "Your husband can't account for his whereabouts at the time Avery went missing."

Erin freezes. She assumed he'd been at work. Where else would he have been? "What?" she says faintly.

Bledsoe fixes his eyes on her. "He says he was out for a drive, from about two o'clock until you called him at about five twenty. No one can verify his whereabouts."

She hadn't anticipated this; she can't even mask her shock. She feels a strange numbness setting in.

"Any idea where he might have been?" the detective asks.

She shakes her head. "If he says he was out for a drive, then he was." But her thoughts are reeling, her stomach clenching.

"That's a long drive," Bledsoe says.

She says, "He really likes his new car."

"How would you describe your relationship with your husband?" Bledsoe asks.

"It's fine." He continues to stare at her, and it annoys her; it's as if he's implying something. She's not going to share the intimate details of her marriage with them. It's none of their business. "I mean, we have ups and downs like any couple, but we're solid."

"And how is your husband with the children?"

"He's an excellent father," she insists.

"Does he ever lose his patience?" Bledsoe asks.

Erin glances at Gully. Why doesn't he let her ask any questions? She finds Bledsoe aggressive, unnerving. She answers carefully; she doesn't like how this is going. "Sometimes. As do I. Any parent does. Do you have any children, Detective?" She's panicking now. What has William said? What has he admitted to? Why didn't they anticipate this and talk before they came in here, when they were in their hotel room? And Michael, they are going to question him. What a terrible position to put a child in—*tell the police the truth or protect your parents.* She feels the room begin to spin.

He ignores her question. "Your husband says he wasn't home yesterday afternoon."

"Of course he wasn't," she answers.

"If he was, we'll find out."

"It wasn't him, it was someone else," she insists, the hysteria coming out in her voice. "Someone must have come to the door, and she let them in. Someone took her. You have to find her!" She turns her panic-stricken gaze to Gully, who is regarding her with sympathy.

MICHAEL BITES HIS NAILS as he sits in the waiting room alone. It's a habit that he kicked recently, but it started again last night with a vengeance. He doesn't care; his world is falling apart. Maybe his last happy moment in his whole life, he thinks, is when the coach praised him at basketball practice yesterday.

He's afraid for his sister. He knows she's a pain and makes them all upset sometimes, that she makes her parents fight. She's been like that for as long as he can remember. He remembers clearly the first time his dad hit her. She was six years old, throwing a tantrum because she didn't get the cup she wanted for supper. His mom got up from the table to take it out of the dishwasher and wash it for her, to placate her. His father was incensed. *Erin, sit down. Stop jumping up to do everything she says. You're spoiling her.* And Avery turning to him and yelling, *I HATE YOU,* and shoving the table so hard that everything spilled. He slapped her face, and everything went quiet. But the quiet didn't last long because then his parents launched into a massive argument. Michael had cried, but Avery had seemed, even then, to enjoy the chaos she caused.

But now, Michael can't stand the thought that she's out there somewhere by herself. She's been out all night. She must be scared, maybe hurt. He feels a sense of dread that he cannot shake. *Why can't they find her?*

It's his fault. If he hadn't sent her home that one time, if he hadn't told her about the key, she probably would have waited for him yesterday. They'd both be going to school today, having a regular day. But instead, his family is in shock and he's sitting in the police station while the detectives question his parents. They're going to question him. He feels sick at the thought. What more do they want from him? He already told them what happened. He's sorry. He wishes he could do it over again, differently. But he can't, and now his little sister is missing.

He hears a door open down the hall, and soon the female detective appears in front of him. They've finished with his mom. It's his turn. He feels a paralyzing dread, like when he had to do a speech last year at a school assembly. But this is so much worse.

Gully says to him, "Michael, we're ready for you now. Come with me, we'll join your mother." Her voice is kind, and she's smiling at him.

He follows her into the small room and sees his mother seated at a table across from Detective Bledsoe. She stands up and he goes to her. She puts her arms around him and kisses him on top of his head. Lately, he'd been telling her not to do that, he's not a little kid anymore, but now he wants all the comfort she can give him.

"Have a seat," Bledsoe tells him. Michael sits down beside his mother. "This won't take long, son, so just relax."

Michael nods silently. He wants to please them.

"When you got home after school yesterday, after basketball practice," Bledsoe says, "was your father at the house?"

Michael is startled. He feels his mother stiffen beside him, as if she's afraid of what his answer might be. He glances up at her, but she's looking straight ahead of her, at the detectives.

"It's okay," Bledsoe says soothingly, "if you change your story now. We just want the truth. Can you do that? Can you tell us the truth, Michael?"

His mother is rigid beside him, but she doesn't say anything. He swallows nervously. "No. He wasn't there. Why are you asking me this?" His voice comes out a little shrill.

"Do you know if he'd been there, earlier, before you got home?"

Michael shakes his head in dismay. They're accusing his father. They think he did something to Avery. The world tilts. "No," he says. "He wasn't there, I swear. There was no one there. The house was empty."

"Okay," Bledsoe says. He waits a beat and then asks, "Did you change anything in the house, Michael? Tidy up, perhaps?"

"What?" He glances again at his mom, who looks appalled and ill. He turns back to the detective and says, rather wildly, "Why are you asking me that? I didn't do anything!"

"Okay, Michael, all right, we just had to ask, okay?" Bledsoe leans back in his chair and says, "You didn't hang up Avery's jean jacket, then?"

"No." He's telling them the truth. He didn't hang up the jacket. He didn't clean up. He didn't see his father. He's told them the truth, but they don't seem to believe him.

"How would you describe your dad, Michael?" the detective asks.

They think Dad did it, Michael worries. *They're wrong. Dad wasn't there. He's telling them the truth.* Finally, he says, "He's good. He's a good dad."

"Does he ever lose his temper with you?"

Michael shakes his head slowly. "No." The detective waits; he wants more. Michael doesn't want to say anything more. He wants this to end.

"Does he ever lose his temper with your sister?"

Now Michael can't look at his mother, he can't bear to. He doesn't know how to answer. He can feel time passing, until his silence is the answer they're looking for and it's too late.

"What did he do when he lost his temper with your sister?"

Michael swallows and says, "Sometimes he'd yell at her."

Bledsoe nods slowly. "Did he ever hit her?"

"Not really."

"It's a yes-or-no answer, Michael."

"He just slapped her sometimes, to calm her down."

"To calm her down," Bledsoe repeats.

"She deserved it," Michael says in his father's defense.

The two detectives shift their eyes to stare at his mother.

Ten

Gully follows Bledsoe, Erin, and Michael out of the interview room. They are all silent. They're done, for now. The revelations arising from these short interviews are disturbing. The father has no alibi. The father has a temper, has a history of losing it with his troubled daughter. He's been known to slap her on several occasions. This has caused friction between the parents, has soured the marriage, something the mother finally—reluctantly—admitted.

Bledsoe is a better interrogator than Gully expected. She was impressed. She can tell he thinks that William Wooler may have done something to his daughter. It's certainly possible. But she worries that Bledsoe will develop tunnel vision, fail to consider other possibilities. She's seen it happen before, with other detectives she's known. She will have to make sure that doesn't happen here.

. . .

NORA COMES DOWN to the kitchen to find Al and Ryan already there, eating breakfast and drinking coffee. She's usually the first one downstairs, but this morning she slept later than usual—she'd been awake most of the night, managing to fall asleep only in the darkest hour before dawn.

Now she pours herself a cup of coffee from the carafe. "Good morning," she says.

They both grunt back a reply.

Al has his laptop open on the kitchen table beside him, while Ryan scrolls on his phone. She hates having technology at the table, but today is different. She wants to scroll her phone, too, but she doesn't want to look too eager, and they know she never looks at her phone before breakfast. She doesn't quite know how to act, what the appropriate level of concern should be.

"What's the latest?" she asks, sipping her coffee, sitting down beside Al. Faith will be getting up soon.

Al looks up at her. "They haven't found her."

Nora's heart sinks.

"They're treating the Woolers' house as a crime scene," Al says.

"What?"

"Look," Al says, pushing the laptop toward her. The sight of the yellow tape across the Woolers' front porch—and what it signifies—distresses her. There are no further details. But it must mean they no longer believe that William's daughter was snatched on the way home from school. Nora's thoughts riot in her head. Did someone come into the house and take her? It defies belief. Nothing like this has ever happened in their town.

"I don't understand," she says stupidly.

"It's pretty clear," Al says. "They think something happened to her in the house. They probably think the dad did it."

She looks up at him in disbelief. "That's ridiculous," she says.

"Is it?" The look he gives her is hard to interpret.

Ryan quickly glances up at the two of them. Nora rises from the table and puts some bread in the toaster. But she does it for something to do; she doesn't know how she'll be able to force it down.

Al and Ryan leave the table and get ready to join the search—they're somber, tired, not as eager as the night before. Nora can't wait for them to leave. Once they're out the door, she searches for any other news on Al's laptop, but there's nothing else. She thinks of what Al said. She wonders if the police consider William a suspect. They always suspect the parents, don't they? She feels a chill of fear. He's a doctor, and highly respected in Stanhope. Well liked. It seems impossible that they might think him capable of doing his daughter harm.

She can't shake her feelings of guilt, that she and William are being punished for what they've done. She's terrified that the police will find William's secret phone. Of course they will, now, if they're treating the house as a crime scene. Collateral damage, that's what she will be. She and her family, destroyed. And then she's ashamed, because a little girl might be dead and she's thinking about how it will affect her.

She gets ready, with shaking hands, for her volunteer shift at the hospital, while Faith gets ready for school, which is sure to be dreadful. There will be lots of tears at school today, perhaps additional support for Avery's young classmates, to help them deal with it all.

Usually, Faith walks to school by herself. But today, Nora walks with her. She wants to hold her daughter's hand, the way she used to, but refrains. They walk past the Wooler house at the top of the street, with its heavy police presence, the crime-scene tape, the curtains drawn—and she thinks of him in there, with his wife, their world collapsing around them. She wonders if he thinks of her at all.

IT'S NOT QUITE nine o'clock Wednesday morning when Gully and Bledsoe finish with the Woolers. The family is being taken back to the hotel by a uniformed officer to retrieve their things; the technicians will soon have finished with the house, and they can return. They still have fingerprints to process, but they've found nothing of interest, no sign that the little girl was harmed inside the house, no evidence of blood hastily cleaned up. William's car has been transported to the crime lab, but they have left Erin's car there. They know Erin was at work until after Avery went missing. They have to hope they will find her somewhere, soon, Gully thinks, and still alive, but with each passing hour, that outcome becomes less likely. It's disappointing that the search has turned up nothing; even the sniffer dogs have come up empty.

Bledsoe says, "We have to consider the possibility that she may have been killed inside the house—strangled or smothered—and the best way to remove her body without the risk of being seen in broad daylight would be through the garage—in the trunk of the car, with the garage door closed. They've got a lock on the garage and an automatic garage-door opener—so the only ones who could have done that are the parents. And we know where the mother was."

Gully nods slowly. It's certainly a possibility that the father killed her and removed her from the house that way. She says, "If someone took her out the back and through the woods, our team would have found something."

But none of the officers doing the door-to-door have found anyone who saw Wooler's car entering or leaving the garage. No one seems to have seen anything the previous afternoon. No one saw Avery come home from school, or outside the house at all, alone or with someone else. There are no cameras in the area. No cameras in the intersections of the streets that lead to the Woolers' house. No one has seen anybody unusual hanging around the house or neighborhood, or a strange vehicle in the area. The tip line set up last night has resulted in nothing useful so far. If Avery got into a car, she could be anywhere by now. They have her description out across the state and the entire country. Everyone has their eyes out for Avery Wooler.

They've arranged with the parents to do an appeal, with them appearing on TV. They will bring them back to the police station for that at noon today. Maybe that will yield something, Gully thinks. She hopes so. Because so far they have nothing. Except for doubts about the missing girl's father.

WILLIAM CAN FEEL the heightened tension between him and his wife and son. It fairly crackles in the silent police car as they are driven back to the hotel. When they arrive, he tells Michael to gather his things in his room. He wants to talk to Erin, and he doesn't want Michael there.

Once inside their room he turns to her, his voice lowered so that

Michael can't overhear from the adjoining room, and says, "What did you tell them?"

She looks at him, frightened, angry, and fires back a question of her own. "Where were you yesterday afternoon? Why weren't you at work?"

He doesn't know what to tell her. How long can he keep spinning the lies? Surely they're going to find the phone any minute now, if they haven't already. Someone from the motel might come forward. But he's a coward—or maybe he's a ridiculous optimist, he doesn't know which. "I was burned out. I didn't feel like being at work—I went for a drive."

"For *three hours?*" she exclaims. "My God! They think you did something to Avery!"

"I didn't!" he says, remembering how his blow knocked Avery off her feet, and then deliberately blocking it all out.

She looks at him, her demeanor cold, almost detached. "They know that you lose your temper, that you slap Avery sometimes."

"You told them that?" Now he's angry at her, feels betrayed. He does lose his temper, he's not proud of it. He's ashamed of it. He's slapped his daughter on several occasions, but it was nothing like what his own father did to him. And unlike his own father, he was immediately swamped with remorse and guilt. And unlike his own mother, who did nothing to intervene, Erin instantly turned on him every time, more furious with *him* than with their rebellious, uncontrollable child.

And then somehow the problem always shifts; it's no longer a problem between the two of them and Avery, because of something she's done, or not done, it's a problem between him and Erin and it becomes not about Avery's behavior, but his. In the end, his wife always makes excuses for Avery, but never for him. She always points out with an annoying air of superiority that *he* is the adult. Avery is what has come between them; they both know it. The constant strain of dealing with her has set them at odds, pulled them apart. It has entrenched resentments, caused untold damage to their marriage. It's ruined them. Erin is more progressive, more patient; he's old-school and flies off the handle. They seldom agree at all anymore on how to handle Avery. They argue about it all the time, nurse resentments and grudges. They both worry about someone finding out, about Avery telling someone at school that her dad hits her, about the impact of it all on Michael. And now the police know their ugly little secret.

Now she's angry too. "Of course I didn't tell them! I'm not stupid. I know how it would look." She takes a deep breath and says miserably, "They put Michael on the spot. He had to tell them the truth. I couldn't call him a liar."

William feels like he's had a blow to the stomach. "Fuck," he says.

"Don't blame our son for this," his wife hisses. "This is on you."

Eleven

William walks up the driveway with his wife and son, past the shouting, surging journalists, past the yellow police tape. *When are they going to take that down?* he thinks angrily to himself.

He feels a stab of fear as he steps inside. The crime-scene team has been here all night. They can't have found the phone or they would have said something. But they've taken his car away, and they're going to go over it with a fine-tooth comb. What is he going to do when they find it? He will have to admit to the affair. He hates what it will do to Erin, especially now. How it will distort everything. And he doesn't want Nora dragged into it either. He will keep her name out of it. They used their phones sparingly, never addressing each other by name in their texts. He should have gotten rid of the damn phone.

They enter the house and find Detective Gully in the kitchen. William doesn't want to meet her eyes, now that she knows how dysfunctional this family is, now that she knows what kind of father he is.

"They've finished up. We can take the tape down," she says. "But there's something we need to discuss."

William's heart is in his throat. He glances at his wife, knowing that this will be what finishes them.

"The television appeal. It will be difficult, and we need to prepare you," Gully says.

GULLY HAS ARRANGED these things before. It's always stressful for the parents, and it shows. Erin is as white as a sheet and looks considerably worse than she did the previous day, Gully notes. Despite her natural stoicism, the strain is getting to her—that, and perhaps the fact that her husband's movements can't be accounted for. William seems agitated, distracted.

They hold the press conference at noon inside a room in the police station, with plenty of seating for the reporters, but still they spill out the door into the corridor. The distraught parents will take turns reading from a prepared statement, which they have formulated with Gully's help, with Michael standing quietly beside them. It will be televised, with photos of the missing girl on the screen and the tip line number running along the bottom. It's a bit of theater, to engage the interest and the help of the public. It's something they do to shake things up, see if anything falls out. It enables the parents to feel like they are doing something to help.

But it's also something they will be judged on. People will have opinions, and they won't hesitate to share them. Social media has made everything exponentially worse. Gully knows that people handle stress and grief in different ways. Some parents cry. Some can't cry because they're in shock. And some of those watching will interpret shock as coldness, as lack of feeling. *What can you do?* Gully thinks. A certain proportion of the public is always going to automatically think the parents had something to do with the disappearance of their little girl and interpret whatever they see in the parents' behavior as confirmation. *And they don't know the half of it*, Gully thinks to herself, remembering their interviews with Dr. Wooler, his wife, and his son earlier that morning.

The detectives know more than they're telling the public. They know Avery was in the house that afternoon, with someone else. They know the father has no alibi, that he has hit his daughter on occasion, that the marriage is strained because of it. They know that Avery wasn't wearing her jean jacket after all. But for now, they're not sharing any of that.

Bledsoe steps up to the mic and introduces himself. "Thank you for coming," he says. "Yesterday afternoon, Avery Wooler, age nine, left Ellesmere Elementary School at approximately three forty-five p.m. and walked home alone. She hasn't been seen since she left the school. She's four foot two inches, about sixty pounds, with blond hair and blue eyes. She was last seen wearing dark-blue jeans, a white T-shirt with daisies on the front, pink sneakers, and a dark-blue jean jacket. If you saw Avery or any suspicious person, activity, or vehicle in the vicinity where Avery went missing, or if you have any information that might be relevant, please call the number on your screen. Now, the parents are going to say a few words. Please be respectful. And they will take no questions."

Bledsoe steps away from the mic and beckons Erin and William forward while Gully watches intently.

Erin speaks first. She has a certain tragic dignity. Her voice is quiet and would be lost without the mic. She stares down at the paper, trembling in her hands. "Our daughter, Avery, is missing. She's a beautiful, smart little girl with her whole life ahead of her. We love her, and we want her back desperately. Please help us find her." She lifts her eyes and cameras flash, making her blink.

William takes the mic from her and reads. "Avery, if you can hear us, know that we love you and want you back more than anything." He seems to falter and then recovers. "If someone out there has our daughter, we beg you, please return her to us. Leave her in a safe place. That's all we ask. She's just a little girl. You can let her go. If you let her go, everything can still be all right."

NORA, IN STREET CLOTHES, but wearing a lanyard that identifies her as a hospital volunteer, hurries down the corridor toward the lounge, her shoes squeaking on the floor tiles, just before noon. She knows they're going to be broadcasting a live television appeal about Avery—everyone has been talking about it, and she knows that they'll have the television on in the lounge. Nora is desperate to see William, even if it's only through a television screen; she hasn't seen him since they parted at the motel, and so much has happened since then. She needs to study his face, try to intuit how he's doing. As she enters the lounge, with the television mounted near the ceiling in the corner, she sees that it's crowded with staff—everyone who can possibly manage it is here.

They are all worried about Dr. Wooler and his missing daughter. Nora sits down in one of the last remaining seats, beside Marion Cooke, one of the nurses she works with regularly, who also happens to live on Connaught Street. Marion glances at her briefly and turns her attention quickly back to the screen. Dr. Vezna looks particularly upset, Nora notes, as do a couple of the nurses. Nora wonders what her own face looks like. She glances around the room. They are all colleagues of Dr. Wooler's; they all like and respect him. He's known to be smart, caring, and hardworking; many of them have been working with him for years. Everyone has been upset at work today.

And then Nora remembers the phone. When that comes out, everyone in this room will know about their affair. She suddenly feels light-headed.

It's completely silent in the lounge as the appeal begins. After the words from the detective, Avery's mother speaks. Nora stares at her, hardly recognizing her. She remembers Erin as a very attractive woman—she has seen her at hospital events—but you wouldn't know it now. And then it's William's turn. Nora can't bear it, seeing the pain and fear on William's face as he reads into the microphone. And then he's speaking as if directly to the person who has taken his daughter, begging for her safe return. She can't believe for a single moment that he isn't sincere. Nobody could doubt him, she thinks, watching him. She glances at Dr. Vezna, who has a hand pressed against her mouth. Others around her are in various states of stoicism or distress. It's like being at a funeral, Nora thinks, but pushes the thought away. She can't bear to think of William's daughter being missing—or dead. She wills herself not to cry. She feels for the tissue in the pocket of her trousers.

Marion, sitting beside her, is one of the stoic ones. But she is the first to get up and leave when it's over. Nora knows how Marion feels about William and suspects Marion wants to be alone.

Twelve

The search presses on, but there is no sign of Avery. Gully knows it's a race against time; with each passing hour, the chance of finding her alive diminishes.

Immediately after the television appeal, however, the tips start to come in. Uniformed officers take the calls and follow up on every one of them, except for the truly outlandish. For a town that prides itself on its sense of community, of looking after one another, there's a surprising number of people willing to tell the police that someone they know is strange or might be a pervert. Like in small towns everywhere, Gully sighs to herself, the mindset can be narrower than in a large metropolis.

Gully is in the large room they've established as the command post when Bledsoe approaches her. She looks up.

Giving her a meaningful glance, Bledsoe says, "You'll never guess what they just found in William Wooler's car."

"Avery's DNA in the trunk," Gully says grimly.

He shakes his head. "No, they're still processing. But they found a pay-as-you-go phone, hidden inside the rear-seat armrest."

Gully is taking this in when an officer approaches the two of them and says, "Someone here to see you."

ERIN IS SITTING, almost catatonic, on the sofa in her living room. She is tortured by thoughts of Avery. Where is she? Is she being held somewhere? Erin can't breathe for a moment. She must stop imagining it. She must cling to hope, focus on getting Avery back.

The police have stopped treating the house as a crime scene, at least. Maybe now they will put more effort into looking for Avery instead of seeing them as possible suspects. But she thinks uneasily about her husband. Why wasn't he at work for all that time yesterday afternoon? What the hell was he doing going out for a drive when he was supposed to be at work? Is he hiding something from her?

"You should eat something," William coaxes her. "You've barely eaten since . . ." he falters, "yesterday."

She doesn't answer, just regards him silently. Michael, unable to bear any of it anymore, has retreated to his bedroom, probably to lose himself in his computer games. She's on the verge of asking her husband again what he was doing the afternoon before, but he speaks first.

"I'm going to make you some toast. And some tea. Okay?" William says solicitously.

He retreats to the kitchen. At least they are being left alone now, she thinks, after the miserable morning. Such an ordeal, all of it—the distressing questioning at the station, coming home from the hotel and preparing for the appeal, the appearance on television. She could feel her hands trembling during the entire thing. She can't bear to watch it. But the TV is on low in the living room, and the appeal plays on the local channel every hour. They are trying. They are all trying.

William brings in the buttered toast and tea and sets it on the coffee table in front of her. The aroma suddenly makes her realize how hungry she is; William is right, she hasn't eaten since lunchtime yesterday. She hadn't been able to touch that muffin this morning.

There's a knock at the door and they both freeze.

"Who's that?" Erin asks, her stomach clenching. She can't possibly see anyone right now. Not even well-meaning friends. She has had William turn everyone away. She wants to hide until all this is over.

"I don't know," William says, and walks over to the living-room window and peers through a gap in the curtains in the direction of the front door. "Fuck," he says vehemently. "It's those fucking detectives." He immediately seems agitated, on guard.

She's taken aback at his reaction. "Maybe they have news," she says. "Maybe they've found her." She feels a sudden alarming combination of hope and fear that makes her dizzy.

William goes to the door and lets them in; Erin doesn't think that she can stand. The toast and tea sit on the coffee table, untouched.

Bledsoe and Gully come into the living room where they have already spent so much time. They sit down in the same armchairs as before, as William joins her on the sofa.

"Have you found her?" Erin asks, her voice unsteady.

Gully shakes her head, and Bledsoe says, "I'm afraid not. Not yet." He looks directly at her husband and lets a long pause develop.

Erin starts to feel frightened. *What's going on here?*

"We have had a tip, though," Bledsoe says, continuing to stare at William. "Someone saw something after all." He waits a beat. "One of your neighbors saw your car, Dr. Wooler, enter your garage at around four o'clock yesterday afternoon."

Erin turns to look at her husband in horror.

WILLIAM IS BACK at the police station in the same interview room he was in earlier that morning. "Do I have a choice?" he'd asked Bledsoe back at the house.

"Not really," Bledsoe had said. "You'd better read him his rights, Gully."

His wife didn't even get up off the sofa as they took him away. She was not on his side. Not anymore. She wouldn't be ever again after this, he thought. They were done. She would hate him. And Michael would too.

William has told them he doesn't need a lawyer because he hasn't done anything wrong. He wonders if this is a mistake, but he already looks bad, and he doesn't want to look worse.

They tell him he's being videotaped, and they begin.

"We have a witness who saw your car going into your garage at around four o'clock yesterday afternoon," Bledsoe says.

At first, he denies it. He wants to deny that any of this is happening at all. He shakes his head. "No. That's impossible. I wasn't there."

"But someone saw you there, William," Bledsoe says. "One of your neighbors saw you. And then he went away overnight on business and didn't come into the station to let us know until this morning. You've got some explaining to do."

William places both hands over his face and begins to sob. He sobs as if he's broken. He *is* broken. He will never survive this. But as he cries, and the detectives watch, he realizes that there is an instinct for survival deep inside him somewhere. Finally, he pulls himself together and wipes his eyes with his hands. Gully pushes a box of tissues at him. They're waiting, as he stares down at the table. They think they've solved the case, the smug bastards, he thinks. Well, it's not that simple.

"I didn't do anything to her," he says. "I don't know where she is." The detectives simply look at him, waiting. "I was there," he admits at last, sensing his own doom. They'll never believe him. "I decided to go home early for a change. I thought the house would be empty. It was Tuesday, and Michael had basketball practice and Avery had choir, and I thought they wouldn't be home until about a quarter to five."

"Go on," Bledsoe nudges, when he stops.

"It's just that I never get to be alone," he says. "There's always people around—I have such a busy practice, I'm run off my feet at the hospital, and everyone's in the house when I'm home, and I just needed some space. I'm only ever alone when I'm in my car." How stupid he sounds. Gully nods as if she understands, but Bledsoe doesn't move at all, not even a twitch. "But when I went into the kitchen, Avery was there." Gully seems sympathetic, so he talks to her. "I hung up her jacket, because she'd thrown it on the kitchen floor." He can't go on.

"Okay," Bledsoe says, "what happened then?"

William swallows. "I asked her what she was doing at home by herself. And she told me she got into trouble and was kicked out of choir. I told her that she should have waited for her brother, but she got really mouthy with me. I lost it and—I slapped her." He stops. It was much more than a slap, but he's not going to tell them that. He's not going to tell them everything.

"And then?" Bledsoe asks.

"I apologized! I told her I was sorry, that I should never have slapped her. That I loved her, and I should have behaved better. But she wouldn't say anything or look at me." He looks Bledsoe in the eye and says, "And then I left."

He can tell Bledsoe doesn't believe him. "That's why I was so certain she must have run away, at least initially," William rushes on. "You see? She was angry at me for slapping her, so she must have left the house again after I did, and someone took her, and you have to find her—"

Gully interjects. "Why didn't you tell us before that you were in the house, that you were the one who hung up her jacket? It might have saved us a lot of time."

"Because I knew how it would look—that you'd assume I'd done something with her, but obviously I didn't."

"It's not obvious to me," Bledsoe says heavily.

William looks back at the detective, afraid.

Bledsoe leans in closer to William over the table. "You were there. You had an argument and you slapped her. No one has seen her since. No one saw her leave the house. I think she left the house in the trunk of your car."

William feels himself go pale. "No." He shakes his head. "No, that's ridiculous. That's not what happened."

Bledsoe leans back in his chair again and says, "You'd think a father who wanted his daughter back more than anything would have told us that he'd been there, that he'd hung up her jacket. An innocent father who wanted to see his daughter alive again wouldn't have lied to the police." He adds, "To his wife."

The detective's face swims before William's eyes. He feels a tightness in his chest.

"We're having your car processed in the lab—every square inch. We'll soon know if your daughter was in the trunk of your car." Bledsoe leans in even closer. "We've already found something else in your car."

William slumps in his chair. He feels like he's had all the stuffing kicked out of him. Finally, he says, "That has nothing to do with my daughter."

Bledsoe says, "An untraceable phone, so carefully hidden. You have a lot of secrets, Dr. Wooler."

"I was having an affair," he says bluntly.

"With who?"

"I can't tell you that."

The detectives wait, staring him down. At length, Bledsoe says, "That car of yours—the Infiniti G37 sedan—it's new, isn't it?" William nods. "The burner phone was unexpected. I can understand how it was missed in the initial search of the car in your garage. There's a secret compartment in the rear-seat armrest, something put there by the carmaker, but not widely known. It's there if you google it. You obviously knew about it. Is that why you bought *that* car, Dr. Wooler?"

William denies it. "I didn't know, I discovered it by accident." It's a lie. He did know. It *was* one of the reasons he bought that particular car. He was just beginning his affair with Nora. He remembers how excited he was the day he drove it off the lot.

"What we're seeing here, Dr. Wooler," Bledsoe says, "is a pattern of deceit."

"I didn't hurt my daughter," William protests. "I was having an affair. That's why I had the phone. That's where I was yesterday afternoon, before I went home. I was in a motel, with another woman. I wasn't driving around, like I said. That's why I lied—I didn't want my wife to know."

"What motel?" Bledsoe asks.

"The Breezes Motel, on Route Nine."

"What time did you leave the motel?"

"About three forty-five. I came home, saw my daughter briefly, and left again. She was fine when I left her."

"What time was it when you left your house?"

"I don't know exactly, about four twenty."

"And where did you go after you left your house?" Bledsoe asks.

William swallows. "Then I really did go for a drive."

"And your cell phone records will confirm that?" Bledsoe says.

He'd turned off his cell phone when he met Nora at the motel. He always did—he didn't want them to be disturbed. He had his pager if the hospital needed to get hold of him. And he turned off his burner phone, too, once he'd texted Nora the unit number of the motel and she'd replied. He hadn't turned his cell back on until shortly after five. He knows how it will look. There's nothing he can do about that. He swallows and says, "I turned my phone off."

A long pause develops, stretches out. At last, Bledsoe says, "Did you now?"

Thirteen

Nora returns home from her shift at the hospital mid-afternoon. She's been scrolling through the news throughout the day whenever she can. But now she turns on her laptop and discovers footage of William being led out of his house by the detectives, surrounded by the press, of his being taken into the police station for questioning earlier that afternoon. It's alarming. She learns that it's the second time he's been questioned at the police station that day. *Why? Why are they focusing on William?* It's been almost twenty-four hours since Avery went missing, and there is no sign of her. The police obviously seem to think William had something to do with it. Nora knows that can't be true. She can't imagine what he must be going through. Terrified for his missing daughter. And suspected, maybe accused.

Her husband and son return home shortly after her, cold and hungry after long hours of searching. They sit down at the kitchen

table while she makes them sandwiches to tide them over till supper. She prepares the food as if in a trance. Ryan is quiet, but Al
tells her what it was like, prodding the ground with sticks, looking for freshly turned earth in the woods—the sign of a shallow
grave—the mood growing more hopeless as nothing is found. "She
must be dead by now," he says. "That's what everybody thinks, you
can tell. They think the father did it—and him a doctor."

She turns on him. "What? What do you mean?"

He looks at her as if in surprise. "It's all over the news," he says.
"They've taken him in for questioning again. My guess is they'll
arrest him soon. The sick bastard."

And as he looks at her, there's something different in her husband's eye, a gleam of something, something nasty she doesn't like.
There's something in his expression. Where is this coming from? Her
heart suddenly seizes—*Does he know? About her and William? Is he
enjoying her suffering?* Maybe he's not as oblivious as she assumed.
Had he followed her, seen them together at the motel? She feels the
tension, suddenly thick in the room. Does he know that William
is her lover—is that what's going on here?

She's becoming paranoid—it's been creeping up on her and now
the paranoia is overwhelming her. It's only a matter of time before
the police knock on her door because they know about her and
William and it all comes out.

She can't bear to look at her husband any longer and turns her
attention to her son. Ryan's a million miles away from her—she
hardly knows her boy anymore, and they used to be so close. She
studies him now, bent over the kitchen table, eating his sandwich.
She wonders what's going through his mind.

. . .

WHILE WILLIAM is at the police station for the second time that day, Erin waits. She can't eat, but her anger gives her nourishment and an energy she hasn't had since Avery went missing. William was seen, here—entering the garage—around four o'clock yesterday. They know Avery was in the house. She's terrified that she is about to learn the truth about what happened to her daughter.

It's like she's split in two, holding two contradictory ideas in her mind at the same time. Part of her simply can't believe it, but another part of her can. She's seen how angry William can get at Avery, how he strikes out at her. She understands it because Avery pushes her to fury sometimes too.

She remembers a birthday party for one of Avery's classmates when she was six years old. Erin took her, anxious about how it might go, because Avery was often difficult, especially around other children. She didn't share well. She didn't seem to know how to get along with other kids. Avery started causing problems right away, pushing another girl roughly in a game of musical chairs and being accused of cheating. Erin was mortified. It got worse from there. She can still remember the embarrassment she felt at the other women's pinched smiles, one woman saying, "Somebody's having a bad day." When the birthday girl started opening her presents, and Avery was grabbing them from her, Erin decided it was time to leave. But Avery refused, throwing a tantrum and hitting her mother. Erin managed to apologize to everyone and keep her cool as they left the house. But once she'd physically carried a squirming, hitting Avery to the car and strapped her in, Erin drove around the corner, pulled the car to the side of the street, and wept uncontrollably, out of frustration, embarrassment, and fury.

Avery's behavior hurts Erin too. It's worn her down, destroyed her confidence as a mother. But the difference between her and William is that William lashes out at their daughter, and she doesn't. What if he'd had enough? And she wasn't there to stop him for once? She can imagine it, she can see it happening—William hitting Avery, or shaking her so hard her neck snaps. Maybe he pushed her, and she struck her head. It would have been an accident. He wouldn't have meant it. He would have tried to save her. He would have felt terrible. He would have lied about it. Maybe William *has* lied to her, lied to the police. What other lies has he told over the course of their marriage? Now she is terribly afraid that Avery is dead, that her husband might have killed her in an uncontrolled moment, and she doesn't know how she and Michael will ever manage to go on.

But they have been married for almost fifteen years. She can't believe that he would do this. It's impossible. Maybe the detectives are making it up about his being seen, trying to trap him in some way.

Erin watches from the living-room window, behind the curtain. She doesn't want to be seen by the reporters outside. As time passes, she knows that one of two things will happen. Either William will come home with a reasonable explanation—perhaps the detectives will admit they invented the witness, to rattle him—or the detectives will come and tell her that he has confessed, and she will know what happened to her daughter.

A police cruiser pulls up in front of the house. She watches William get out.

. . .

GULLY HAS SPOKEN to the officers who interviewed Avery's teachers at the elementary school. They all agreed that Avery is very bright, but there were behavioral problems, challenges. She was defiant. She told lies. The staff was pretty sure that an act of vandalism—stuffing a toilet in the girls' bathroom with paper and causing a flood—was done by Avery, who claimed she'd seen another girl do it. But other than getting a better picture of what Avery was like, they got nothing. None of her teachers had noticed anyone hanging around the school that day or in the preceding days. No strange men skulking outside the school fence, following her home. No strange vehicles on the street. No one taking an interest in Avery.

In any event, they now know Avery's father was in the house with her yesterday afternoon, that he was the one who hung up her jacket. If he's telling the truth and *didn't* harm her, then she must have left the house again and met with foul play. Gully knows Bledsoe thinks William Wooler killed his daughter and got rid of the body. But she's trying to keep an open mind—at least until forensics is finished with Dr. Wooler's car.

She's just been to the Breezes Motel and discovered that the security cameras there haven't been in working order for some time. They don't know the identity of William Wooler's lover. No one at the motel remembers ever seeing her, just him. The desk clerk recognized him. He used a different name and paid in cash. He was there yesterday afternoon, as usual, but the clerk didn't know when he left. It would be good to talk to this other woman, Gully thinks, if only to learn more about William Wooler, his state of mind that day. Maybe his lover knows more than his wife.

Now she heads back to the Woolers' neighborhood. Maybe she'll learn something from Avery's only friend, Jenna, who lives across the street. She must be home from school by now.

Gully parks outside the Wooler residence and walks across the street to the Setons' house. She rings the doorbell and waits, thinking about what's going on in the Wooler house behind her. She imagines William telling his wife what he told them. She can't begin to imagine what Erin Wooler will feel then.

The door is answered by a woman in her late thirties, with a pretty, pleasant face. "Mrs. Seton?" The woman nods. Gully pulls out her identification and introduces herself. "I'm investigating the disappearance of Avery Wooler." The woman's face becomes serious. A girl with long dark hair approaches and stares at Gully from beside her mother. "And you must be Jenna," Gully says, smiling warmly at her. The girl nods.

"Come in," the woman says, opening the door wide. She leads her into the kitchen, and Jenna sits down at the table. "The police officers were already around and spoke to all of us yesterday. Unfortunately, none of us saw anything."

Gully says, "I'm really here to talk to Jenna, if that's all right?"

Jenna's mother glances at her daughter protectively. "Would that be all right, Jenna? Are you okay talking about Avery?"

"Yes," Jenna answers, but she looks nervous.

Gully sits down across from her while her mother watches them, leaning against the kitchen counter, arms folded.

"You're friends with Avery, right?" Gully asks.

Jenna nods. "We're in the same grade. In the same class."

Gully smiles encouragingly. "Did Avery ever tell you anything she was worried about?" Jenna shakes her head. "Did she ever mention whether someone was bothering her?" She shakes her head again. Gully lowers her voice. "Did she tell you any secrets?"

Now Jenna hesitates, then says, "Yes. But they're secrets, so I can't tell you. I promised not to tell."

Gully glances up at Jenna's mother, who looks worried.

"You can tell me, though," Gully says, "because I'm a police detective. And I'm trying to find Avery and bring her home safe. We're all very worried about her."

Jenna bites her lip and glances anxiously at her mother. "But you can't ever tell Avery that I told you."

"I won't, I promise," Gully says.

"Because if you tell her, she'll kill me."

"I understand," Gully reassures her.

Jenna's face turns pink. "She said she had a boyfriend."

"A boyfriend?"

Jenna nods. "He's older than us."

"How much older?" Gully asks.

Jenna shrugs. "I don't know. She wouldn't tell me who he was." She adds, "She liked to tease me like that." Her skin flushes deeper. "But she said he did things to her. Grown-up things."

Fourteen

When Michael hears his father come home, he creeps out of his room to listen unobserved, at the top of the stairs. He doesn't know why the detectives came back for his father; he'd had his headphones on in his room and hadn't even known the detectives were here, but his mother told him where his father was. He wonders if this is his fault, too, for telling the truth about his dad slapping Avery. It's all his fault. He wants to run away. Be someone else. Anybody but Michael Wooler. But he's been waiting, his headphones off, anxiously listening for his father's return.

It isn't hard to hear what his parents have to say, because they are raising their voices. He's troubled to hear his father crying. He's never heard his father cry. He's even more troubled to hear him admit, through sobs, that he was home yesterday afternoon and saw Avery. That the police know. That they seem to think he had something to do with her disappearance.

"Did you?" his mother asks, in the coldest voice he's ever heard. Michael almost passes out.

"What? Are you out of your mind?" his father rails. "Of course not! How can you even ask me that? I saw her, and I left again. We had an argument. I slapped her, that's all. I felt terrible and I left. She was fine when I left her. I swear to you."

"You lied to the police! You lied to *me!*" his mother screams. "How can I believe anything you say?" She turns the full force of her anger on him. "This is all your fault—*you left her here, alone, and now she's gone!*" There's a long, terrible silence, and then his mother cries, "What were you even doing here?"

His father says, his voice anguished, "There's something else you should know."

Michael wants to run back to his room and cover his head with his pillow. He doesn't want to hear any more. But he can't move; he's frozen in place.

His father sounds utterly miserable. "I've been having an affair. The police know."

Michael's entire body is trembling as he sits through another long pause.

"Who is she?" his mother asks, her voice so full of venom it's almost unrecognizable.

"I can't tell you. But it's over now. I was with her yesterday afternoon. She ended it. That's why I came home."

Michael hears a resounding *smack*; what can only be the sound of his mother slapping his father's face. "Get out," she cries. "Get out and never come back!"

Michael runs back to his room and puts his headphones on to shut it all out.

DETECTIVE BLEDSOE looks back at her in disbelief. "Do you think she was making it up?"

"Who? Jenna or Avery?" Gully asks.

"Either."

Gully sighs heavily. "I think Jenna was telling the truth. But Avery? I don't know, to be honest. Avery seems to have a history of telling lies. But it could be true." She takes a breath, lets it out. "Look, she's nine. She's not allowed to walk home from school alone because there's a busy street to cross, and she apparently can't be trusted to wait for the light. But we know she's allowed to play on the street, and in the woods behind the house, and at that tree house, unsupervised. It's possible someone has been taking advantage of her. If so, it's probably someone close by. She has so few friends—it makes her vulnerable." Gully pauses, thinking about the lonely girl who had written in her diary. "It's a lead we need to follow up."

Bledsoe shakes his head. "Our priority right now is Wooler, and where he might have taken her. We've been trying to pin down his movements that day, now that we know he was at the house. He says he left at about four twenty. By the time his cell was back on shortly after five, he was here"—he points to a map on the wall—"on Route Nine. When his wife called him at five twenty, he was here"—he moves his finger south—"about twenty minutes north of Stanhope, not far from the Breezes Motel, actually, and we've confirmed he arrived home at five forty, so he went straight home after he spoke to his wife. If he killed her, he didn't have much time to get rid of the body—an hour, roughly. We'll shift our search to where he could have dumped her, given what we now know. That will narrow things down." He looks at Gully. "They've already started, but I'd like you to get out there."

NOW, AS NIGHT FALLS, the darkness seems to bring despair with it, Gully thinks. Avery has been missing more than twenty-eight hours. The search of the woods and fields and the immediate neighborhood near the Wooler house has ended. Now efforts are being concentrated in the area along Route 9, which William Wooler could have reached between when he left the house at approximately 4:20 and received his wife's call at 5:20.

Gully joins the search that spreads out along the highway. There's a mix of commercial properties, empty lots, dumpsters, and housing, petering out to empty land, much of it wooded, on either side of the highway. The river lies close by to the west. He might have dumped her in a field, in the woods, or in the river. Efforts are redoubled.

As Gully searches, she finds herself hoping that William Wooler is innocent, because if he isn't, Avery's body is likely out here somewhere. She hopes desperately that Avery is still alive, that she's just a runaway, that she'll turn up, that they'll find her in time. But she knows the awful statistics—that about 75 percent of children who are abducted and killed are murdered within the first three hours of when they were taken, 88 percent within twenty-four hours. She knows the odds are against them.

ALICE SETON HAD told her husband about the detective coming to their house. She'd called him at work as soon as the detective left and Jenna was busy in her room. He didn't like it at all. That made two of them.

Now Pete is home, Jenna and her brother are in their bedrooms, and they're discussing it in quiet voices in the living room. She tells him again what Jenna said, about Avery having an older "boyfriend."

Her husband shakes his head and says, "That's sick."

She agrees; she feels the same revulsion.

"I don't like that they're friends," Pete says.

And then they both feel uncomfortable, because Avery is missing, possibly dead, and a friendship between the two girls is probably not something they're going to have to worry about now. He amends, "I just mean I don't think she's a good influence, if she was saying things like that to Jenna."

Alice nods. She knows what men are like, how they prey on women and girls. Pete's a good man, of course. Lots of men are. But there are plenty of bad ones out there. And she really fears that one of them may have been taking advantage of Avery, and it's horrible, just horrible, even to think about.

Alice says, "Someone might have been molesting her. That's obviously what the detective thought." He looks back at her, his face filled with disgust. "And what if whoever it was took her? What if he has her right now—locked away somewhere?" Alice says. "It scares me. It makes me afraid for Jenna. What if it's someone from around here?" Pete puts his arm around her shoulders. Alice hesitates and then says, "There's that boy down the street."

"What boy?" her husband asks.

Fifteen

Ryan isn't working this evening either. After spending most of his day volunteering in the search for Avery, he spends the rest of his time holed up in his room. Most of his friends recently left for college. He's at loose ends. He wishes he'd been able to go away to school this year too.

He thinks about what was going on between his parents, earlier, in the kitchen. His dad seemed almost to be toying with his mother somehow, when he was talking about Dr. Wooler. It was weird, the way his dad was looking at her—as if he were trying to hurt her. Why would he do that? He keeps worrying at it like a sore tooth, but the only reason Ryan can think of is that his father thinks something is going on between Dr. Wooler and his mother. Something more than that they just work at the same hospital. The idea upsets him.

But it might explain the way his mother's been acting ever since Avery Wooler went missing.

. . .

AL BLANCHARD WATCHES the eleven o'clock news in the living room with his wife. He doesn't usually watch the late news, but he wouldn't miss it tonight. He keeps a furtive eye on Nora, slumped against the arm of the sofa, deliberately ignoring him. She doesn't seem to want him here. There's a new coldness between them, an overt animosity, a change from the usual indifference. She didn't like what he said earlier about the missing girl's father. Well, she wouldn't, would she?

He knows what William Wooler is to her. He realizes he'd been waiting for this all his married life. A beautiful woman like her; he couldn't believe his luck when she'd married him. He should have paid her more attention, shouldn't have taken her for granted. He should have addressed the restlessness in her somehow before she'd found a lover, before she'd crossed the line. He's pretty sure that Wooler has been the only one, and that it started last summer. She'd been a good wife up until then. A good wife and a good mother. He himself has always been faithful, has never so much as looked in another woman's direction. In their marriage, she was the one who seemed to have a midlife crisis, perhaps afraid of losing her youth, her attractiveness. If it had been him, he would have just bought a new, sportier car. What is the women's equivalent? Surely they don't all have an affair when they start to fear their youth and beauty are leaving them. He's just lucky, he thinks bitterly.

He should have taken her to Europe last summer. She was unhappy in the spring, despondent—well, they were all under a terrific strain at that time. And then she'd started volunteering at the hospital, and she'd seemed to come out of it and gradually became brighter again, more cheerful. Sometimes he'd catch her looking at herself in the mirror, straightening her shoulders, lifting her chin, tilting it this way and that. She'd always gone regularly to the gym, but then she bought new makeup, some new clothes to wear at the hospital. She started smiling more, humming while she washed the dishes. At first, he'd congratulated himself on not wasting the money on a trip to Europe after all—he doesn't really like to travel. What a fool he was. And now she's in love with someone else. Someone the police think murdered his own child. And he's enjoying it. He's enjoying seeing her suffer. It's a just punishment, isn't it? For what she's been doing?

When they go to church on Sundays, and he sits beside her in the pew, he doesn't listen to the sermon anymore. Instead, he thinks about what's going through her mind. Is she thinking about her lover? About what they do in that motel room? Is she asking the Lord for forgiveness? *Does she feel guilty at all about the sin she's committing?*

Sometimes, beside her in church, he wonders if they're both imagining the carnal activity that goes on in that motel room. Then he starts to look around the church and wonder how many of the women there are cheating on *their* husbands, and how many men are cheating on their wives, and still showing up at church every Sunday. He knows there is sin everywhere. He just didn't think it was in his own house.

The truth is, Al has been afraid to confront her all these weeks because where his wife is concerned, he is a coward. He was afraid she would look at him, make a cool calculation, and decide that she'd rather leave him and get a divorce. They'd have to live apart and share the kids. She could continue to carry on seeing William Wooler and not have to bother with him. She'd probably be happier.

But now, Al thinks, maybe Wooler will end up going to prison for murder. Wouldn't that be perfect? Al feels terrible about the little girl, but if this had to happen to anyone, he's glad it's happened to William Wooler. And Nora will learn an important lesson. *The wages of sin is death.* If the man she chose to fall in love with is a murderer, Al doubts his wife will ever cheat again.

The newscaster is now turning to the Avery Wooler disappearance, and Al directs his attention to the television. There's footage of William Wooler coming out of the police station that afternoon, being accosted by media, looking shocked and haggard. Then a reporter standing live outside the police station, her hair blowing in the wind, says that a witness has come forward claiming to have seen Dr. William Wooler's car entering his garage at approximately 4:00 p.m. the day before.

Al is surprised; this is new. They didn't mention anything earlier about Wooler being home yesterday afternoon. They seemed to believe Avery had gone missing on the way home from school. If someone saw Wooler at the house that afternoon, that changes everything. He must have kept that from the police, and now he's been found out. That must be why they're treating the house as a crime scene.

He glances at his wife. She's staring at the television, rigid, her face washed out in the pale light. He almost feels sorry for her. It must be hard, he thinks, realizing you've been sleeping with a murderer. That you're in love with a monster.

. . .

NORA STARES UNBLINKING at the television. She's so cold all of a sudden, as if all the warmth has gone out of the room. It can't be true what they're saying, that William was at home that afternoon. Why didn't he tell them that in the first place, if it's true? What's going on here? William couldn't have hurt his daughter. Not the William she knows.

She clenches her hands together in her lap, quietly panicking. She doesn't want Al, sitting in the nearby chair, to see how much this upsets her. She's almost convinced now that Al already knows about her and William, or at least suspects. The police will find his phone. The police might knock on her door any minute, wanting to talk to her. Al will know everything then. Never in all her worst imaginings of their affair being discovered did she imagine it unfolding like this.

If they come, what will she tell them? She won't be able to deny the affair. But she can tell them the truth—she doesn't believe for a minute that William harmed his daughter. She will defend him to her last breath. But her own life, at least as she knows it, will be over. What will happen to her? To her children? She will have destroyed her family, in the most shameful and scandalous way, and they will hate her for it.

Finally, she turns off the television and they go upstairs to bed. It's not the first time that she wishes she and Al slept in separate bedrooms. For the second night in a row, she finds it hard to fall asleep, staring wide-eyed at the ceiling, thinking about William. But this time she's asking herself why he went to his house yesterday afternoon, and why he lied about it.

Sixteen

It's late, and Gully should probably be at home, getting some much-needed sleep. But she's called in at the station after being out with the search, trying to warm up with a hot chocolate, when Officer Weeks approaches her.

"Just had a call on the tip line," he says. He seems excited. "Caller says she saw Avery get into a car at the end of the street yesterday, outside her house, where Connaught turns into Greenley, at about four thirty in the afternoon."

Gully's fatigue evaporates and her pulse begins to race. "She's sure it was Avery?"

"Said she recognized her. Said she couldn't see the driver but knew whose car it was. Belongs to a man who lives on the Woolers' street." He adds ruefully, "She wouldn't give her name, and hung up on me."

"Shit," Gully says. Gully hates these anonymous callers. It could be a prank. But it could be a lead, and they need to check it out.

Why did the woman wait so long to call? It's been more than a day since Avery went missing. If the woman is telling the truth, she must be local, to have recognized whose car it was. She probably lives on the same long street.

Gully checks her watch. It's after midnight, but she'd better call Bledsoe at home. "What's the man's name?" she asks Weeks.

"Ryan Blanchard."

NORA IS LYING sleepless in bed, on her side, staring at the digital clock on her night table while Al snores loudly beside her. It's 1:11 in the morning. When she hears the doorbell ring, she nearly jumps out of her skin. When it rings again, she quickly rises from the bed, pulling her robe on. Al is still sound asleep as she leaves the room. It's the middle of the night. Who else could it be but the police?

She moves down the stairs in trepidation. She opens the front door and sees two people in plain clothes on her doorstep, a man and a woman, as the cold of the autumnal night creeps in. The man holds up his badge and introduces himself as Detective Bledsoe. She recognizes him from the television. She doesn't catch his partner's name, she's too frightened for it to register. She holds her robe tight to her neck. She feels so vulnerable in her nightclothes.

"Mrs. Blanchard?" the detective says.

"Yes."

"Sorry for the late hour. May we come in?"

She lets them in. What else can she do? She feels herself growing colder and colder and pulls her robe more tightly around her. She begins to tremble. She finally brings herself to face them, flooded with shame. Adultery is a sin. And now everyone will know.

"We'd like to talk to your son, Ryan," Bledsoe says. "Is he here?"

"What?" she asks. They're not making sense. Why do they want to talk to Ryan?

"We need to talk to your son. Is he home?" Detective Bledsoe repeats.

"He's in bed."

"Can you get him up, please?"

She turns away from them and makes her way upstairs and opens the door to her son's room, her mind all over the place. She's thinking, *Not again*. She can't face Ryan getting into trouble for drugs again. She flicks on the light. He doesn't respond. She moves over to the bed and shakes him by the shoulder and says urgently, "Ryan, the police are here. They want to talk to you."

He looks up at her groggily. "What? Why?"

"I don't know."

On the landing, Al appears at their bedroom door. "What's going on?" he asks, rubbing the sleep from his eyes.

Nora says, "The police are here. They want to talk to Ryan." She sees the immediate concern on her husband's face.

Her husband grabs a robe and the three of them go downstairs. Nora keeps her eyes on her son, in T-shirt and pajama bottoms, his hair sticking up at odd angles. But what she notes most is how worried he looks when he sees the detectives standing in the downstairs hall.

"Let's go into the living room," Nora suggests, functioning on automatic pilot, something awful in the pit of her stomach. None of this feels real. She can't do this. Not again.

They all sit down and face one another.

Detective Bledsoe says, "Ryan, do you mind telling us where you were Tuesday afternoon?"

Nora's simmering anxiety escalates to genuine fear. *What is going on here?* She glances at Al, who looks alarmed. Then she looks back at Ryan, who suddenly seems very young and overwhelmed.

"I, um, I have to think," he says.

"Take your time," Bledsoe says, as if humoring him. Nora immediately dislikes the detective.

"My shift at work was canceled yesterday," Ryan says, stumbling over his words. "I usually work one to nine, but they've been cutting back lately."

"So where were you?"

"I was here, at home for a while." He turns to Nora. "I was here when you left, remember?"

She nods. "That's right. He was home."

"And what time did you leave, Mrs. Blanchard?"

"I went to run a few errands around two or two thirty," she says, feeling the heat rise in her face with the lie. She'd gone to the motel to meet William. But they aren't here about her and William, she realizes. This is much worse.

"And what did you do, Ryan?" the detective asks.

"I, uh, I hung out here for a while, then I went out in my car."

"Alone?"

Ryan nods. "Yes." His face is flushed. He's not meeting the detective's eyes.

"What time would that be?" Bledsoe asks.

"I don't know exactly. Sometime around four thirty?"

Nora sees Bledsoe give the other detective a sharp glance.

"Where did you go?"

"I drove out of town, just killing time."

"Where, exactly?"

"I don't know, east—onto the rural roads. I had nothing to do."

"What car did you drive?" the detective asks.

"I have my own car, it's a 2015 Chevy Spark."

"Anyone see you? Did you talk to anyone?" Bledsoe asks.

Ryan swallows. "I don't think so. I didn't talk to anybody. I don't know if anyone saw me."

"Why don't you go get dressed," Bledsoe says. "We'd like to bring you down to the station for further questioning, if that's all right with you."

Nora looks on in shock, unable to grasp what is happening. All she knows is fear.

Seventeen

Ryan is petrified. His mouth is dry, and he can feel himself trembling. He had hastily thrown on a pair of jeans and a clean T-shirt and his jacket and been brought down to the station. It's the middle of the night, and the houses on the street were dark; no one was watching, at least. He went voluntarily—he wasn't cuffed or anything. His mother is here, somewhere in the station, but they wouldn't let her in the interview room with him, no matter how much she insisted, because he's not a minor anymore. They wouldn't even let her in the detectives' car with him. She'd had to follow in her own car. She'd demanded to know why they wanted to question him, but they wouldn't say anything. Now she's out there somewhere, and he's in here, shaking and afraid.

The two detectives sit down across from him. They've read him his rights. It all feels completely surreal, like a bad dream. They start the videotape. His right leg begins to bounce up and down involuntarily. He's afraid he might piss himself. Somehow he manages to say, "Am I under arrest?"

Detective Bledsoe answers him. "No. But we thought we should read you your rights before we question you, given the circumstances."

"What circumstances?" He's trying to keep the panic out of his voice.

"We have a witness who saw Avery Wooler getting into your car, at around four thirty Tuesday afternoon."

Ryan feels like he might pass out. He says, "I want a lawyer."

They have to turn off the tape.

ALONE IN THE WAITING ROOM, Nora struggles to keep it together. This can't be happening. She wishes Al were here, but someone had to remain at home with Faith. She tells herself it's all a mistake, that it's better to cooperate and do what the detectives ask and get it over with. And the detectives had been pleasant enough, insisting that they just wanted to talk to Ryan, ask him a few more questions. She thought they'd be done in under an hour, and they could go home.

Once they'd arrived at the station, however, things had seemed to take a darker turn. They wouldn't let her be with him. That frightened her. She doesn't know what's going on in that room. Her son is an adult now, in the eyes of the law, but to her, he's still just a child. Her child. Even after all that had happened last year. But he'd been a minor then, and it had been different.

They've been in there more than half an hour already. She hears rapid footsteps coming down the hall in her direction and looks up. At first, she doesn't recognize him, because she's never seen him in anything but a business suit. But it's Oliver Fuller, criminal attorney, called out in the middle of the night, dressed in jeans and sneakers and a denim shirt, and carrying that familiar briefcase. He spots her in her chair and walks over to her.

"What's this about, Nora?" he asks.

"There's been some kind of mistake," Nora says. "I think they're asking him about that missing girl."

The attorney looks grim. He turns away, walks down the hall, and knocks on the door of interview room 2. The door opens and he disappears inside. Nora feels her world collapsing. She can hardly breathe. She pulls her cell phone out and calls Al to tell him that Oliver Fuller has arrived.

IT'S AFTER TWO O'CLOCK in the morning, and Gully could use a coffee. At least the attorney has now arrived. There are introductions all around. "I need a moment with my client," Fuller says, and Gully and Bledsoe leave the room.

They turn to the lunchroom for coffee, avoiding Ryan Blanchard's mother, sitting anxiously in the waiting area. Gully can't help feeling sorry for her. She seems like a nice enough woman, a caring parent. Gully hopes for her sake that her son isn't a kidnapper and possibly a murderer. But there's another woman out there whose daughter is missing, and her life has been horribly upended. Gully has to consider her too.

"What do you think of him?" Bledsoe asks her.

She shrugs. "I don't know yet."

"He was awfully quick to call a lawyer."

"You can't blame him for that," Gully says, although she'd noted it too. She's bothered by the fact that they don't know who this witness is. If Ryan Blanchard doesn't give them anything, they'll have to let him go.

They hear the door open down the hall, the attorney beckons, and they return to the interview room.

They videotape the interview. After the introductions for the tape, Bledsoe begins. "Ryan, as we told you earlier, we have a witness who saw Avery Wooler get into your car at the corner of Connaught and Greenley, at approximately four thirty Tuesday afternoon."

Gully watches the boy stare straight ahead, his face unnaturally pale. His Adam's apple bobs as he swallows.

"Who is this witness?" the attorney asks.

"We don't have to disclose that at this time."

"Let me ask you this," the attorney says. "Are you able to produce this witness at will?"

Fuck, Gully thinks. He's got them. Bledsoe doesn't answer.

"I see," Fuller says. "So you have nothing on my client except that he willingly admitted that he drove down the street *that he lives on,* on the afternoon that Avery Wooler went missing." He asks, "Are you detaining him?"

"No."

Fuller stands up, turns to his client. "We can go, Ryan." He says as he's leaving, "Let's not have any more nonsense, Detectives."

ERIN WOOLER WANDERS restlessly around the house, unable to sleep, pale and distraught, as if she's some kind of tortured ghost, unable to find peace. The October wind wails around the house.

It's after two in the morning, but every time she closes her eyes, she sees Avery—and the pictures in her mind are impossible to bear. She looks in on Michael again; he is mercifully, finally, asleep. He'd seen his father pack a bag and leave the house. William has gone back to the Excelsior Hotel. Michael must have heard everything; he knows as much as she does about what his father has done.

It twists her heart in knots that Michael still seems to think that somehow this is his fault. She's tried to reassure him that he's not responsible for other people's decisions, for other people's actions. Her mind drifts to something she read once about plane wrecks— that it's never just one mistake, but a series of mishaps that lead to disaster. That's what they have here—a series of mishaps that have led to disaster. If only Avery hadn't misbehaved in choir. If only Michael hadn't sent Avery home that one day and told her where to find the key, she might have waited for him. If only her husband hadn't come home early that day; if only he hadn't been having an affair; if only he'd been at work like he was supposed to be, instead of with his lover; if only this other woman hadn't broken it off, he might not have come home at all. If her husband isn't guilty, he certainly left Avery here, alone in the house. If only Avery hadn't opened the door to someone, or left the house again, to be snatched by some monster. If only, if only, if only.

AL IS STANDING in the living room, staring at his wife and son, who have just returned from the police station and are sitting together on the sofa. He's never seen Ryan look so shaken, not even when he had the problem last spring with the drugs. He hadn't been able to go to college this fall because he'd had to perform community service. Now, the boy looks sick and frightened. *Should they be frightened too?*

Nora meets his eyes; she's obviously scared, but she's pretending she's not. She's pretending that everything is fine now. "So that's it, then?" Al asks. "Fuller thinks they don't have a witness at all, that they were just making it up? Why would they do that?"

Ryan glances up at him. "He thinks that someone called in a tip anonymously, saying they saw her get in my car. But it's not true. I never saw her that day."

"Why would someone do that? Call in a fake tip?" He looks at the two of them in disbelief. But maybe he shouldn't be so incredulous; he knows what people can be like. People lie all the time. Just look at his wife. People can be vindictive and manipulative. Maybe even more so in a smaller town, where everyone seems to know everyone else's business. But who would have it out for his son? "Who would do that?" he repeats, his doubt in his voice.

"I don't know!" Ryan cries loudly.

He seems defensive, and so young. He's just a kid, really. Al remembers uneasily how Ryan has denied things before and then the truth came out. His parents were frightened then, too, and disappointed in him. But possession of drugs is a common enough problem with teenagers. His son is not a kidnapper. His son is not a child molester. He likes girls his own age, that's clear enough. He dated Debbie for almost a year, until she went off to college at the end of August. Someone is lying, and it's not his son. Not this time.

"It's obvious the father did it," Al can't resist saying. His wife looks up sharply at him but remains silent. He wonders if she feels as protective of her lover now.

They all hear it at the same time, a sound on the stairs, and turn to see Faith coming down the stairs in her nightie. "What's going on?" she asks.

It breaks Al's heart to have to tell her. She took it so hard when her brother was in trouble. She had some problems with the kids at school, and her schoolwork suffered. They'd been worried about her. She was just getting her stride back. And now this.

Eighteen

William is back at the Excelsior Hotel, without his wife and son this time, sitting in the only chair in the room in the middle of the night, thinking about his situation. He had caught the furtive glances when he checked back in, alone this time. He knows what they're saying on the news. It was obvious that his wife had kicked him out; he'd felt his face burn with shame.

William Wooler is now a pariah. He used to be respected in this town. How quickly things change. His wife hates him. Her face as he told her what he'd already admitted to the police—the disbelief, disgust, rage, hatred. She'd thrown him out of the house, probably for good. His son must hate him too. He must have overheard their harrowing argument, so he knows what a lying, deceitful shit his dad is. Michael had watched him pack, numb horror on his face. William has taken indefinite voluntary leave from work. The police think he's a killer. The media think he's a killer. Is there anyone anywhere who will believe he is innocent? Will the hospital, or the patients in his practice, ever want him back?

His thoughts turn to Nora. Does she believe what they're saying? Does she think he murdered his daughter? He would give anything to turn the clock back, for none of this to have happened.

He thinks about calling her. He can't call her home phone because someone else might pick it up. She's probably thrown away her secret burner phone by now, but maybe she hasn't. He could try calling her tomorrow, when her husband is at work, like he used to. He could use a pay phone, if he can find one; he doesn't want to risk calling from the hotel, and the police took his cell. He wants her to know that he's kept her out of his troubles, that he's honorable. He wants her to know that he loves her. He wants to tell her that he's innocent, and he wants her to believe him.

THE NEXT MORNING, Thursday, Gully is having her second coffee after only three hours' sleep. The search teams, out there in the rain, have turned up nothing. This afternoon they will be at forty-eight hours missing. Her heart sinks at the thought. She feels like she has a ticking clock inside her mind.

Officers have been to every storage facility within the area that William Wooler might have reached. They have shared his photo, but no one remembers a man looking like him taking a storage unit and paying with cash. If Wooler did it, wherever he might have hidden the body, he hasn't been anywhere since to move it—they know because they've had eyes on him. If he disposed of the body in the short amount of time he would have had, he did a very good job of it. What might they have overlooked?

Their next step will be to shift the search to the rural area to the east of town, where Ryan Blanchard claims to have been. They don't have enough to get his cell records to confirm where he was. They need more than just an anonymous witness, even though a child's life is at stake.

"Gully?" an officer interrupts her.

She turns her head. "Yes, what is it?"

"Someone here to see you. A Mrs. Seton."

Jenna's mother. Gully stands up and follows him out to where she's waiting, sitting primly in one of the plastic chairs. Alice Seton's face seems relieved when she sees her. "Mrs. Seton, what can I do for you?" Gully asks, hoping that Jenna might have remembered something. She hasn't brought the girl with her.

"Please, call me Alice. Can we talk?"

"Of course," Gully says and leads her down the hall to an empty interview room, where they sit down. Alice takes a quick look around the room, as if expecting more somehow, but there's not much to see. "What is it?" Gully asks.

Alice shifts in her chair. "I'm not sure I should even be here," she begins.

"If you have anything that you think might be relevant to Avery's disappearance, you must share it with us. It's up to us to decide if it's meaningful or not."

Alice nods. "I know. That's why I'm here. I just—I feel a little uncomfortable about it, you know? I don't have any proof or anything."

Gully nods. "That's okay, just tell me."

"I was shocked when Jenna said that Avery told her she had a boyfriend. I mean, my daughter's the same age. It made me really uncomfortable—you don't like to think of that kind of thing at this age."

"Yes," Gully says, wishing she would get to the point.

"Well, there's this boy. He's about fifteen or sixteen, I think." She hesitates.

"What boy?"

"Adam Winter. He lives on the other side of the street from us, a few houses down from the Woolers. And . . . he's a bit *weird.*"

"Weird how?"

"He's just different. Like autistic, maybe? I don't know. He won't talk to you or look you in the eye. He goes to a special school. I see him around, but he's always by himself. He doesn't seem to have any friends." She pauses. "Avery doesn't really have any friends either. I mean, I know she and Jenna are sort of friends, but Jenna doesn't really like her, she's just nice to her. Avery's a bit . . . sometimes she's hard to like."

Gully has to bite back her distaste at the other woman's sanctimonious attitude. "Did Jenna say anything about this boy Adam?" Gully asks.

"Not really. I asked her if it could be him and she said she didn't know." She continues. "But this boy, he's very good-looking. Maybe Avery had a crush on him? I saw them together once. They were talking on the street. I thought it was a bit odd because he doesn't really talk to anyone."

"Any idea what they were talking about?"

"He was showing her this drone he had. He's really into that drone."

"A drone," Gully says.

"Yeah, it's like this robot that flies."

"I know what a drone is."

"Anyway, I was wondering if maybe he could be the 'boyfriend' Avery was talking about. I thought I should let you know." She adds, "And he *is* odd. I've told Jenna to avoid him."

"Thank you, Mrs. Seton," Gully says, standing up. She's eager to get rid of her and get back to work.

But Alice doesn't get up just yet. "I saw something last night," she says.

"Yes?" Gully prompts.

"I was up quite late and saw you and the other detective take Ryan Blanchard away in a car. Is he under suspicion? Do you think *he* might be the one who took Avery?"

Gully shakes her head. "I can't discuss that."

Finally, Alice stands and grabs her bag, and says, "I mean, you just never know, do you?"

WHEN GULLY is finished with Alice Seton, Bledsoe sees her and waves her into his office. She can tell that he's not happy.

"What is it?" she asks, sitting down in front of his desk.

"We got the preliminary forensics back on Wooler's car. Nothing." He slaps the report down on his desk in disgust. "Literally nothing. He must have vacuumed the whole thing out."

"When would he have done that?" Gully asks. "He wouldn't have had much time."

Bledsoe turns to her. "If he did it, this fucker is smarter than he looks. He's dumped her body someplace we can't find it. Maybe

he stopped at a car wash and vacuumed out his trunk. Get someone checking all the car washes in the area—maybe there's camera
footage or maybe someone will remember him." She nods. "Who
keeps their trunk that clean? It's been vacuumed recently, that's
for sure."

Nineteen

Gwen Winter is a single mom. She has one child, Adam, and she loves him more than life itself. But Adam has autism, and life is not easy for either one of them. She worries about his future. It's a constant battle, navigating the world on behalf of a child with autism, and she is exhausted all the time. Her husband left them when Adam was only four; he wasn't up to the challenge. He couldn't deal with the meltdowns; the public embarrassment; the judgment; the lack of a normal life, doing normal things. Life with Adam wasn't what they'd expected when they decided to start a family. They couldn't do the same activities other families did without thinking—not with Adam's sensory issues and his behavioral problems. So Mark left and she has had to do it all. The problems with the schools have been the worst. It's better now that Adam's in a special school, where they seem to understand him better. He's less upset, calmer. And there are kids there who are also on the spectrum, who share his interests. Bright kids who experience the world differently.

She hears a knock on the door and looks up from her computer—she works from home as a bookkeeper; the dining-room table acts as her office. She doesn't get many people knocking on her door during the day. It might be the police again, going up and down the street, about that missing girl. She opens the door and sees a woman she doesn't recognize standing there. "Yes?" she says.

The woman shows her a badge, but she barely gets a chance to glance at it. Gwen immediately thinks something's happened with Adam. She's had so many complaints over the years.

"I'm Detective Gully," the woman says, "Stanhope Police. May I come in?"

"Yes, of course," Gwen says, her heart pumping faster.

"We're investigating the disappearance on Tuesday afternoon of Avery Wooler."

Gwen nods. This isn't about anything Adam did, then, it's just routine—they're probably seeing if they missed anything. The uniformed police officers were already here the night Avery Wooler disappeared, but she'd had nothing to tell them. She hadn't seen anything, and neither had Adam. Gwen leads the detective into the living room, and they sit down.

"I understand you have a son, Adam," the detective begins.

Oh, here we go, Gwen thinks, immediately on the defensive. Years of this have worn her down. *It's about your son, Adam . . .* How many times has she heard that? "Yes," she says tightly. "What about him?"

"Did he know Avery?"

"I think that's highly unlikely." She can't remember him ever mentioning her; she'd never seen her with him. He's much older than the missing girl. "Adam keeps to himself."

The detective sighs. "We've learned that Avery told a friend that she had a boyfriend—someone older than her. And someone has mentioned seeing Avery with Adam recently," the detective says gently.

"Oh, really? I doubt it. He's not her boyfriend. Who said so?" She doesn't bother to disguise the bitterness in her voice.

"I'm not at liberty to say."

She shakes her head. "No one around here understands Adam. This is a small-minded town. I've been thinking about moving, but I've got Adam in a good special school near here, so . . ."

Detective Gully nods sympathetically.

"Adam is a gentle boy at heart. He would never harm anyone." And it's true, she knows it. Despite the tantrums, the loss of control, the meltdowns, he wouldn't actually *harm* anyone. He's not made that way.

"Even so, I must ask—where was Adam on Tuesday afternoon, do you know? From around four o'clock on?"

"He was home with me," she says. "I picked him up from school. We usually get home shortly before four."

"I understand he has a drone," Detective Gully says. "Does he use it a lot?"

"Yes," she answers. "It's his current obsession."

"Does it have video capability?"

"Yes."

"I'd like to see the footage," the detective says. "We might see something we've missed."

Gwen nods and says, "Adam was outside in the back flying his drone that day, until it started to rain. But if he'd seen anything, he would have said something. And I've asked him. He didn't see anything."

"I'd still like to have a look."

Gwen explains, "He doesn't like anyone to touch his things— especially his drone and his laptop. He has autism; he gets upset."

"I understand," Detective Gully says. "But can you bring Adam and his drone and his laptop to the station when he comes home from school today?"

"Okay. Yes, of course."

"Thank you. "I won't take up any more of your time."

Gwen watches the detective's back as she walks to her car, then closes the door.

GULLY DRIVES BACK UP Connaught Street and parks outside the Woolers' house. She glances across the street at the Seton residence, thinking about Gwen Winter and how different Alice's and Gwen's experiences of motherhood have been.

Gully gets out of the car and approaches the Wooler residence. Bledsoe is at the station, directing the investigation. They are both inclined to dismiss as a prank the anonymous claim that Ryan Blanchard picked Avery up in his car. They have no corroboration of it, and his attorney shut them down pretty smartly. The boy seemed frightened, but who wouldn't have been? Gully's following up on the "boyfriend" angle. She wants to talk to Michael again. It's just possible he might know something about this older boy, if he even exists. He might be a figment of Avery's imagination, or a lie. Gully suspects Michael didn't go to school today, not when it's all over the news that his father has been questioned about his sister's disappearance—and changed his story. Poor kid.

When Gully arrives at the Woolers' door, Erin answers. Her face is tear-streaked and wild looking. She stands there looking at Gully for a moment as if she's staring out from the edge of an abyss.

"What is it?" Erin asks. "Do you have any news?"

Of course, Gully thinks, she's terrified that every time someone comes to her door, it's to deliver bad news. Gully wonders if there will ever be good news. She says calmly, "No. Not yet. May I come in?"

Erin turns away in despair and walks inside, leaving Gully to enter and close the door behind her.

"I kicked William out," Erin says. "He told me everything he told you—all of it."

She looks ghastly, Gully thinks, like a tragic character in a Shakespeare play, beset by too many troubles.

Erin says, "I feel like I don't know him at all."

Gully feels terrible for this woman, living through the worst thing that can happen to any parent—a missing child—only to learn that her husband has been lying to her. "What did he tell you?"

Erin says wearily, "He told me he was home, that he saw Avery. That he left her here alone. That he's been seeing another woman, and that he was with her in a motel. That's why he wasn't at work."

Gully nods sympathetically. They haven't been able to trace this woman—all they know is she has a pay-as-you-go phone, and she didn't pick up when they'd called it from William's burner. They'd like to talk to her, if only to see if she can help them better understand William Wooler and what might have happened that day, but he isn't talking. After a respectful pause, Gully asks, "You don't have any idea who it might be?"

Erin shakes her head. "No idea at all," she says, and seems to shrink, becoming smaller in front of her.

Gully leaves the armchair and comes over to sit beside Erin on the sofa, resting a gentle arm on her shoulder. "You must be strong, Erin."

Erin looks at her and nods. "I know. I have to think of Michael."

"Actually, I wanted to talk to him. Is he home?"

She nods. "No way he was going to school."

Gully really wishes she didn't have to do this. She says gently, "A friend of Avery's told us that Avery said she had a boyfriend. Someone much older than her."

Erin looks back at her in surprise. "A boyfriend? Hardly. She's nine years old!" She asks, "Who told you that? Probably Jenna—Avery doesn't really have any other friends."

Gully says carefully, "We're concerned that Avery may have been taken advantage of by someone older. Jenna said Avery told her they did 'grown-up things.' It could be that she was being molested. She was lonely, vulnerable."

Erin looks back at her in revulsion. "My God," she cries, "could it get any worse?" Her voice rises in despair. "What else was going on right under my nose?"

"I'm sorry," Gully says.

"Oh God," Erin says, "I can't deal with this."

"So you don't have any idea who that might be, if it's in fact true?"

Erin shakes her head and covers her face with her hands.

"Can I talk to Michael?" Gully asks.

Erin nods wearily. "He's upstairs. I'll get him." She seems to steel herself, then rises slowly from the sofa and climbs the stairs as if she's aged decades since her daughter went missing. She returns with Michael trailing behind her, a tall, gangly boy who looks like he's about to face a firing squad. He seems even paler than before, with his wheat-colored hair and dark circles under his eyes.

Gully stands. "Michael, I was hoping I could talk to you about your sister, would that be okay? Your mom can stay with us."

Michael nods and sits down on the sofa beside his mother, and Gully sits again in the armchair across from them. She leans in closer to Michael. "Did Avery ever say anything to you about having a boyfriend?"

Twenty

"No," Michael says automatically, before he even thinks about it.

"Take your time," Detective Gully tells him, her voice soothing.

He's glad it's her and not the other detective. The other detective scares him. He feels hollowed out, after everything that's happened. He can hardly think straight. He glances at his mother, who is watching him in dread, as if expecting to hear something terrible. He can't do that to her. He must protect his mother—she might be all he has left. Besides, he doesn't know anything. He blurts out, "She's only nine."

"I know," Gully says. And waits.

"She never said anything to me about a boyfriend," Michael says.

"I know this is hard, but it's important," Gully says to him gently.

"We've discovered that Avery claimed she was seeing an older boy, that they did 'grown-up things' together."

He feels his face flush with embarrassment.

"Did you ever see her with an older boy?" Gully asks.

He thinks hard. He can't believe Avery was doing anything like that. She's just a kid. But it makes him uncomfortable because he knows how guys talk about girls.

He shakes his head. Then he hesitates, suddenly remembering something. He says, "Just once." And stops himself cold.

"Who did you see her with, Michael?" the detective presses.

He doesn't want to say, because he doesn't like where this is going. But Gully is waiting, and his little sister is missing. He swallows nervously. "It was at the tree house, in the woods." Gully nods, encouraging him. "I was in the woods one day a few weeks ago, and I went to the tree house and Avery was there. At first I thought she was alone. But she wasn't."

"And . . ." Gully prompts him.

"They weren't *doing* anything," he insists.

"Who was with her, Michael?"

"Derek. Jenna's brother."

MIDMORNING, WILLIAM FINALLY locates a pay phone at the local community center. He keeps an eye out, paranoid that he's being watched. He'd snuck out the back of the hotel to avoid the reporters. For once the police seem to be leaving him alone—no one has asked him down to the station for questioning yet today. He thinks about Erin and Michael, and worries about how they're doing. He will call them soon, if they will even talk to him.

He doesn't want the detectives to connect him to Nora. He must protect her, and she must believe he is innocent, even if no one else does.

He dials Nora's secret phone, grateful that he remembers the number, and holds his breath. He hopes she has her phone on her; he knows she keeps it turned off and hidden when she's not alone, but she keeps it with her when she's home by herself. Or maybe she's thrown it away.

Perhaps she won't answer. And he won't know whether it's because someone else is there or because she thinks he's a murderer and never wants to speak to him again. But she picks up.

He finds himself hesitating. There's a long pause—long enough that he wonders who is on the other end of the line. Has her husband found her phone? Her son? Whoever it is doesn't say anything. Maybe it's Nora and *she's* wondering who's on the other end of the line. Would the police phone the number to see who answers? All this goes through his mind in a flash. "Nora?" he says at last, risking all.

"Yes."

He takes a deep breath, which catches on a sob. "Nora," he gasps.

"What's happening?" she asks, and he can hear the wariness in her voice.

He knows they can't talk long; he feels so conspicuous at this pay phone. "They found my other phone. I want you to know—I had to tell them I was having an affair, but I kept your name out of it. I will never tell them it was you I was seeing. I promise."

"Thank you," she says. She sounds deeply relieved.

He knows how worried she must have been; she would know

they'd find his hidden phone. William says, "I could never do anything to hurt you, Nora."

There's a silence. He rushes to fill it. "I didn't do anything to Avery. You can't believe the news, the police," he says urgently. "I didn't hurt her, I swear. Someone has taken her."

"I know," she whispers.

His heart lifts, just a little. "The detectives—they always think it's the parents. They've got us under a microscope," he says bitterly.

"It's not just you," she says, her voice unnatural, strained. "They're looking at my son."

"What?" He doesn't think he heard her correctly. "What did you say?"

"Someone called in an anonymous tip that they saw Avery getting into Ryan's car that afternoon. But it's not true. Who would do something like that?"

He feels a clutch at his heart. Is she accusing him? Of having someone call in a false tip, just to take the heat off him? He would never do that. But if he did, the last person he would point the finger at is Nora's son. He could never hurt her.

"Who would make up a malicious lie like that?" she repeats.

"I don't know," he says. He tries to think. He doesn't know anything about Nora's son, except that he's eighteen and didn't go off to college this year like he was supposed to—something to do with community service he has to complete because of a drug charge. She'd let that slip one day.

"I should go," she says.

"No—not yet," he pleads.

They stay on the line, breathing together, saying nothing. Unsure of each other.

Finally, William says, "I know it's impossible, but I wish I could see you."

"It's impossible," she agrees dully.

He's suddenly swamped by despair. He's lost everything. And the police are probably going to charge him with murder.

"I think Al suspects us," she says.

"How would he know?"

"I don't know. Maybe he followed me one day. Or maybe somebody at the hospital suspects something and told him. He's being weird."

"No, we've been so careful," William protests.

Her voice catches. "He's convinced you killed Avery."

"No! Nora, I didn't." She doesn't say anything. "Don't get rid of your second phone," he tells her. "I'll call you again—for as long as I can," he says. "I'm staying at the Excelsior. Erin has kicked me out." And then he immediately regrets it because she asks him the question he's been dreading.

"William, why did you lie to the police?"

NORA HOLDS HER BREATH. She had to ask. Everyone is asking, Why did William Wooler not tell the police he was at home that day? But now he has been found out. *He was seen. There was a witness.*

She wonders if he's going to hang up. But finally he answers.

"It's complicated," he begins, his voice unsteady. "After you ended things with me, at the motel, I was really upset. I thought no one would be home, and I wanted to be alone for a bit, to process it. But Avery was home." He pauses; she can hear him swallow. "She'd gotten into trouble at school, and we had an argument and

I stormed off, went for a drive. And then later, I knew how it would look if I admitted I'd been home. I couldn't account for my time because I'd been at the motel with you. So I panicked and didn't tell them when I first had the chance, and then it was too late . . ." He adds, "God, I was so stupid. I just didn't think."

It sounds almost plausible, she thinks. "I have to go," she says and hangs up.

She sits on the edge of her bed for a long time. She's alone in the house—Al at work, Faith at school, Ryan doing his community service. She begins to cry. William had sounded horrible—on the edge of losing it. But he'd protected her. How does she feel about him now? Does she believe him?

That's the thing. She's not sure she does.

Twenty-one

Ryan Blanchard moves like an automaton through his morning shift at the homeless shelter, keeping his head down. He doesn't want to be noticed. He still finds it embarrassing to be here, in a place he doesn't belong. He's middle class, college bound; the shelter, and the lost and downtrodden people in it, make him uncomfortable. He feels out of place here, freshly showered, in his clean, good-quality clothes. In a flash of maturity one day, not long ago, he'd realized how privileged he was, born to well-off parents who took good care of him. But it was like a glancing blow, quickly shrugged off. Mostly he resents having to be here—the smells, especially, are hard to take—urine, vomit, and body odor so thick and so embedded into their filthy clothes that it makes him gag. And the visuals are pretty awful too. Seeing people reduced to nothing, to rags. He can't wait for his probation to be up and his community service to be finished. Two hundred hours. He's counting them down.

It could have been much worse. He knows he's here because of his own actions. But acknowledging this, even to himself, is painful, so he usually quickly thinks about something else—about his friends at college, going to parties, meeting girls. But he's not thinking about any of that today. Today, he's thinking about last night at the police station. Remembering how antagonistic that Detective Bledsoe was, how piss-scared he was. A drug charge is nothing compared to a kidnapping or murder charge.

When it was over, he was alone with his attorney for a couple of minutes. Oliver Fuller had looked him in the eye and said, "This is some serious shit, Ryan."

"I didn't do it," he insisted.

Fuller merely nodded. "Just keep your nose clean. With any luck, the witness won't come forward."

He looked up then, frightened. "What do you mean?" He didn't understand. "I thought there was no witness?"

"There's obviously an *anonymous* witness, one they can't produce. But if they come forward and go on the record—"

"But I didn't see her! She didn't get into my car, I swear," Ryan said, panicked. "They're lying!"

Fuller had said, "Let's go see your mother."

And then when they got home there'd been the inquisition with his father, and Faith coming down the stairs. They'd had to tell her what was going on; she's not stupid. He'd seen the fear in his parents' eyes—he recognized it. It was the same look they'd had when they'd been blindsided by his arrest for possession of Oxy. They simply couldn't believe it. Their boy, with drugs.

Only this time their fear and revulsion were amplified because it's a child missing, possibly dead. The look in their eyes was almost feral. He knows they no longer trust him. He shocked them with the Oxy. They thought it was so out of character. But they don't know him, and they don't know everything. They don't know how it is, how many of his friends do Oxy, and other shit too. They don't know how it feels, all the pressure building in your head, how good it feels to let go of it. But his other friends didn't get caught. He can think of at least two people who should be here with him, cleaning up piss and vomit in the homeless shelter. But he kept his mouth shut.

He relives it all as he mops floors, washes dishes, changes bedding. *How did he get here?* He doesn't know who he is anymore. His life is so different than it was a few months ago that it makes no sense to him at all. Fuller had managed to keep him out of jail. His parents had paid a fine, and he'd gotten probation and community service—and a criminal record. It could have been worse; he could have gone to jail for up to a year, for a first offense.

It hasn't been easy; it feels like each day is a struggle against temptation. Sometimes the pressure, the tension, is too much.

Is he going to end up like the people in here? It's all he can do not to panic and run out the door, desperate for freedom and fresh air.

GULLY OBSERVES the scowl on Bledsoe's weary face. They've just learned that William Wooler had had his car completely cleaned and detailed at Euro Autobody the previous Sunday, only two days before Avery went missing. That would explain why his car was so pristine.

"Fuck," Bledsoe mutters. "So if he took her anywhere, he must have wrapped her in plastic or something."

Gully chews her lip thoughtfully. They'd found a roll of plastic sheeting—vapor barrier—in the Woolers' garage in the initial search. No way to tell if William had used some of it to wrap the body in before he placed it in the trunk. But he could have. That might be why they found no trace of Avery there. Or maybe he didn't do it.

Gully feels her spirits flagging. She's had very little sleep. "The boyfriend angle," she begins. "I might have a lead." She tells him what Michael told her about Jenna's brother, Derek. "We know that Avery liked to go to the tree house. They've already searched it, but there was no obvious sign of Avery coming to any harm there." She pauses and adds, "They found some discarded condoms beneath the tree house. Apparently it's a place kids go."

Bledsoe nods tiredly. "You'd better talk to this kid Derek."

"I'd like to take a closer look at the tree house first," Gully suggests.

ERIN STANDS AT the living-room window, staring out from between a crack in the curtains. It's midday, broad daylight. There are still some reporters out there, although fewer than before. Let them take her picture, a terrified mother—the ghouls. She doesn't care anymore. She knows that some of them have left and are staking out the hotel where William is staying. She'd seen them on the news.

Her phone rings, but she doesn't recognize the number. She answers.

It's William. He speaks quickly. "Someone is claiming they saw Avery getting into Ryan Blanchard's car on Tuesday afternoon," he says. His voice is stressed, almost unrecognizable.

"What?"

"There's an anonymous witness. I don't know if it's true or not."

"How do you know?"

He doesn't answer her question. "I got a new phone this morning. You've got the number now, if you need me. I have to go," he says then, and quickly disconnects.

She sits down, stunned by this new information. Would Avery get into Ryan's car? Why would she? She doesn't really know him. Unless . . . unless she *does* know him. Maybe *he's* the older boyfriend that Gully is looking for. It's too much. Erin runs to the kitchen and retches into the sink. She stands over the stainless steel, heaving, but there's nothing in her stomach.

She wants her daughter back, that's all. Even if William's innocent, she's done with him. She just wants Avery back, safe and sound.

She drifts back to the front window and stares at the Setons' house across the street. Her stomach curdles. What if it's true? What if someone was molesting Avery, abusing her, and she didn't have a clue? It sickens her. What kind of mother is she, not to know? Not to be able to see that something was wrong? She knows Avery doesn't tell her everything; they aren't close that way. Avery has always had a core of resistance in her. She's hard to connect with on an intimate level, except on the very rare occasions when she lets her guard down. Erin remembers Avery sobbing to her some months ago, telling her that she was lonely and had no friends. It had broken her heart. Her immediate response was to try to fix it somehow. Arrange playdates? Try getting Avery to join a sport, a club? But all those things had already been tried repeatedly, and had failed repeatedly. In the end she did nothing—just offered support and gentle suggestions on how to make and keep friends. It was the last time Avery had confided in her. She'd let her down. And maybe *because* she was lonely and vulnerable, someone was able to take advantage of her.

The grief and guilt are becoming too much for her to bear. She hadn't protected her daughter.

Maybe William is telling the truth about slapping her and leaving her alone in the house. That *is* his way—he loses it and then retreats in shame. Maybe someone else took Avery. She thinks again about the Blanchard boy. William says someone saw Avery getting into his car on the afternoon she disappeared—if that's true, then William is innocent and Ryan is the guilty one. She knows the Blanchard boy's had trouble with the law before. She wants to go over to the Blanchards' house and get Ryan in a room alone and shake him violently until the truth spills out.

And Jenna's brother, Derek—could Derek have been molesting Avery? She's always thought Derek was a nice enough boy. But he would have seen Avery more than anyone, whenever Avery spent time over at their house.

She hates hiding inside, waiting. She must do something to find her daughter.

Twenty-two

The sodden ground squelches beneath Gully's boots as she walks through the woods on her way to the tree house. She has an off-duty police officer with her, one who was involved in the search of the area; he knows where to go. As she follows him deeper through the trees, cold water drips off the branches and down her neck beneath her jacket, giving her a chill.

They soon come to a small clearing, and the officer in front of her stops. An enormous oak tree rears up in front of them. Its leaves are almost gone, fallen to the ground, so the tree house is clearly visible. It sits in a notch of the tree, made from salvaged, mismatched wood. It has four walls and a rusted tin roof and a door with hinges. A crude window is cut out of the side facing them. There's a rope ladder hanging down the broad trunk. One that could be pulled up by the people inside if they didn't want to be discovered, Gully thinks.

The officer says, "As you know, it was thoroughly searched. No obvious sign of the girl, her clothes, anything."

Gully walks around the tree, observing it from all sides. Then she says, "I'm going up to have a look."

Gully is fit and athletic, and she climbs the ladder with relative ease. When she arrives on the platform in front of the door, she pauses and gazes down below. Heights have never bothered her. The vantage point is good from here—you could see someone coming, probably hear them too. She opens the door—there's a small piece of wood nailed to the tree house that you twist to open the door. Inside, she sees a dirty futon, some soda cans. Gully stands there for a while trying to imagine what went on in here. Avery was here, with Derek Seton. The two of them, alone. Michael discovered them. He says they weren't doing anything. But how would he know? He said they dropped the ladder for him, so it must have been pulled up. They had time to stop whatever they were doing. What was fifteen-year-old Derek doing with a nine-year-old girl?

But even if someone like Derek—or Adam Winter, or anyone else for that matter—was molesting Avery in the tree house, it's unlikely she was killed here. There was no sign of a struggle here. There was no sign of her body or her clothing found in these woods, no indication of her having been dragged or transported through here. What would the killer have done with her?

Where the hell is Avery Wooler?

Gully climbs back down. Avery could have been molested in the tree house. With the ladder pulled up, there would be plenty of privacy. She'd better talk to Derek Seton. As they turn away from the tree house, Gully gets a call. It's Bledsoe. "What's up?"

"She's willing to come in, the witness who saw Avery getting into Ryan Blanchard's car."

"Jesus, that changes things," Gully says.

"It does." She can hear the excitement in Bledsoe's voice.

Bledsoe tells her that the woman hadn't given her name on the call but had said she was coming to the station to tell them what she knew and that she'd be there in half an hour. Gully's excited now—this could be the first real break in the case.

"With any luck," Bledsoe says, "we can pick up Ryan Blanchard this afternoon. Have another go at him." He adds, with obvious satisfaction, "Wipe the smirk off his attorney's face."

Gully arrives at the station, but the witness doesn't. The half hour passes, then an hour.

"She's fucking with us," Bledsoe says in frustration.

"She's either lying," Gully says, "or she's afraid to come forward, to identify herself for some reason." She wonders what that reason might be—if there is one, it must be good. She's as frustrated as Bledsoe.

They speak to the officer who took the call on the tip line. It's the same officer who took her first call, Officer Weeks, and he assures them that it was the same woman. She wouldn't give her name on the phone but admitted she was the one who had called earlier. She wanted to know why Ryan Blanchard hadn't been arrested yet. He'd explained that they couldn't do much based on her information, unless she came forward—an anonymous tip wasn't enough. She'd reluctantly agreed to come in. "But she's obviously had a change of heart," the officer concludes, clearly disappointed. He adds, "She told me that when Avery got into the car, she was wearing a T-shirt and jeans; she didn't say anything about a jean jacket. I pressed her for more details, thinking she'd add the jean jacket. She didn't, but she said Avery had her hair in one braid down her back."

Gully turns to Bledsoe. "Erin didn't mention anything about that. I'll call her." She quickly makes the call and Erin picks up. "Erin, it's Gully," she says. "Do you remember how Avery was wearing her hair on Tuesday?" She waits, mentally crossing her fingers.

"I think—I think I braided it for her," Erin answers.

"One braid or two?" Gully asks.

"Oh God, have you found her?"

"No, but please, just tell me."

"One braid, down the back."

"Thanks, Erin, I'll keep you posted," Gully says and disconnects. She turns to Bledsoe. "Her mother did her hair that morning—one braid, down the back." She asks, "Do we have enough to get a search warrant for Ryan Blanchard's car?"

Bledsoe says, "It's unusual to get a warrant based on a tip from an anonymous witness. But it can be done—if the witness has details that make him credible, and I think that's the case here. The girl's been missing for about forty-eight hours. I'll find a judge."

Gully turns away and almost collides with an officer who's approaching her.

"There's someone here to see you," the officer says. "Gwen Winter and her son. She said you asked them to come in?"

"Yes, good." She follows the officer out to the front desk and greets Gwen and her son, Adam. He's a tall, good-looking boy, but he won't meet her eye when she talks to him. He's carrying his drone protectively, and his mother has his laptop in a case.

"Come over here, with me," Gully says, and leads them to a quiet area. She calls over another uniformed officer, one with more technical expertise than she has. "Adam, you understand why we want to look at your drone footage?" Gully asks.

"I'm autistic, not stupid," the boy says bluntly. Then he proceeds to put down his drone carefully and pulls out his laptop and sets it on the desk in front of him. "I didn't need to bring the drone—I've already downloaded everything onto my laptop. But I'd be happy to show it to you—"

"Maybe after we look at the footage," Gully says.

"Okay." He gets everything started, makes a few clicks, and says, "I've had this drone for seven weeks tomorrow. I've flown it almost every day, so I have lots of footage, but you're probably most interested in what my drone might have seen when Avery Wooler disappeared, right?"

"Yes," Gully says. "Let's start with Tuesday."

He makes a few more clicks and then they are all looking at the footage on the screen of his laptop. It's like seeing below from an airplane. The image is very crisp and clear. *This is amazing*, Gully thinks. She looks at the time signature on the screen. The drone took off on Tuesday at 4:05. Her heart begins to race. There is Adam's house on Connaught Street below.

"Where were you when you flew this thing?" Gully asks.

"In my backyard. It can go about a half a mile in any direction from where I'm standing. I can see what the drone sees, and I didn't see anything happen to Avery. I would have said."

But maybe they'll see *something*. Gully focuses on the screen in front of her.

Twenty-three

Erin Wooler doesn't even wash her face or change her clothes. She hasn't showered since Avery went missing. She doesn't care what she looks like. She looks frantic, she knows that. She grabs her keys and knocks on her son's bedroom door, opening it. "I'm going out for a bit," she tells him from the doorway. When she tells him that, he looks frightened.

"Why, where are you going?"

She comes into the room and sits down on the bed. "I'm just going to speak to your father, at the hotel. We have things to discuss."

"I don't want to be here by myself," Michael says plaintively.

She thinks about that. There are still reporters outside their door, like so many swarming insects, and Michael will be alone inside. "Just don't open the door to anyone. *Anyone*, okay? Even if it's the detectives. I'll lock the door behind me. If the detectives come, tell them through the door to call me on my cell; I'll have it with me." She gives him a firm hug and kisses the top of his head. He seems so young, suddenly, that she wonders if she should stay. But she thinks of her missing daughter, and gets up and says, "I'll be back soon, I promise."

She goes back down the stairs clutching the rail, her head swimming. She hasn't eaten much in the last couple of days or slept either. But she has fear and rage simmering through her veins, and it's enough.

She puts on her jacket, takes a deep breath, and opens the front door. She's immediately blinded by the flashing of cameras, assaulted by the clamor of voices. It's a crazy tumult on her doorstep, and somehow it matches exactly what she's feeling inside. It doesn't faze her. She stands still and gives them a stony stare and says nothing. Her suffering confers on her a kind of dignity. They are so surprised to see her suddenly there, alone and vulnerable on her front doorstep, that they fall silent and still, as if waiting for her to speak. Instead, she makes her way down the front walk, and they step aside, allowing her passage. It's a bizarre moment, Erin thinks, but this is all bizarre. It's as if it's happening to someone else. She feels detached, there and not there.

She reaches the driveway, and they move for her so that she can get to her car. But she walks past her car and turns right at the end of the driveway. She walks quickly, with purpose, her heart pounding. They start to follow her then, cameras clicking, calling, *Where are you going? Has there been any news? How are you feeling, Mrs. Wooler? Where is your husband?* She ignores them.

MICHAEL LISTENS TO his mother leave the house; he hears the front door open—the shouting of the mob of reporters—then the door closes behind her and the journalists are muted again. He wants them to leave his mother alone. Maybe he should have gone with her. He hurries to the front of the house and slips into his parents' room; their window looks out onto the street. He sees his mother walk past her car and head down the drive. She's not going to the hotel to see his father like she said. *Where is she going?* His stomach lurches; she must be going to Derek's, because of what he said. He feels sick now. But no, she turns right and keeps going, past the Setons' house. He watches the mob of reporters and camera people follow her, at a slight distance. It makes him think of the story of the Pied Piper of Hamelin; his mother is the piper and the journalists are the rats following her down the street. He wonders what makes him think of that, until he remembers that the Pied Piper stole children, that must be the connection. Avery has been stolen. And he begins to cry—broken, ugly crying that he wouldn't want anyone to see, to hear. But he keeps watching through his sobs and is shocked to see his mother turn up the driveway at the Blanchards' house.

GULLY'S EYES are glued to the laptop screen. The drone hovers for a while over the Winters' house as it begins its flight. Then it travels along and over the street, moving north toward the field at the top of the street, where it turns east onto Greenley. The drone circles over the empty field to the north of the Woolers' and eventually heads over the woods along the river.

The drone is nowhere near Connaught Street at 4:30, when Avery is supposed to have gotten into Ryan Blanchard's car, or for that matter, at 4:20, when Wooler's car left the garage. *Shit.* Gully has to swallow her disappointment. She wasn't expecting it to be that easy. Adam had already said he hadn't seen anything.

Even so, Gully has the other officer sit with Adam while they go back through the previous days of footage, working backward from Tuesday, to see if they can find anything that might relate to Avery—maybe they'll see Avery with Ryan, or with someone else. "And let's get a copy of everything, okay?"

NORA HEARS a disturbance outside and looks out the living-room window to investigate. She sees a woman she recognizes as Erin Wooler—but a very different-looking Erin Wooler—turning up her driveway, followed by a pack of media. She feels a wave of panic. Erin must know. She must know, somehow, that Nora is William's lover. He swore he wouldn't tell, just this morning, on the phone. She believed him. Or did Erin find out some other way? And now she is coming up Nora's walk, followed by all those reporters, and this can't be happening, she wants to hide. She *will* hide. She won't open the door. She'll pretend she's not here. Even though her car is sitting there in plain view in the driveway.

Now Erin is pounding forcefully on the front door. Nora covers her ears with her hands, slides down the wall to crouch on the floor, and closes her eyes tight. The photos of this will be everywhere— Erin pounding angrily on her door. But she won't open the door, and Erin will have to go away, taking the reporters with her.

The pounding on the door intensifies, the door is rattling in its frame, and now the doorbell is ringing incessantly. She hears Ryan coming down the stairs and opens her eyes.

"What's going on?" Ryan asks in alarm, looking at her strangely.

She stares at him in dismay; she'd forgotten he was home. Thank goodness Faith isn't home from school yet. What must he think of her, finding her crouching on the floor with her eyes shut tight and her hands over her ears? She has no time to answer. She hears the front door flung open. *Shit.* It wasn't locked. How dare Erin just barge in here? Nora scrambles to her feet, comes out of the living room, and faces Erin Wooler, standing in their foyer. Erin thrusts the door closed behind her.

Nora stares at her. Erin is almost unrecognizable. Her attractive face has become gaunt in such a short time. She is without makeup, her hair unwashed; she's wearing track pants and an old hoodie. She looks like she's almost out of her mind. Nora observes all this and is frightened. And percolating beneath the fear is shame, shame that she's brought more pain to this suffering woman. In that moment, Nora feels that she deserves to go to hell. Perhaps that is where Nora is right now, and Erin too.

Nora trembles before her, but Erin barely looks at her. She turns her attention to Ryan, now in the foyer with them.

"What are you doing here?" Ryan demands.

Nora notices that he looks frightened of her as well.

"Where is she?" Erin asks, her voice threatening. "Where is my daughter?"

Nora is hit by a wave of nausea.

"What?" Ryan stammers.

"She was seen getting into *your* car," Erin cries, her eyes wild. She comes up very close to him and cries, more loudly, "What did you do with her?" And she pushes him aggressively, both hands against his chest.

Ryan falters but recovers his balance. "I didn't do anything with her," he protests. "That's a lie. She didn't get into my car. Someone made that up."

Nora watches in disbelief as Erin pummels Ryan violently with both fists. Ryan backs up to get away from her and loses his balance, landing on the floor at the bottom of the stairs.

"Get off him!" Nora screams, animated out of her stupor now, rushing to the side of her son. She glances up at Erin as the other woman stands over him, breathing heavily, her eyes murderous. Beyond her, Nora can see the journalists pressed up against the windows, hear them outside baying for blood. She feels the bile rising in her throat. This can't be happening. They can't be seeing this.

She turns back and leans over Ryan. He's not hurt at all and waves her off. He sits up, looking warily at Erin. But she's harmless now, weeping raggedly, a figure of raw pain. Nora begins to cry too. And that's when the police arrive.

Twenty-four

G ully knows that something is amiss when they pull up outside the Blanchards' house and see reporters wedged in together in the dead flower beds, hands cupped around their eyes, peering in the large living-room window.

"What the hell?" Bledsoe says, and he's out of the car as soon as she's got it in park. She's close behind him. They race up to the house, calling to the crowd to get away, to step back, ordering them to retreat to the sidewalk. Gully sees Bledsoe knock on the door before quickly opening it—they have a search warrant, after all. Glancing over her shoulder, Gully sees the search team arriving, the white van now parking on the street.

When they step inside, she's not prepared for what she sees. Erin Wooler is sobbing and gasping, and Nora Blanchard is hovering protectively over her son. She looks at the two women, a world of pain between them.

"What's going on here?" Bledsoe asks.

"She assaulted my son!" Nora says wildly.

Gully closes her eyes briefly, opens them again.

"What are you doing here, Erin?" Gully asks her gently. But Erin doesn't seem capable of speech. "I'll take her home," Gully says to Bledsoe. "I don't imagine you want to press charges," she says to Nora and Ryan, hoping she's right. They glance at each other, as if uncertain what to do. Gully takes advantage of their hesitation. "That's that, then. Come, Erin, I'll take you home." She wants to defuse the situation.

"Who called you?" Nora asks. "Why are you here?"

Bledsoe answers, producing the requisite document. "We have a search warrant."

Gully watches the color drain from Nora Blanchard's face. Ryan looks even worse. She leads Erin away.

ERIN ACCOMPANIES Gully in a daze.

She can't believe what she just did. She completely lost control. It was like she was out of her mind, outside of her own body. She might be charged with assault. They could charge her if they want, but the Blanchards have bigger problems right now. She's glad they're going to search Ryan Blanchard's car and house, like they searched theirs. They must find Avery. That's all that matters. She doesn't care about anyone, or anything, else.

They make it to the detective's car. They can't walk back down the street with this rabid bunch following them, shouting questions, taking photographs, not after what just happened. She and the detective don't speak on the short drive back down the street. Gully gets her safely inside the house and sits her down on the sofa.

She looks at her with concern. "Can I get you anything, Erin? A cup of tea, maybe?"

Erin shakes her head. She's angry that Gully hasn't been forthcoming with her—that she didn't tell her about the witness who saw Avery get into Ryan's car. She doesn't tell her anything. Erin doesn't give a damn about police protocol—she's Avery's mother, and she has a right to know what they know. Michael comes down the stairs, looking worried. He looks like he's been crying.

"What happened? What were you doing at the Blanchards'?" His voice rings with anxiety.

She swallows. She doesn't want to tell him what she did. He doesn't need an out-of-control mother right now. But he needs to know what's going on. "Your sister may have gotten into Ryan Blanchard's car. There's a witness—an anonymous witness." She turns to Gully. "Isn't that right? Isn't that why you called me a little while ago to ask how Avery was wearing her hair that day? Isn't that why they're over there right now with a search warrant?"

Gully asks, "Where did you hear that?"

Erin says wearily, "William told me." She turns to Gully. "How would he know that? You didn't tell him, did you?"

Gully shakes her head. "No."

"Who else would know?" Erin asks. Gully doesn't answer. Erin says, suddenly struck, "The *Blanchards* would know." She breathes out heavily, like she's been punched in the stomach. "Oh God. It's Nora Blanchard, isn't it? She's the other woman."

AL BLANCHARD IS AT WORK Thursday afternoon when he gets a frantic call from his wife.

"The police are here," she says breathlessly. "You have to come. I can't handle this by myself." She sounds like she's barely keeping it together.

"Wait, why? What are they doing there?" His heart pounds as he thinks of his son. Of him sitting on the living-room sofa in the middle of last night after returning from the police station, denying that he had anything to do with Avery Wooler. But there was some small part of Al that was afraid. It's like he's living the nightmare of the drugs all over again. The fear, the confusion. He's afraid that he doesn't really know his son at all. Doesn't trust him. Doesn't *believe* him. He knows his wife is a liar, that she has deceived him. And he knows his own thoughts run awfully dark at times lately—thoughts he wouldn't share with anyone. Perhaps Ryan has fooled them all.

"They have a search warrant," Nora says.

He collapses into his chair, as if he's had the wind knocked out of him. He seems to be having trouble breathing. They must have found the witness then. They must know who it is. Who would say this about their son if it wasn't true? Why would anyone make that up? What if it's true and Ryan took that missing girl in his car somewhere and did something to her, and then didn't want her to tell anybody and panicked? And then—and then he'd deny it, of course he would. He'd cover it up. He'd pretend it hadn't happened, like he did with the drugs, he'd deny it until he couldn't deny it anymore—

"Are you coming?" his wife says into the phone.

"Yes. I'll be right there." He's surprised at how calm he sounds.

On the drive home his mind is a seesaw—he tries to think of anyone who might want to harm his son with a lie like this. His drug buddies? But that doesn't make sense, because Ryan didn't name anyone, didn't say who he got the drugs from. Maybe someone wants to hurt not Ryan, but him. Or his wife. What better way to hurt someone than to suggest that their child is a pervert and a killer? But Al has no enemies, and neither does his wife. The idea is ridiculous. They are just normal, average people; they don't make enemies. He would like to know who it is. He would like to know who claims they saw his son take Avery Wooler.

When he arrives, his alarm increases. There's a pack of journalists outside his house, who swarm his car in the driveway when they realize who he is. He flees inside, his hands covering his face as the cameras flash. When he gets inside, his wife and son are in the living room, and he's confronted by the two detectives who'd been in his house late the night before. Bledsoe and Gully.

Bledsoe says, "We'd like to ask all of you to come down to the station to answer a few questions, if that's all right."

His wife regards him with fear in her eyes. But it's the expression on Ryan's face that hits him hardest. Ryan looks absolutely terrified.

WILLIAM WOOLER IS CLOSETED in his hotel room late in the afternoon. He's sitting on the bed with his new cell phone, following the news feeds. Because the police had taken his cell phone—and his laptop—he'd had to slip into a local store this morning after calling Nora to get a new one. Now, in disbelief, he watches footage of his wife—looking like a madwoman—storming her way into the Blanchards' house. There was some kind of altercation inside. This is his fault. He shouldn't have told her about the anonymous witness saying they saw Avery get into Ryan's car. This is what he has wrought. His wife has lost her mind.

But it doesn't matter now whether he told her. Because he has the TV on and there's a reporter standing in front of the Blanchards' house explaining that the police are exercising a search warrant.

She says, "Police have revealed that an anonymous witness, whom they deem to be credible, claims to have seen the missing girl get into Ryan Blanchard's car at approximately four thirty on the afternoon of her disappearance."

It must be true then, he thinks—someone really must have seen Avery get into Ryan's car. William leans back against the pillows, suddenly breathless. How is it possible that Nora's son might have taken his daughter?

Twenty-five

Gully and Bledsoe have separated the members of the Blanchard family. Each is in a separate room, waiting to be interviewed. They are taking up all three interview rooms; it's not a large police station. The mother has arranged for their young daughter to be picked up by the parent of a friend. Ryan has his lawyer, Oliver Fuller, with him, and they are closeted together privately for now. In the meantime, Gully and Bledsoe will speak to the parents. Ryan's car has been transported to the forensics lab.

They begin with the mother, Nora Blanchard. She's distraught, understandably, and Bledsoe tries to put her at ease. "I know this is hard," he begins.

She stares at him as if he has no idea how hard this is. Gully's with her on this one—Bledsoe doesn't even have kids. He can't possibly imagine what she's going through.

"We want to ask you again about the whereabouts of your son that day."

"I told you," she answers. "He was at home. His shift had been canceled. We were both in the house until I left to run some errands sometime around two o'clock."

"Where did you go?" Bledsoe asks.

Gully notices that the question seems to make her uneasy. That's no surprise if Nora Blanchard is William Wooler's lover, which now seems likely. How else would William have learned about the witness, if not from Nora? And Nora is an attractive woman; she and William would make an attractive couple.

Nora says, "I did some shopping, ran some errands, you know."

"What time did you get back?" Bledsoe asks.

"It must have been sometime around four forty-five, before Faith got home from soccer at five. Around there, anyway. I've told you all this already."

"And Ryan wasn't home?"

Nora shakes her head.

"His car wasn't there?"

"No. He already told you he went out in his car around four thirty." She sounds impatient.

"What time did he get home?"

"It was after six, maybe closer to six thirty."

There's a knock on the door of the interview room, interrupting them.

"Yes?" Bledsoe calls, looking over his shoulder at the door.

A uniformed officer beckons him out, and Gully is immediately curious. A moment later Bledsoe returns and sits back down. "Guess what they just found at your house?" he says.

Nora Blanchard goes rigid.

"A pay-as-you-go phone, hidden behind the air vent in your bedroom." He adds, "How about that?"

Gully watches the other woman's face collapse and can't help feeling sorry for her.

NORA FALLS APART, sitting on the hard wooden chair in the interview room. With everything that had happened—Erin attacking Ryan, the journalists taking pictures of it all through the windows, the search warrant, and all of them being hustled off to the police station like criminals—she'd completely forgotten about her hidden phone. She can't believe she's been so stupid. She should have gotten rid of it, but she wanted to keep that connection with William. Now they know. And Al will know for certain, his suspicions confirmed. She will be publicly shamed, because they won't keep this quiet, why would they? Such an interesting twist to the case—the father of the missing girl and the mother of the prime suspect, lovers—how the media will love it!

She looks back at the detectives, who are waiting for her to say something. "It's mine," she manages finally.

"We know." He adds, "William Wooler had a hidden burner phone too. And the only number he called on it is the one to the phone we found hidden in your house." He pauses. "You two are having an affair."

"We were," she admits, looking down at the table, defeated, ashamed. "I ended it."

"Such a small world, isn't it?" he says. She remains silent, miserable. "How did your son, Ryan, feel about you sleeping with William Wooler?"

She lifts her head. "He didn't know," she says.

"Kids usually know more than their parents think," Bledsoe says.

Nora's heart trips as she asks herself the question. Could Ryan have known she was having an affair with William? They can't think he took Avery to punish William? To punish *her*? No, that's not possible, she can't believe that. Ryan wouldn't be capable of it.

Oh God. The bile rises in her throat, and she swallows it back down. Her head swims, and she grabs the edge of the table. Gully pushes a glass of water toward her. She drinks the taste of bile away; her hand that's holding the water glass shaking. They wait.

"He didn't know," she says at last. This is the ultimate betrayal, she thinks, worse even than sleeping with another man. She will surely rot in hell for this. "But I think my husband did."

FAITH BLANCHARD has been picked up after soccer by Samantha's mother, Mrs. Slagle. Faith doesn't want to go to Samantha's house after practice, she wants to go home. She's anxious and wants to be with her mother. Samantha chatters beside her in the back seat of the SUV, happy about the change of plans.

Faith isn't listening. She's remembering the awful tension in the living room last night when she woke up and they had to tell her what was going on. If she hadn't woken up, they probably wouldn't have told her anything, they think she's still a baby. They'd told her that the police had questioned her brother about Avery because someone had called in a false tip. Even then she wondered if it was true. She's been feeling sick to her stomach ever since. And now she's heard that the police are at their house, and that's why Samantha's mother has picked her up, to keep her out of the way.

She's still angry at her brother about last spring, what he put them all through. The house had felt like a storm was brewing, and everyone was worried, herself included, that Ryan would go to jail. Her mother cried a lot in secret, and her father was very quiet. Ryan was sullen and unapproachable. And Faith was upset and humiliated because some of her classmates knew about it—even though Ryan was a minor and his name was supposed to be kept private—because Katie's dad was a police officer and she heard him talking about it, and Katie has a big mouth. Other kids made fun of her, of her family. But they'd somehow got through it, and Ryan didn't have to go to jail. He just had to miss going to college this year and work in the homeless shelter. She knows he's not happy about it, but he deserved it, she thinks. Now she wishes he had gone away to college.

Because now there's this. She's worried sick. Her stomach hurts. It's happening all over again. Only this is a million times worse.

She catches Samantha's mother watching her in the back seat through the rearview mirror. Faith glares at her, and Samantha's mom averts her eyes, embarrassed.

Twenty-six

Al Blanchard waits anxiously in the empty interview room, wondering what the hell is going on. He hates not knowing. How long can they keep him here? *Can* they keep him here? And then he remembers Oliver Fuller telling them, before, that if they detain someone, or have them in custody or arrest them, they must read them their rights. No one has read him his rights; he thinks he's here voluntarily, that he's free to leave.

But just as he stands up, the door opens, and Detective Bledsoe and Detective Gully enter the room. He quickly sits back down.

"Sorry for the wait," Bledsoe says, pulling out a chair opposite him. Gully sits down too.

"Do I have to stay here?" Al asks.

"No," Bledsoe tells him. "You're free to leave. But it would be helpful to us, and perhaps to your son, if you could answer a few questions."

"Of course," Al says, deciding to cooperate. There's no point getting confrontational.

"Where were you on Tuesday afternoon?" Bledsoe asks.

"What?" It's not the question he was expecting; he thought they wanted to talk about his son. The detective doesn't repeat the question. Al says, automatically, "I was at work."

"And is there anyone at your place of employment who can confirm that?"

No, there isn't. Because he remembers now that of course he wasn't at work on Tuesday afternoon. "Actually," he says, "sorry, I just remembered. Tuesday I was out of the office. I had a meeting with a client from one till shortly after two."

"And what did you do after that?"

"Why are you asking me this?" Al says.

"Please just answer the question."

Al swallows.

He takes his time answering. He doesn't want to lie to the police. "I didn't go back to the office," he admits reluctantly. "I—I stopped at a motel."

"What motel would that be?"

Al can feel the blood rushing to his face. He's feeling increasingly uncomfortable. "The Breezes Motel, on Route Nine."

"And what were you doing there?" Bledsoe asks, glancing at his partner.

Al shifts in his seat. He doesn't want to tell them. He feels his anger and his shame growing. How can he be in this position, being asked this? He remembers who has put him here. His wife. Finally, he answers, trying to pretend it doesn't bother him as much as it does. "If you must know, my wife is having an affair. I suspected her some time ago, so I followed her one day. She goes to that motel every Tuesday afternoon. To meet William Wooler." He feels the heat rise up his neck. "So every Tuesday, I park in the back behind the dumpster, and I watch for them to come out." And then he suddenly feels everything inside him give way and he begins to cry. Oh, the embarrassment of it, the humiliation. The shame. They wait till he pulls himself back together.

"What time did they come out?"

He wipes his eyes roughly with his hands. "It was about three forty-five." He adds, "Earlier than usual."

"And what did you do then?" Bledsoe asks.

"Nothing. I just sat in my car behind the dumpster until it was time to go home. I left there about five thirty." He confesses, his misery and shame complete, "That's what I do every Tuesday. I told work that I have an appointment every Tuesday afternoon at three, and I don't go back." He adds, his voice breaking, "And then I go home and pretend I've been at work."

GULLY AND BLEDSOE take a moment alone before interviewing Ryan Blanchard. They have suggested that Nora and Al go home, but they have chosen to remain and wait for their son. It might be a long wait. Or it might not.

"You just never know what people are really up to, do you?" Gully says, thinking of Al Blanchard sitting in his car behind the dumpster, every Tuesday afternoon, while his wife and William Wooler were having sex in a motel.

"It gives him motive," Bledsoe says darkly.

Gully nods. "It does."

"We only have his word for it that he stayed there till five thirty. We already know there aren't any working surveillance cameras on that motel," Bledsoe says. "Maybe that particular day he'd had enough and followed Wooler home to have it out with him. But then William left again and maybe Al saw Avery leave the house and took her. Maybe he thought he could take the daughter and everyone would think William had done it." He adds, "Revenge— the oldest motive in the book."

"Assuming Wooler didn't kill her himself, and assuming Ryan Blanchard didn't pick her up in his car." She adds, "And there's still the boyfriend angle. I need to talk to Derek Seton."

"Yeah," Bledsoe agrees, sighing heavily. "We'd need Al Blanchard's cell phone records to pinpoint his location and eliminate him as a suspect, but I don't think we have enough for a warrant."

Gully muses, "It's too bad Nora didn't seem to have much insight into William Wooler—or into his relationship with his daughter."

"Other than to tell us that he could never have done it—and to admit he was upset that she'd just broken off their relationship. Maybe that was enough to tip him over the edge?" Bledsoe says. "Let's talk to Ryan—it probably won't take long, with his attorney here. If he doesn't say anything, we'll have to let him go—for now."

Twenty-seven

The tension in the car as the three of them drive home makes Nora want to throw open the passenger-side door, leap out, and walk home by herself. She knows the detectives talked to Al after they talked to her. Al must know now for certain, if he didn't before, that she and William were lovers. The air is charged between them. They're not going to discuss it with Ryan in the car, but it will come up later tonight, when they are alone, and she's a little frightened. How angry will he be? She's seen a side of him lately that she hasn't seen before. The angry little jabs whenever William Wooler's name comes up. Something seething beneath the calm, detached surface. How will she respond? What will she tell him? That it's over, and she's sorry and she'll make it up to him? Or will she tell him that it's not over, she's not sorry, and she's in love with William? She doesn't know. All she knows for sure is that her two children are the most important things in the world to her, and they need her.

More frightening even than an enraged husband and the end of her marriage is that the detectives seem to believe that Avery got into Ryan's car that day. Nora no longer knows what to believe. She wants to ask Al later whether he thinks Ryan knows about her and William. Maybe Al told him.

"What did you say to the detectives?" Al asks Ryan, glancing at him in the back seat through the rearview mirror as he drives.

"Nothing," Ryan says.

"What do you mean, nothing?" Al says. "You must have said something." There's an edge to his voice.

"I didn't. Oliver told me to say nothing, so I didn't say a word."

"What did they ask you? What did Oliver say?" Al presses, as Nora listens anxiously.

"Nothing, really. Nothing new."

Nora wishes she could believe him. But this is what he was like before, shutting down, shutting them out, not wanting to tell them anything, until it was too late.

AS EVENING DESCENDS, Erin locks herself in the bathroom and has a hot bath. She leans against the back of the tub and closes her eyes. If it's true that Ryan Blanchard took Avery, or anyone other than her husband—that will make it easier, in the end, for her and Michael. It will be easier to have someone else to blame. But they're no closer to finding her daughter. She does the rough calculation in her head—Avery's now been missing for about fifty-one hours. Ryan was taken in for questioning, but she knows they let him go—she saw it on the news. They don't know who the witness is, so they let him go. They should be hammering at him until he breaks down and tells them where Avery is, Erin thinks in fury. But, of course, he's got a lawyer, and she knows how it works. They won't get anything out of him. He's protected by his rights. Even though her poor daughter is out there somewhere, and Ryan may know where she is. Where is the humanity in that? Where is the fairness, the justice? What about her rights, and her daughter's? It's fine to be a defense attorney and do your job, until you look at it from other eyes—from the eyes of a mother whose child has been taken by a monster.

GULLY KNOCKS ON the Setons' door, following up on Derek Seton. Maybe the search of Ryan Blanchard's car will turn up something. But maybe it won't. They need to find Avery. And every hour that she is missing is making people around here become more unhinged. The calls from the public about suspicious people are increasing. She remembers the shocking scene earlier that afternoon—Erin standing over Ryan after knocking him to the floor, his mother hovering over him protectively, those hyenas from the news outlets pressed up against the windows. They all need the truth.

Alice Seton answers the door and seems surprised when she sees Gully. "May I come in?" Gully asks.

"Of course," she says, letting her into the vestibule. She lowers her voice and says conspiratorially, "Was it Ryan Blanchard?"

It seems everyone is glued to the news. "You know I can't discuss the case with you," Gully says.

Alice nods, shrugs. She says, "It's just—Jenna's so traumatized by Avery's disappearance. All her classmates are frightened, understandably so. We all just want whoever took Avery caught as soon as possible." She pauses and asks, "What can I do for you?"

"I'd like to talk to your son, Derek," Gully says.

Alice seems taken aback. "Well, okay, but I don't think he knows any more than his sister. And he's not friends with Ryan at all."

Gully follows her into the living room. It sounds like the family is having dinner in the kitchen. "I'm so sorry to interrupt your meal," she says.

"It's okay, we've just finished," Alice says.

Gully says, "Either you or your husband must be present, as he's a minor. But maybe one of you could take your daughter upstairs?"

Alice regards her for a moment and then says, "Yes, of course. I'll get Pete to take her. Give me a minute." She returns to the kitchen, and Gully hears quiet voices, then a boy's voice rising in protest. Then they all come out. Mr. Seton nods at her as he and Jenna go upstairs. Jenna looks back over her shoulder at the detective, eyes wide.

Derek is a nondescript-looking boy—average height, messy brown hair, a few pimples across his forehead. Gully smiles at him as he sits down beside his mother on the sofa. Gully pulls a chair up closer and begins. "I'm sorry to bother you," she says. "But you know how important it is that we find Avery."

The boy nods back at her, looking nervous. Alice is watching her, clearly wondering what Gully is up to.

"Do you know Avery?" Gully asks.

Derek looks at his mother as if to say, *Why is she asking me this?* Then he turns back to Gully and says, "Yes, of course. She's a friend of Jenna's, sort of."

Gully notes again how they always seem to make it clear that Jenna doesn't really like Avery. It makes Gully feel a sudden surge of sympathy for Avery.

"Did you ever hang out with her, with her and your sister?"

He shakes his head, glances again at his mother, rigid beside him. "No. They're, like, nine."

"Do you think she might have had a crush on you?" Gully ventures.

The boy flushes to the roots of his hair. "No."

"What's this about, Detective?" Alice Seton interrupts.

"I'm just trying to get to the bottom of this story that Avery told your daughter, about having an older boyfriend. Perhaps it was a figment of her imagination," Gully suggests. "Perhaps she merely had a crush on an older boy, and Derek is an older boy that she might have come into contact with."

"Well, that's ridiculous," Alice says. "Derek had nothing to do with Avery."

"But that's not exactly true, is it?" Gully says, looking directly at Derek.

Derek stares back at her and swallows. He doesn't look at his mother now. A silence stretches out uncomfortably.

"What are you talking about?" Alice asks, her voice tense.

Gully's genuine sympathy for Alice in this situation is tempered somewhat by the other woman's earlier eagerness to point the finger at Adam Winter simply because he's *different*. She knows that it's not necessarily the ones who seem different that you need to be afraid of—it's the ones who can carry off normal without anyone suspecting a thing. Gully ignores her. "Derek, were you ever in the tree house in the woods with Avery?"

The boy swallows again. "I don't remember."

"Of course you remember," Gully says gently. "Avery's brother, Michael, found you there with her a few weeks ago." She adds, "You were alone with Avery in the tree house, with the ladder pulled up. What were you doing in the tree house with Avery, Derek?"

He looks petrified now. "Nothing."

Alice looks as if she might faint.

"What were you doing there with her?" Gully asks again.

Derek begins to tremble. "She was just there. I went to the tree house one day when I had nothing to do. I thought no one was there. I climbed up, but when I opened the door she was inside. I didn't expect to see anyone. We just talked for a bit. It was awkward. I was going to leave and then Michael came. She saw him out the window and called down to him."

"And then you put the ladder down for him."

"I guess, I don't remember," Derek says.

"I'm just wondering why the ladder was pulled up at all," Gully says.

Twenty-eight

Alice observes her son, her heart in her throat. This has all gone very weird, very fast. She thought Gully was here to ask her son some routine questions, but that's not the case at all. Gully seems to be accusing Derek of molesting a nine-year-old girl. Alice struggles to hide her dismay as she observes him. Her son is shaking; he looks frightened, and suddenly she feels sick to her stomach. She wants her husband here with her; she doesn't know how to handle this. She wants to go get him, but she doesn't dare leave. She's so stunned that she doesn't even call out his name to have him come join them.

"Why was the ladder pulled up, Derek?" Gully presses.

"It wasn't," he says.

"Michael says it was. He says Avery put it down for him."

"She must have pulled it up then," Derek says. "It wasn't me." His skin is flushed a dark red.

"I know why teenagers go to that tree house, Derek," the detective says, as Alice watches in disbelief. Derek remains miserably silent.

Alice swallows, her throat dry. She thought the tree house was for younger kids. She doesn't want to know about this.

"Derek?" Gully prods.

Alice is suddenly terrified that Derek will say something he shouldn't. Something that she can't bear to hear. She must stop this. "Peter!" she calls out loudly, turning toward the stairs. "Can you come down here, please?"

Gully sits back in her chair, as if annoyed at the interruption.

There's a poisonous silence as they wait for Peter to appear. Her husband hastens down the stairs and arrives in the living room, taking in the atmosphere. He looks questioningly at her; he knows he's walked into something.

"Detective Gully seems to be accusing Derek of something," Alice says, her voice low. She sees the sudden alarm on her husband's face.

"Sit down, please," Gully tells him. "And I'm not accusing anyone of anything."

He sits down on the sofa, on the other side of their son, glancing briefly at her over Derek's head. She watches his face as the detective explains the situation. The same incredulity, the same fear. Then they all turn their attention back to Derek.

Derek says, "I don't know what the other kids do. I never touched her. I just went to the tree house one day and she was there, playing by herself. I felt sorry for her, so I talked to her a bit and then I was going to leave, and Michael showed up. She must have pulled the ladder up, I didn't. I never touched her! Why do you believe Michael over me?" he cries.

"Michael has no reason to lie," Gully says simply.

"My son is not a liar," Alice says sharply.

Then Gully asks Derek, her voice casual, "I'm just wondering—where were you on Tuesday afternoon?"

Alice feels as if she's been yanked out of her own life and dropped into someone else's. The detective is asking her son for an alibi. This can't be happening. Her husband seems too shocked to speak.

"I left school at three thirty and came home."

"Anybody in the house with you?"

Alice's alarm grows. She knows no one was home that day. Pete was at work, she was out running errands, and Jenna was at choir practice. She picked her up at school after choir and took her to buy shoes.

"No," Derek says.

"I got home with Jenna shortly after five," Alice says. "Derek was at home, like he says."

"Okay, thank you," Gully says, getting up. "I think that will do for now."

When Gully leaves, Alice closes the door behind her and returns to the living room, where her son and her husband are suspended in a deeply uncomfortable silence.

Derek looks up at her then and cries, "I didn't touch her, I swear. I don't know why they think that!" And he bursts into tears.

Alice believes him, of course she believes him. She wants desperately to believe him. She sits down beside him and pulls him into a hug. "Of course you didn't," she says soothingly, glancing over at her husband, who is still shell-shocked, his face gray.

"What if they think I had something to do with—?" Derek cries.

"They can't think that," Alice says. She refuses to believe it.

THE POLICE SEARCH TEAM has finished at the Blanchards' house. They have sole possession of their home again. Nora wonders what they found, if anything, other than her hidden phone. Supper is much later than usual, and quiet, but emotionally charged. Even Faith seems unnaturally subdued, Nora thinks, observing her daughter. But it's no wonder, with everything that's going on.

"How was your time with Samantha?" Nora asks her.

"Fine," Faith says, avoiding her eye. Nora gives up on any possibility of conversation. Her daughter knows they were all at the police station that afternoon, stretching into the early evening—that's why she had to go to her friend's. She knows their house was searched, that Ryan's car has been taken away. They told her that the police had to do it because of that anonymous caller. But there was nothing to worry about because the caller was making it up, and the police would soon realize that. But Faith clearly isn't buying it, Nora thinks, because they are all obviously petrified and trying to hide it.

They are all anxious to leave the table. Al pushes his plate away first, stands up, and leaves the kitchen. Nora hears him go into the living room and turn on the television. Ryan gets up without a word and trudges up the stairs to his bedroom. Nora hears his door close.

"I have homework," Faith says, and grabs her backpack from the floor near the door and goes upstairs to her room.

Nora sits alone at the kitchen table, as if paralyzed. She must talk to Al. She forces herself to get up and clear the dishes, taking her time. When she can put it off no longer, she goes into the living room. Al is waiting for her. He sees her come in and increases the volume on the television—he's watching a basketball game, and the noise will mask their conversation. Unless it becomes very heated. But then, she thinks, maybe it's better if everything comes out now. Her infidelity might soon be in the newspapers anyway. She doesn't trust the police.

She sits down beside him on the sofa. Who will fire the first salvo? She decides to wait. Her nerves are drawn so tight she feels as if she might snap.

"You've been sleeping with William Wooler," he begins, eyes firmly focused on the television. His voice is low but laced with bitterness and disgust.

"Did the police tell you?" she asks, her voice dull.

"I already knew." He pauses. "And now everyone will."

"I thought you might," she says. She's surprised she sounds so calm, because she's churning inside. "Did you have me followed?"

"No. I followed you myself."

Her stomach lurches. The thought of it, of Al following her to the motel, of him watching, seeing her with William. She never noticed him. And they thought they were unobserved. What fools they were.

"When?" she asks, finally looking at him. She wants to know how long he's known.

"Every Tuesday for the last couple of months."

That astounds her. She feels her mouth drop open.

"That surprises you, does it?" he says, turning to face her. "That I can pretend as well as you can?" He leans closer to her so that his face is just inches from hers—as if he's leaning in for a kiss—and hisses, "I parked there, behind the dumpster in the back, every Tuesday afternoon and waited for you to come out of that sleazy motel with your lover and back to your car. And do you know what I did while I sat there, while you were in there with *him*? Breaking your marriage vows? Destroying our life together? Let me tell you," he spits. "I imagined what you were doing in that room, in that bed—all those things you won't do with me. I imagined you naked with him, enjoying yourself, enjoying your *sin*."

She looks back at him, mesmerized. He's not so detached now, he's fully present. He seems so different, so angry, so menacing. She wonders how she ever married him, how she ever loved him. "I'm sorry," she whispers. "It was wrong," she admits, her voice breaking. It was a sin. Her mind flits to thoughts of hellfire and damnation. She doesn't want to believe in hell, and she doesn't, not really, not most of the time. But sometimes she fears hell really does exist, and she is going there. Maybe Al will be there with her. *Maybe that's what hell is, other people,* she thinks as she stares at him for a long moment. "What now?" she asks finally.

"I should throw you out," he says viciously.

She recoils. Then she asks, "How long were you going to pretend you didn't know?" She wonders, if the disappearance of Avery hadn't brought all this about, whether he would have gone on pretending for the rest of their lives. But now he can't pretend; other people know. The police know. The news media will find out somehow, and then everyone will know. There's nowhere to hide. She feels sick to her stomach.

"I don't know," he says, and covers his face with his hands and begins to sob.

She watches in pity, but she can't bring herself to comfort him. Not now. It sickens her to think of him hiding behind the dumpster every week while she was making love to William, and then coming home and pretending he had no idea. But who is she to judge, considering what she has done? "We have to think of the kids," she says finally, when he has pulled himself together. He nods. She has to ask him. "Does Ryan know? Did you tell him?"

He turns to her then, the disgust he feels for her plain on his contorted face. "Why the hell would I do that?" He narrows his eyes. "And why would you ask me that?"

And now it's her turn to fall apart. She gives in all at once to her reeling emotions. They overwhelm her. "This is my punishment, mine and William's, for what we did. His daughter is missing, and we've been found out." She feels her voice rise with her hysteria. "The police think Avery got into Ryan's car, that he took her." She stares back at her husband—he is the only one she can say this to. She lowers her voice to a whisper. "What if he did?"

"How can you even suggest that?" he whispers back harshly.

"If he knew, and he wanted to hurt William—"

"No! He didn't know. And he wouldn't do that," Al insists.

No, she can't believe that her son would ever want that kind of vengeance. He doesn't have it in him. But she wonders again if Al might. What if Al took Avery, in an act of revenge, and this is *his* punishment, the police thinking his son is guilty of the father's crime? Oh God—is she losing her mind? They are churchgoers. Al is devout, but she is unsure—sometimes she believes, and sometimes she doesn't. But she knows that if God *does* exist, He is not always benevolent, and He works in mysterious ways.

Twenty-nine

Gully drives back to the station in the dark, drained by the events of the last two days. She'd like nothing better than to go home and get some much-needed sleep. But Avery is still out there. The ticking clock inside Gully's head allows her no rest. She thinks about her interactions with William Wooler, the Blanchards, and now Derek. Everyone here is lying, she thinks.

She's troubled by her conversation with Derek Seton. She doesn't know what to make of him. He was rattled. He might have done something to Avery in that tree house. He could be the older boyfriend. But she doesn't think he took Avery Wooler. How could he have? Even if he'd seen her on the street after her father had left the house, and lured her into his own empty house and assaulted her, what would he have done with the body?

She almost goes through a red light. *What would he have done with the body?* If he *was* molesting her, and no one was home, could he have invited her in? He was right across the street. Might he have strangled her, if she threatened to tell? Avery could be in the house. He could have panicked and shoved her in a crawl space until he got the chance to move her, later, perhaps into the woods, or the river, after the searches were called off. It's a large house, it probably has hiding places. His mother didn't get home with Jenna until shortly after five.

Gully pulls over and reaches for her cell phone.

RYAN LIES ON his bed and stares at the ceiling. He knows his parents are talking in the living room about what happened at the police station. His dad has turned up the volume on the television, like he does when he doesn't want them to be overheard. Like he used to do when Ryan was going through his drug problems and his parents had to talk. Ryan can't hear anything but the tinny, distant buzz of the television. They're worried about him. They don't trust him. Why would they? The police think he took Avery. Even his own lawyer seems to think he might have done it. He's scared shitless.

Ryan thinks about running away, disappearing. Changing his name somehow, never seeing any of them again. But they'd probably find him, and running away would amount to a confession. All he can do is wait it out, trust Oliver to do his job and protect him. He turns over and cries silently into his pillow.

GULLY ARRIVES BACK at the station and makes her way directly to Bledsoe. He shakes his head at her. "We'd never get a warrant to search the Seton place," he says. "We don't have enough. So he was in a tree house, once, weeks ago, with the missing girl—we can't search the house based on that."

Gully nods tiredly. "I know." She pauses. "Maybe I'm losing it. I need some sleep." She rubs her eyes.

He nods at her. "Go home, Gully."

But her mind is still working. "I could ask them if they'd consent to a search, without a warrant."

"There's no way they'll say yes to that."

"They would if they believed their son."

"No, they wouldn't," Bledsoe says. "Christ, do you really think he could have done it?"

"I don't know. There was something about him," Gully says. "I'm not convinced he hadn't been doing something inappropriate with her in that tree house." She takes a deep breath, lets it out. "Let's say Avery's father is telling the truth—he hits her then leaves the house at four twenty or thereabouts. What if she leaves the house again—she goes out the front door, onto the street. Let's say the witness who says she saw Avery get into Ryan Blanchard's car is lying—maybe she saw Avery on the street, without her jacket and her hair in a braid, but didn't see her get into Ryan's car, and made that up for some sick reason—maybe even because she saw her with Derek and wants to protect him? The Setons' house is right there, across the street. Derek was home by then. He could have seen her, seen that she was alone. If he *was* molesting her, he could have coaxed her into his empty house. His mother was out, his dad at work. What if he knew his mother was going to pick up his sister at four thirty and take her shoe shopping, and that they probably wouldn't be home until after five? They wouldn't have had much time. But maybe she threatened to tell this time, and he panicked and had to shut her up. But he can't get rid of the body—he doesn't have time and has no way to do it. He's only fifteen; he can't drive. So he has to hide the body somewhere in the house until he can get rid of it later. She could be there still."

"It's been two days," Bledsoe says. "If that's what happened, any chance the parents know? That he told them and *they* got rid of the body?"

Gully considers, shaking her head slowly. "I don't think so. Both parents seemed genuinely shocked when I was over there. But you never know." She adds, thinking it through, "If he confessed to his parents, they *could* have put the body in the trunk of their car while it was in the garage with the door closed and driven her out right under our noses, while we had police all over the Wooler house across the street."

They stare at each other for a long moment.

"We're not going to be able to search that house unless we get more," Bledsoe says finally, throwing himself into a chair. "Let's look deeper into this boy—any younger girls at school complain about him? Find out. In the meantime, we should have preliminary forensics back on Ryan Blanchard's car sometime tomorrow. They didn't find anything in the house, besides his mother's hidden phone."

"They're really something, these small towns," Gully can't resist saying. Bledsoe gives her a wry look. Gully remembers how she was concerned, in the beginning, that Bledsoe would focus solely on William Wooler and willfully blind himself to anyone else. To his credit, that hasn't happened; he has proved to be more thoughtful, more open-minded than she expected. What they have instead is too many suspects and no real evidence. Gully says, "I could pay Alice a visit in the morning, after the kids go to school and the husband goes to work. See if she'll let me look around, see if I can get anything more out of her."

Bledsoe nods and looks at the clock on the wall; he's obviously aware of the time passing, the clock running out on Avery. They all are. "This anonymous witness," Bledsoe says. "It's got to be someone on the same street. She recognized Ryan's car, and she had to have been nearby to see it at four thirty on Tuesday." He pauses and says, "Hang on a sec." He steps outside his office and gestures to Weeks, who's manning the tip line, to join them. He asks Weeks, "This anonymous caller—you've spoken to her twice now. Do you think you'd recognize her voice if you went door-to-door on Connaught Street and spoke to all the women?"

Weeks considers and says, "I don't know. There's nothing distinctive about it, but maybe. I'd be game to give it a shot."

"It's worth a try," Bledsoe says. "We need to identify this witness. She's either lying and fucking with us, or she's telling the truth—and we need to know which."

WILLIAM WOOLER FEELS like a wounded animal, trapped in a cage. He can't leave his hotel room without being accosted by reporters. They've discovered the back entrance he used this morning to slip out to a pay phone to call Nora, and when he tried to use it earlier this evening, to grab a bite to eat, they were waiting for him. He retreated into the hotel and ordered room service.

He calls Detective Bledsoe for an update.

"We're making progress," Bledsoe says. He doesn't elaborate.

William had seen the news about the anonymous witness, Ryan Blanchard being taken in for questioning, the house being searched. He knows his wife knocked Ryan down in his own house. He can hardly imagine Erin, usually so calm and reasonable, doing something like that, but there are photographs to help him. And these are desperate times. Maybe her own sudden, violent loss of control will help her to understand his. He wonders if she believes he's innocent now. "Am I still a suspect?" William asks.

"Yes," Bledsoe says bluntly. He pauses. "We found Nora Blanchard's hidden phone. We know it's her you were seeing. We've spoken to her."

William closes his eyes for a moment, opens them again. "At least you didn't hear it from me," he can't resist saying. Nora must be going through hell. "Is that going to make the papers too?" he asks.

"We'll try to keep it quiet," Bledsoe says. "But no promises."

Thirty

The next morning, Friday, Gully is sitting in her car outside the Wooler house shortly after 8:30. But it's the Seton house across the street that she has her eye on. Peter Seton has already left in his car for work, and she now sees Derek and his little sister, Jenna, leave the house for school. Derek notices her in the car, that's fine. She gives him a little wave. He grabs his sister's arm and marches away down the street and around the curve out of sight. Gully gets out of the car and knocks on the Setons' door.

Alice Seton looks like she hasn't slept much since Gully saw her last. She can't blame her. It must be awful, wondering what her son might have done. Gully doesn't have children, not yet anyway, and times like this make her question whether she'd be better off not having them at all. Maybe it's not worth it; you never know what might happen, how they might turn out.

"Alice," Gully says. "Can I come in?"

The other woman stares back at her resentfully and says, "No, I don't think so."

Gully nods. "Okay." So much for the consent to search idea. She fixes her eyes on Alice Seton's. "We've applied for a search warrant." It isn't true, but she wants to see Alice's reaction. And there it is—pure fear.

"I think you should leave," Alice says firmly, but her pallor betrays her.

"I'm going," Gully says. As she walks to her car, she wonders what Alice will do next. Call an attorney? Maybe they did that last night. Or maybe, Gully thinks, now that she's finally alone in the house, Alice's thoughts will run along the same lines as Gully's, and she will tear the empty house apart, looking for Avery Wooler. She can't get inside the house, Gully thinks, but she can have someone keep an eye on it and see what happens next.

ALICE CLOSES the door behind the detective and latches the deadbolt. She feels weak with fear. The long night awake, with all these disturbing thoughts running through her mind—it has taken its toll. Peter had eventually fallen asleep—she doesn't know how—but she'd gone over and over it all in her head. What the detective said. How Derek reacted.

He'd practically fallen apart. Is that what an innocent boy would have done? Or is that what a guilty boy would have done? She doesn't know.

Peter refused to believe any of it. Later, in bed, he said they had to stand by him. Derek was a good kid, not a child molester. He'd never lied to them. She nodded in agreement, but then Pete had fallen asleep, and in the long, dark, desperate hours before dawn, she'd given way to doubt and had let her mind run away with her.

It's horrible to think your own son might have molested a little girl. She was so quick to point the finger at Adam Winter, and now . . .

She makes her way back to the kitchen and dumps her cold coffee down the sink. She and Pete had talked to Derek at length after the detective left, and he'd stubbornly repeated to them what he'd said to the detective. But she has a gnawing doubt. Why was he in that tree house? It could have happened just like Derek said, but why was the ladder pulled up, if, in fact, it was? That was what the detective seemed to be fixated on. The ladder would only have been pulled up if they didn't want anyone to surprise them. One of them pulled it up. Why? Why didn't Derek just leave when he found Avery there? He doesn't even like Avery.

But she knows what kids do. The show-and-tell. *Show me yours and I'll show you mine.* It might have happened. It might have been fairly harmless. Avery might have exaggerated. She might even have initiated it. But Derek is old enough to know better. That's the thing—the age difference. It makes it inexcusable.

And then, the rest of it. Gully asking him where he was that afternoon. She knows how it looks, Derek home alone in this house at the time Avery disappeared, right across the street. She knows what they must be thinking—that if Derek was molesting Avery, he might be the one to have harmed her. But that's ridiculous. Even if he—for fuck's sake, he's not a *murderer*.

What about the witness who saw Avery get into Ryan Blanchard's car? Why won't that person come forward? Maybe because Avery never got into Ryan's car at all.

And now Gully was just here, on her doorstep, saying they're going to get a search warrant, and Alice doesn't know what to do. Why would they get a search warrant unless they thought they might find something? What are they expecting to find?

And then it hits her. They think Avery might have been in this house that day, and that she might not ever have left.

She sinks into a kitchen chair as her legs collapse beneath her, her breathing ragged. For a long moment she can't think at all. But then her mind clears. She must look, before the police do. She will search the entire house, and she will find nothing. Then she will know that Derek had nothing to do with this. He could not have killed Avery and disposed of the body anywhere else, because the search parties have been everywhere—except inside people's houses. And then the police can come in and do their thing, and they will have nothing to worry about. And they will deny and deny and deny that Derek ever touched her. And chances are, Avery's never coming back to say anything different.

Alice knows this is insane, but she's going to do it anyway. She'll start with the basement. She gets up and grabs a flashlight out of one of the kitchen drawers.

MIDMORNING, ERIN WOOLER is standing at her living-room window, dead-eyed, staring at the empty street, as if willing her daughter to come home. There's no one else out there now; the reporters have all given up, gone away. Nothing happening here.

Erin hasn't left the house since Gully brought her home after she attacked Ryan in the Blanchards' house yesterday afternoon. She wonders where all the reporters have gone. Nobody else's daughter has been kidnapped. She knows, because she watches the news religiously, hoping there will be a break in the case, fearing what it will be. Detective Gully has been good about checking in with her regularly, but she hasn't spoken to Gully yet this morning. She watched her knock on Alice Seton's door and talk to her briefly, but Gully didn't come over and talk to Erin. Probably because there is nothing to report. She'd noticed another car take up a position on the street; she wondered what it was doing there.

Erin knows they are still looking for Avery—the TV reporters tell her so, many times a day. They still have search parties out, beating the bushes, looking in ravines and dumpsters; they are looking for her everywhere. But if they'd gotten anything out of Ryan Blanchard, he wouldn't have come home. And she knows he came home—she saw the footage of him leaving the police station last night on the television. Maybe the reporters are now stationed in front of the Blanchards' house, farther down the street. She goes to the front door and steps outside, looking down the street. Yes. There are reporters clustered outside their house. She slips back inside.

She feels so alone, so powerless. She wishes she had someone to talk to. She doesn't know what happened to her daughter. Perhaps William had nothing to do with their daughter's disappearance. But she will never forgive her husband for his other, grievous sins—for slapping Avery; for then leaving her home alone to come to harm, if that is what he did; for lying about it. For his affair. She believes it's Nora Blanchard he's been having an affair with; of course it would be her. She's so beautiful. And William is so shallow.

She picks up her phone and calls her husband's new cell. He

picks up immediately. When he answers, she says, not bothering to hide her hostility, "It's Nora Blanchard you've been sleeping with, isn't it?"

He doesn't deny it. She waits for him to say something, and when he doesn't, she hangs up the phone.

Thirty-one

"We're not aware of any complaints of that kind about Derek Seton," the school principal, Ellen Besner, says. Gully nods.

"If anything like that had come to the attention of one of the staff, they would have had to bring it to me," the principal says, "so I don't think it's necessary for you to ask each of them directly."

Gully agrees. She doesn't want to do any unnecessary damage, and she knows that teachers are required to report any suspected abuse. She will leave it at that. She knows that teachers gossip, like everybody else. She has tried to be discreet, but she knows how people talk—even school principals. If Derek is innocent, she doesn't want to cause him any harm.

"Thank you for your time," Gully says, rising. As she does, her cell phone buzzes. She leaves the principal's office and answers. It's the plainclothes officer she'd had stationed outside of Alice Seton's house. "Yes?" Gully says.

"Alice left the house, driving her car out of the garage a little while ago. She drove to the grocery store. I'm in the parking lot now watching her load groceries into her open trunk."

"Okay. Thanks," Gully says, ending the call. Alice Seton isn't disposing of a body, obviously.

MARION COOKE WATCHES the police officers coming down the opposite side of the street. They have knocked on her door before, on the day Avery Wooler disappeared, and she told them that she saw nothing that day. She admires their persistence, asking the same questions of the same people, expecting to hear something different, or something more.

It's one of her days off from the hospital. She goes about her housework, every now and again peering out the front windows to see where they are now. They will be here soon; she lives eight houses down from the Woolers, and four houses up from the Blanchards on the other side of the street. She cleans and watches as they make their way to her house. Should she simply not answer the door this time? They've already spoken to her, so maybe they'll let it go. But she decides she will answer the door, or they might just come back. She pops into the bathroom to freshen up, so that she looks presentable.

When the knock comes, she's ready. "Hello," she says to the two male officers in dark uniforms on her front step.

"Good afternoon, ma'am," says the older one, showing a badge and introducing himself and his partner. "We're investigating the disappearance of Avery Wooler. Do you mind if we ask you a few questions?"

"Some other officers have already been here," she says, but she smiles slightly, to show that she really doesn't mind, that she understands it's necessary.

"I know, I'm sorry, but we have to be thorough." She nods. The officer says, "Perhaps you've remembered something. Did you see anything on Tuesday, the day Avery Wooler disappeared? Anything that you've remembered since you last spoke to the police?"

She shakes her head, frowning with regret. "I'm sorry, no. I'd like to help, I really would, but I didn't notice anything. It's so awful about that little girl. I'm a nurse, I work with her father at the hospital. I hope you find her. I hope she's all right."

Now the younger officer is observing her closely, his eyes alert. She finds him unnerving.

He speaks up for the first time. "Do you know the Blanchards at all?" he asks, out of the blue.

She's taken aback. "The Blanchards?" she repeats. "I know them to speak to; I don't really *know* them. Nora Blanchard volunteers at the hospital, so I know her a little."

"Do you know what kind of car Ryan Blanchard drives?"

She shakes her head. "No, I don't think so. I've never paid much attention."

"I think you do," the younger officer says. His voice is kind, unthreatening. "I think you've been calling the tip line, haven't you, without identifying yourself. I recognize your voice."

She freezes. *Shit.* She didn't want this to happen. She didn't want to be identified, that's why she called from a pay phone. Fortunately, there are still some left in Stanhope, though very few. Marion thinks about denying it, but she knows the young officer is certain. She denies it anyway.

"No," she says. She feels her face coloring. "I never called the tip line."

"We'd like you to come with us to the police station," the other officer says.

No. She doesn't want anyone to see her being taken to the police station in a cruiser. She can't risk that. "I'll come in, but not with you, not in a police car. I'll go in a few minutes, in my own car." The two officers look at each other; it's not like they have much choice, short of arresting her. They already know who she is and where she lives.

"Okay." He adds, "If you don't show up, we'll just come back."

GULLY WAS GETTING another coffee in the lunchroom when Bledsoe tracked her down.

"They've found her," he almost crowed. "We have our witness. We know who she is—Weeks recognized her voice. She's coming in." All Gully's tiredness had evaporated; she felt like she'd just had ten coffees.

Now, Gully studies the woman across from her at the table in the interview room. She's probably in her late thirties or early forties, wearing jeans and a cashmere sweater. She looks fit, as if she takes care of herself. Her nails are professionally done, but kept short, in a subdued shade of pink. Her brown hair has highlights and a good cut. Gully doesn't know quite what to make of this woman. She seems respectable. She's a nurse, lives in a nice, well-kept house, and looks well put together. But what kind of person calls a tip line, twice, with important information about a missing child, but refuses to come forward and identify herself? And then tries to deny it? As Gully studies her, Marion Cooke shifts uncomfortably in her seat.

Bledsoe begins. "Ms. Cooke, one of my officers believes you are the person who called and spoke to him on our tip line, not once but twice, claiming to have seen Avery Wooler get into Ryan Blanchard's car. He recognized your voice."

"He's mistaken," she says. "I never called the tip line. I didn't see anything."

But she seems nervous, Gully thinks, her eyes flitting back and forth between the two detectives.

Bledsoe persists. "You live on Connaught Street. You would presumably know Avery by sight and recognize Ryan Blanchard's car. What I don't understand is why you refused to give your name, and why you now refuse to admit it. But I can hazard a guess." He looks her in the eye and says, "You were lying."

She says, "No."

Bledsoe leans in close, lowers his voice. "A lie like that can get you into a lot of trouble." He adds, "You could be charged with falsifying an incident, which is a serious charge." She swallows, tears her eyes from his, and looks down at the table. "Did you see Avery get into Ryan Blanchard's car on Tuesday afternoon?"

Now she lifts her eyes and looks up at them, as if coming to a decision. Gully waits, realizes she's holding her breath.

Finally, she says, "Yes."

Bledsoe lets out a long breath and looks down at some notes in the file on the table in front of him. "Okay. You said you were sure it was his car, but you didn't see him specifically."

She nods.

"Where were you when you saw this?"

"I was on my front porch."

"You waited more than a day to make the first call. And then you refused to identify yourself. And then you denied it. Why?"

She swallows again. "I should have called right away. I realize that now. I regret that I didn't. But I guess I hoped she would turn up and she would be all right. That's what I told myself. Then, when she didn't, I called, from a pay phone." Gully and Bledsoe wait. "I didn't want my name mixed up in any of this. I didn't want to be in the news."

"And why is that?" Bledsoe asks.

"Because of my ex-husband," Marion says miserably. "I escaped a very abusive relationship a number of years ago. I had to get a restraining order against him. I don't want him to know where I'm living now. I thought if I came forward as a witness, my name and photo would be in the news, and he would find me." She looks back at them. "I didn't want to risk him hurting me. I hope you can understand that."

Gully finds her convincing. Her explanation makes sense. How unfortunate, she thinks wearily, that the one person who last saw Avery alive was too afraid for her own life to come forward.

"We can try to protect you, keep your name out of it," Bledsoe says.

"Can you?" She looks back at him desperately. "Can you really do that?"

The relief she so obviously feels at this makes Gully feel genuinely sorry for her, even though she's angry that she didn't come forward voluntarily, and sooner. It might have made all the difference.

.   .   .

MARION COOKE IS uneasy as she leaves the police station after signing her written statement. She'd parked her car on the street and now she walks that way. It's after four o'clock, but she doesn't want to go home yet. She decides to walk around downtown for a while, to clear her head. As she walks, glancing in shop windows, her thoughts turn to what might happen now.

Thirty-two

Nora Blanchard opens her front door just before five o'clock and feels the world tilt. It's the detectives, Bledsoe and Gully, back again, and they look grim.

"Is your son home?" Bledsoe asks.

She wants to lie, tell them he's out—anything to prevent what she knows is going to happen next. But Ryan is already coming down the stairs; he must have heard the knock. Or maybe he's been watching for them out his window, expecting them.

Nora can't speak. She feels a terrible dread. Ryan comes and stands beside her.

Bledsoe looks at Ryan and says, "The witness has come forward, the one who saw Avery get into your car on Tuesday afternoon at four thirty." He adds, "We're taking you into custody. You're under arrest." Bledsoe reads him his rights again.

Ryan turns white as the cuffs go on. He bursts out, "They're lying!"

Nora finds her voice. "It's not true! Who is this witness?" she cries. But they ignore her. As they take her son away, Nora calls after him, "I'm coming with you, Ryan. I'm right behind you. I'll call Oliver. I'll get your father. We'll be there with you."

GULLY DRIVES, OCCASIONALLY glancing via the rearview mirror at the white-faced boy sitting handcuffed and silent in the back. Bledsoe is beside her, probably running through his mind how he's going to conduct the interrogation. They know they can't talk to him until his attorney, Oliver Fuller, is present. For that reason, they probably won't get anything out of him. But Bledsoe will try to scare him, then offer him hope—offer him something to make him talk. A lot depends on what happens in the next hour or two. Gully takes a deep breath. She knows they can't fuck this up.

The attorney wastes no time getting to the station. They are soon all seated together in the interview room—Bledsoe and Gully on one side of the table, Ryan and Oliver Fuller on the other, like before. The interview is being videotaped. The cuffs have been removed.

"This is serious, Ryan," Bledsoe begins. "A girl is missing." Ryan stares straight ahead, not meeting the detectives' eyes. But he's trembling like a leaf. "We have a credible witness who will testify that they saw Avery getting into your car at approximately four thirty on Tuesday afternoon. And no one has seen her since." He pauses. "We know you didn't get home until sometime between six and six thirty. What were you doing in that time?"

Gully studies Ryan Blanchard, trying to read him. Did this trembling boy do something to Avery?

"What is the name of this witness?" the attorney asks.

"You'll find out in due course," Bledsoe says. "But we know who it is. The witness is very credible and has been into the station this afternoon to make a written statement."

Gully sees a flicker of concern cross the attorney's face.

"We all know that eyewitnesses are notoriously unreliable," the attorney says. "Have you any other evidence?"

"Not yet. But I'm sure we'll find it."

Bledsoe seems confident, but Gully knows that so far, they've found nothing in Ryan Blanchard's house or car. No bloodstained clothing, nothing that belonged to Avery. They've been through all the drone footage and have seen nothing of Avery ever being with Ryan—or anyone else. They've got the preliminary forensics back on Ryan's car, and come up empty. If the girl was in his car, it was probably for a short time, and he could have cleaned it afterward. There are no signs that she was assaulted or killed in that car. But he could have driven her out to the country somewhere, attacked her, murdered her, hidden her body. They have his cell phone records so they know roughly where he drove that afternoon. That rural area is being searched as they speak. But if they don't find her, and if he doesn't talk, it makes it bloody difficult to get the evidence they need.

"Here's the thing, Ryan," Bledsoe says, leaning forward and fixing his eyes on the frightened boy. "If there's any chance that Avery is still alive, it is in your best interest to tell us where she is. Things will go much easier for you if you do."

Ryan says, "She never got in my car, I swear." He turns to his lawyer. "Why don't they believe me? Why do they believe this other person? Whoever it is, is lying!"

Bledsoe continues as if the boy hadn't spoken. "And if Avery isn't still alive, it is still in your best interest to cut a deal. Do the decent thing and tell us where she is. Give the parents some closure." The boy appears to be struck dumb. Bledsoe sits back in his chair again and says, "Tell us what happened, Ryan. Was it an accident? You didn't mean to kill her, did you?"

"Stop!" the boy screams. He raises his hands to cover his ears.

The attorney studies Ryan briefly and says, "I'd like a moment with my client."

AFTER A FEW MINUTES, the attorney beckons them back in. Gully reenters the interview room with Bledsoe and looks at the boy in the chair. He's obviously been crying, and she allows herself to hope. Perhaps he's ready to talk. Maybe they can end this.

They sit. The attorney looks grim, resolved.

"Well?" Bledsoe says.

"My client denies any involvement with the missing girl. She did not get in his car that day. He is innocent."

"Is that right, Ryan?" Bledsoe says tiredly.

Gully can see his fatigue, and it hits her then, how tired she is too. They've been running on adrenaline, and now she realizes how empty her tank is.

Ryan says tearfully, "I had nothing to do with her. Whoever said she got in my car is lying."

"But the witness is a fine, upstanding citizen," Bledsoe can't resist saying to Ryan, "and you're a known drug offender."

"That's enough," the attorney says, a knee-jerk reaction.

"Oh, right, you were his attorney on that, weren't you?" Bledsoe shoots back. Then he turns back to the boy. "You've got a good lawyer, Ryan—good for you. But we're going to hold you for now."

Bledsoe pushes back his chair noisily and stands, while the attorney rests his hand on the boy's back in a gesture of comfort. Gully knows Ryan's never been in jail before. She's looked into his file. He was a minor when he was arrested for possession, and he was released to his parents. But now he's an adult, and he's suspected of kidnapping and possibly murder.

Gully hears the attorney speaking quietly to Ryan. "It's okay. You'll be held overnight here. They can't hold you for too long before bringing you in front of a judge and charging you. But if they don't find any physical evidence, they'll never be able to convict."

Gully wonders if the attorney believes Ryan is innocent. She can't tell.

MARION COOKE LIVES alone in a bungalow with two bedrooms on the main floor and a guest suite in the basement with its own bathroom. It's small, but nicely redone. She's never had children, so the house is quiet, clean, and uncluttered. The guest room in the basement is generally empty. She does, occasionally, have her sister come stay.

Marion spends a long time downtown before she drives home, still feeling on edge.

She places her handbag on the kitchen counter and unlocks the door from the kitchen to the basement. She flicks the switch on the wall to light up the stairs and the area around the bottom. She listens for a second, cocking her head. Silence. The television isn't on. That's unusual.

She heads down the steps. The basement is divided into two separate areas, a bedroom with a small bathroom at the front of the house, and a larger main room behind it, where the windows—barred long ago to prevent break-ins—don't let in a lot of light. Her guest is in the bedroom, where there is no window at all.

Marion knocks on the door to the bedroom and calls, "Avery?"

Thirty-three

Ryan stands up, his legs trembling beneath him. None of this feels real. He's afraid to look his attorney in the eye in case he doesn't believe him. Ryan knows he didn't pick Avery up in his car. He's innocent. But what really frightens him is that the truth doesn't seem to matter. He knows that innocent people get convicted all the time of crimes they didn't commit. For a moment he can't move, even though his lawyer is urging him forward.

He stumbles, putting one foot ahead of the other. His parents are waiting outside this room, down the hall. Will he see them before they take him away? In handcuffs? He wants to see them, he wants his mother to hug him and tell him that everything's going to be okay, that he'll be home soon, that she'll make everything better. He wants his dad to fight for him. But he doesn't want them to see him like this. He's afraid he'll blubber like a baby.

His parents are there in the waiting area when they bring him

out. His mother looks like she's been sitting at the bedside of someone who is dying. His father is clearly frightened. Ryan wonders if
they actually think he took Avery Wooler and killed her. How
could they believe that of him? He made some stupid choices. He
wishes he'd never done the drugs, that they'd never lost faith in
him. He made one mistake, and now the whole world is prepared
to believe the worst of him.

They let his mother and father hug him. His mother won't let
go. She causes a bit of a scene, and he's grateful, because it takes
attention away from him and his unstoppable tears. He meets his
father's eyes one last time as he's taken away.

An officer brings him downstairs, and as the door closes behind
him and they descend he can still hear his mother's wails. In the
basement are the cells. At the moment, they're empty. Stanhope
doesn't have a lot of crime.

"The drunks will come in later," says the officer directing him
from behind, "especially on Friday night." He pushes him into a
cell, releases him from the handcuffs. Checks for a belt and removes
the shoelaces from his sneakers. He locks him in and walks away,
the sound of his steps on the concrete fading. Ryan looks at the cell
as if he's looking into the future. He lies down on one of the beds
curled into the fetal position and stares at the wall, too stunned to
keep crying. Waiting for morning, and what will happen to him next.

AVERY HAD HEARD the front door open upstairs and then
footsteps crossing the house to the kitchen, then coming down the
stairs to the basement. She listened carefully, fully alert; it sounded
like only one set of footsteps, and she relaxed.

"Avery?" Marion says, on the other side of the bedroom door, pushing it open.

"Where have you been?" Avery demands, sitting up straighter on the bed. Avery had heard the police officers come to the door, hours ago. She couldn't hear much of what they said, but she knows that Marion spoke to them and then they left. Marion had gone out afterward and had been gone a long time.

"I had to do some shopping," Marion says. "I needed to get a few things."

Avery asks, "What did the police want, earlier?"

"They're just asking everybody the same questions over and over again, hoping they might have remembered something."

Marion couldn't have said anything. If she had told the police that Avery was hiding in her basement, she wouldn't still be sitting here, would she?

"Don't you trust me anymore?" Marion asks.

Avery ignores the question. "What did they ask you?"

"The same things as before. Did I see anything unusual, any strangers or strange cars in the neighborhood around the time you disappeared or in the days preceding."

"What did you say?" Avery asks. She wants to know everything.

"I told them I was home, in the house. That I didn't see anything unusual that day." She adds, "They didn't get anything out of me."

Avery slumps down again on the bed. Things are not going her way, not anymore. She'd watched on the small television across from the bed as her father was taken in and out of the police station, looking like he didn't know what had hit him, looking like he was going to be arrested. It was very satisfying. She wanted him to suffer. She watched the news on TV and read the newspapers that Marion brought her, holed up in her basement. Avery was a celebrity. She would be even more of a celebrity when she turned up again, having survived a kidnapping, with her unknown kidnapper still out there somewhere.

She'd enjoyed it when she found out that her father had lied about being home that day—*liar*—and that he now seemed to be living in a hotel. It looked like he was going to be arrested, that he would learn his lesson and she could reappear and go home. But then suddenly they were interested in Ryan Blanchard. She didn't even know him. Then it was on the news that the police had an anonymous witness who said they'd seen Avery get into his car. It wasn't true. "I'll make us something to eat," Marion says. "I'll bring it down here and we can watch the seven o'clock news."

MARION MOVES AROUND the kitchen, boiling water for pasta and grabbing a jar of sauce out of the cupboard. Soon it will be time to put an end to this. It's been three days.

Avery had been outraged when she heard on the news last night that someone claimed to have seen her get into Ryan Blanchard's car. *How can that be?* Avery had said. *I never got in his car. Somebody is lying!*

Those detectives believed her, Marion thinks. No one will think Marion Cooke, a respected nurse, is lying about what she saw.

Marion arranges two plates of pasta on a tray, with cutlery and two glasses of milk, and carries it down to the basement. Avery has already turned on the television on the wall in front of them. It's almost seven o'clock. They wait through the commercials. Are they going to say anything about the witness? Marion wonders. Are the police going to release her name? They said they wouldn't. But they will probably arrest Ryan Blanchard now, and that will make Avery angry. She doesn't want Avery to know it was her. Not yet. She doesn't want Avery to know that the pact between them was never real at all.

Marion is tired of having Avery in her house; she wants this to be over. She wishes she hadn't opened the door today to the officer who recognized her voice.

The newscast begins, and as expected, the lead story is about the girl sitting beside her. "There have been new developments in the Avery Wooler disappearance," the anchorwoman says, her voice serious. "Police today have taken into custody eighteen-year-old Ryan Blanchard. Police have confirmed that a witness, who claims to have seen Avery getting into Ryan Blanchard's car on Tuesday afternoon, has now come forward. Blanchard lives on the same street as the missing girl. The nine-year-old girl hasn't been seen since she disappeared Tuesday afternoon, despite a massive search involving hundreds of volunteers and police officers."

The screen now shows footage of Ryan Blanchard being taken out of his house in handcuffs and bundled into an unmarked car.

"No," Avery says. Marion glances over at her; the girl's face is flushed with anger.

"No, it isn't true!" She turns to look at Marion. Marion shakes her head, trying to appear sympathetic while still listening to the news for anything about the witness.

"People in the neighborhood expressed both shock and relief..." the anchor continues, but she adds nothing that hasn't been said before.

Marion glances at Avery. She's obviously furious. When she's angry, she's a bit scary. "Maybe it's time you went home," Marion suggests casually. She doesn't mean it. Avery can't go home. She'll never go home now. Marion has her own agenda, one that Avery doesn't know about.

"No."

Marion has learned how stubborn the girl is, how petulant.

"I wanted him to be sorry," Avery complains. "I wanted him to be blamed!"

"I know," Marion says.

"And now you want me to leave," Avery says sulkily. "I like it here."

Marion feels a surge of annoyance. Of course she likes it here, living like a spoiled princess, having food brought to her, watching all the attention her disappearance is getting on television, reading about herself in the papers—it all feeds her enormous narcissism.

But it's not up to her, Marion thinks. None of this is going to end the way Avery Wooler thinks it is.

Thirty-four

Avery glares at the woman beside her. Marion wants her to leave. Nobody ever wants her. It infuriates Avery to be rejected, and now Marion, her helper, her secret friend, seems to be rejecting her too.

She's scared, Avery thinks, having her here when there's a massive search going on. She's probably worried about being arrested if she's found out. Well, maybe she *should* worry, Avery thinks. Because Marion shouldn't be mistaken about who has the power here. It's not Marion. Marion agreed to help her, but she'll throw Marion under the bus if it suits her.

Avery is the one in charge. Because she knows that if she tells the police that she was in Marion Cooke's basement the whole time she was missing, then Avery won't be the one in trouble—Marion will. Marion will be held responsible; Avery is only nine years old. Marion should know better. Grown-ups shouldn't let missing girls stay in their basement while the whole world is looking for them.

She has known this from the beginning, but it just seems to be occurring to Marion now, Avery thinks. Maybe she's not that bright. In fact, she was a bit surprised that Marion agreed to help her at all. Maybe she *is* kind of stupid.

Avery used to play in the woods behind their street, and she was behind Marion's backyard one day when Marion called out a hello. Avery was lonely, playing by herself.

"You're Dr. Wooler's daughter, aren't you?" she asked. She seemed friendly.

"Yes," she admitted. She came closer.

"I'm Marion," she said, smiling. "I'm a nurse. I work with your father at the hospital."

"Oh," Avery said, losing interest.

"Would you like some cookies? I just baked some."

Avery considered.

"Chocolate chip," Marion added.

Avery had been told not to speak to strangers. But she loved chocolate chip cookies, and this woman wasn't really a stranger. She was a neighbor, and she worked with her dad.

"Sure." Avery followed her into the house through the door into the kitchen. The house was more modest than her own home down the street. Marion seemed to want to know all about her, asking her questions about school, about her family. Avery thought it was a bit strange, all the interest, but adults were like that. Lots of questions. Different from kids. She didn't mind. Hardly anyone showed an interest in her. So she told her about her mom and dad, how they fought about her.

"Is that right?" Marion asked. "Why do they fight about you?"

"Because I'm difficult," Avery said.

"You seem like a perfectly nice girl to me," Marion said, smiling.

After that, through the summer, she often went to Marion's house, through the woods behind the houses, into her yard to her back door, mostly for the cookies. She never told anyone; it felt pathetic not to have friends her own age. And when she wanted somewhere to hide out for a while after her dad hit her, the only person she could think of was Marion.

She wonders if Marion still thinks she's a perfectly nice girl now. Probably not. She turns to Marion, still sitting on the bed beside her.

"You're afraid we'll be found out," Avery says.

Marion looks at her. "We won't be found out."

She seems awfully sure of herself, Avery thinks.

MARION GATHERS UP the dirty dishes and makes her way back upstairs. She puts the tray down on the counter and silently locks the door to the basement. She keeps it locked at all times so that Avery can't come up to the rest of the house. But Avery knows the rules and hasn't tried to leave the basement in case she'd be seen; she doesn't know the door is locked.

Marion leans against the door.

The girl downstairs may be smart, but she's only nine years old, and she doesn't know everything. She has no idea what's really going on here. Avery, hidden away in her basement, has no idea what she's walked into. She doesn't know that she's in over her head.

She doesn't know that Marion is obsessed with Avery's father. The fact is, she's been in love with him for a long time, her days and nights filled with thoughts of him. Looking forward to seeing him at the hospital, living only for that. It was enough, somehow, to nurture this fantasy of the two of them falling in love, of being together, her and the handsome doctor—even though she knew he was married, that he had a family. But lots of handsome men—doctors included—leave their wives and their families to marry someone else, someone younger and more attractive. She's not kidding herself that she's more attractive than his wife, but she's at least comparable; she's seen his wife at hospital events. She has gone through the last year or more trying to get his attention, but he always regarded her with complete indifference. She thought perhaps he was a good man, loyal to his wife, one who wouldn't stray, despite the easy charm, and that made her idolize him even more. And made him more of a challenge.

When she recognized his daughter lurking outside her backyard fence, she'd invited her in, bribed her with cookies. They got to talking, because Marion wanted to know as much as possible about Dr. Wooler and his family. She befriended the girl, but she had never mentioned it to anyone. She certainly wasn't going to tell Dr. Wooler that she was chatting to his daughter on a regular basis. He might think she was stalking him.

She could have gone on like this indefinitely, sustained by her hopes and fantasies, merely seeing him at the hospital. She had her own soap opera running in her head. And it would have been enough, if it weren't for the day, just a week ago, that she saw him with Nora Blanchard.

Thirty-five

Marion had been in a supply closet at the hospital, gathering up supplies, when she heard someone come quietly into the outer room. Then she heard a man's footsteps and the sound of the door quietly closing. For a moment, she didn't move. But then she heard Dr. Wooler's voice, deep and husky. It sounded seductive. "Come here."

Now frozen, Marion heard a woman moan and the unmistakable sound of kissing. She heard sharp breaths, and gasps and more moans, and she felt her entire world falling apart. Dr. Wooler was not a good man, loyal to his wife. He was cheating on his wife, and it wasn't with her.

She felt the most colossal rage in that moment. He'd always acted as if she didn't exist, as if he didn't see her, even when she was speaking to him, when she was trying her very best to engage his interest, and here he was, in the arms of another woman. She could hardly breathe. She had to know who this other woman was. She crept to the partly open door of the supply closet and peered out. Dr. Wooler was in an amorous embrace with someone she immediately recognized—Nora Blanchard, a volunteer at the hospital, and one of her neighbors. Of course. The most beautiful woman around. It wouldn't be anyone else. Marion stood silently behind the door in turmoil, watching through the crack for several minutes, enduring it, until they finally broke apart, breathing heavily, smiling at each other and rearranging themselves. "I'll leave first," Dr. Wooler said. Nora nodded. "See you soon," he said, and gave her a last kiss, another longing look, and left.

Marion stood, rigid, behind the door, unable to decide what to do. Should she confront Nora? She wanted to go out there and smack her face, claw her short nails across it, disfiguring her, leaving scars. She was overcome with feelings of rage and jealousy, disappointment and worthlessness. She watched the other woman—so perfect, so desired—smooth her hair as she waited a bit before she left. She was so beautiful. Seeing Nora had always made Marion feel plain, but now she was filled with self-loathing. She couldn't compete with that, and it made her miserable. *See you soon*, he'd said. They were obviously having an ongoing affair. They were clearly in love; there was so much passion there, passion that she'd imagined for herself. Now she imagined him leaving his wife, leaving his family, but not for her, for Nora Blanchard.

Marion didn't go out and confront the other woman. She simply stood behind the door in the supply closet until Nora left. And then she had gone home ill in the middle of her shift. That had happened just days before Avery showed up at her back door with the welt on her face. Marion let her in and listened to her story that her father had hit her. She wasn't sure she believed Avery, because why would he even be at home at four in the afternoon? He'd be at work. But someone had obviously hit her, and it was clear she was angry at her father; perhaps it *was* true. Marion was still angry at him herself.

Avery explained her childish plan to run away and hide for a while to pretend she'd gone missing and asked if she could stay with Marion. She wanted her father to be sorry. She wanted her father to be blamed. Marion, too, wanted to see William Wooler hurt. The only thing she wanted more was to see Nora Blanchard hurt, and she saw an opportunity.

So she'd let Avery stay, hidden in her basement. She told Avery she was not to come upstairs, ever, in case she was seen through the windows, and like a wicked old witch, Marion quietly locked her in.

Marion would visit her in the basement, and together they'd watched the search unfold and Dr. Wooler's fall from grace on television. Marion enjoyed watching him suffer, maybe even more than Avery did. It served him right—for ignoring her, for cheating on his wife, for choosing someone more beautiful than her. She welcomed the scrutiny Avery's disappearance brought to Dr. Wooler, because she knew they would investigate him. She hoped they would find out that he was having an affair with Nora and that it would blow his life apart. She hoped it would destroy Nora's marriage, and her family, and her comfortable life. But there was more. Because she'd seen Ryan Blanchard drive down the street that day, just before Avery turned up at her back door. And she knew she could do something that would rip Nora's heart right out of her chest.

She waited till she'd seen William suffer sufficiently, then she'd slipped out to a pay phone and called the tip line and claimed to have seen Avery Wooler get into Ryan Blanchard's car. And when they didn't immediately arrest him, she'd done the same thing again, adding some details about Avery's appearance. She'd said she was willing to come in, but she'd lied. She wasn't going to identify herself as the witness till Avery was disposed of.

It was unfortunate that the police had discovered her before she wanted, but she had her story about an abusive ex-husband ready. Now Ryan Blanchard has been taken into custody, and Nora must be going out of her mind.

As soon as things quiet down a bit, Marion will get rid of Avery. And then she will come forward publicly and stand by her story till her dying breath.

ALICE SETON HAD SEEN Ryan Blanchard being taken into custody on the seven o'clock news. She can't help it—she feels relieved. Jenna doesn't know what her brother, Derek, has been accused of, and Alice and Peter want to keep it that way. Maybe, with Ryan in custody, that will be the end of it.

Alice has not confided in her husband about what she did earlier that day. She did tell him that Detective Gully had arrived at their front door that morning and threatened them with a search warrant. They both hope that is now on hold. She felt weak with relief when she heard they'd taken Ryan into custody.

But she hasn't told her husband what she did once Gully left in her car. How she lost her mind and tore the house apart, looking for the body of a dead girl. How she'd gone through the house—the crawl space, the furnace room, the attic, everywhere, anywhere you could hide a body, even the shed in the back. She'll never tell a soul. It's something she will take with her to her grave.

She's so ashamed that her imagination took her there. Ashamed that she could think that of her son, even for a moment. At one point during that dreadful, crazed morning, she'd glanced out the window and noticed a car. It was still there when she looked later on. She realized she was being watched, which only fed her paranoia. But finally, when she'd searched everywhere and found nothing, when she was certain that the police would find nothing, she sat down, wrote out her grocery list, and went shopping. There was nothing to find. She was sure of that.

And now it's going to be all right because Ryan is in jail. She spares a thought for Nora Blanchard, whom she knows a little, because their daughters go to the same school. What she must be going through. What they *all* must be going through in that house.

She thinks of her own son. This has been very distressing for him. For all of them. He'll get over it, in time, Alice tells herself. This will all pass, and they will never talk about it again.

Thirty-six

Erin Wooler wanders around the house like a ghost who can't move on. She's relieved that they have arrested Ryan. She remembers his face when she knocked him down—she thought he looked guilty.

She has to put her faith in the police, trust that they know what they're doing. They have found the witness, at least. She wants to know who it is. All she knows is that it must be someone who lives around here, probably on this very street, or how else would they have seen what they saw, and recognized the car? Why are they keeping the witness's name secret? She would like to know who it is. She'd like to know who waited *so long* to tell the police who took her daughter. Maybe she should feel grateful to the witness for finally coming forward, but all she feels is colossal rage at the delay. Why didn't this witness tell the police what they saw the moment they saw it? What possible acceptable reason could there be for a nine-year-old girl to be getting into a man's car like that? And it was only a short time later that the police were called and a full search was on. So why the hell didn't they go to the police with what they knew? If they had, there might have been time to save her daughter. She'd like to confront this witness, the way she confronted Ryan, and ask, *Why?*

They will never recover from this if Avery never comes back. Erin wonders just how much damage all this will do to her son. To all of them. How it will change them. She already knows that she has changed. She will never be able to look at the world the same way, ever again.

She's so worried about Michael. She goes upstairs and taps on his bedroom door, pushes it open. Her son is sitting on his bed with his laptop, looking pale and afraid. "Do you want something to eat?" she asks.

"No."

"You didn't eat anything at supper," she tells him.

"Neither did you."

She takes a deep breath, lets it out. "If I make a sandwich, will you share it with me?"

"Okay." He looks relieved, and she realizes then how anxious he must be about *her*, on top of everything else.

"Come downstairs and I'll make us a grilled cheese." It's his favorite.

WILLIAM WOOLER SITS in the chair in his hotel room staring blankly at the walls. He can't stop thinking about Ryan Blanchard and what he might have done to Avery. All the ways he might have hurt her, and then probably killed her. He has to face it—Avery might never be coming back to them. He weeps into his hands.

Putting a face to her kidnapper has made it all the more horrible. The witness has come forward; it must be true. He wonders who it is, and why they aren't releasing the person's identity. He'd stared at the television in revulsion and disbelief, watching them take Ryan away. A good-looking kid. He looked so *normal.*

His thoughts turn to Nora. He doesn't blame her. He can't blame her. Kids turn out the way they're going to turn out, despite their parents' best efforts and intentions. He knows this because of Avery. He and Erin have done everything they can to love her and help her, but she is who she is, and they can't change that; they can only hope to encourage her in the right direction. But look at Michael, there's nothing wrong with him. They were brought up by the same parents, in the same household, yet they couldn't be more different.

If Ryan is a child molester, kidnapper, or, sickeningly, a *murderer*, he can't blame Nora for it, or her husband either. They didn't make him that way. He was born that way; William is convinced of it. He loves Nora, but now there's baggage. At this thought, he laughs out loud, long and bitterly. Baggage. You could say that.

NORA HAD HAD to be held back by her husband as they took her son away. She wouldn't let go of him, was crying and wailing. The police officers had to prize her off her son, gently at first, and then more forcefully.

When he'd gone, down to the cells, she had slumped in her husband's arms, a dead weight. Her legs couldn't support her, and he had half carried her over to a chair. She stopped wailing as a kind of stupor set in.

Now Oliver Fuller is trying to get her attention, trying to get her to focus. He's telling her that it's not over. That Ryan will probably come home in a day or two. She tries to focus on what the attorney's saying. He's telling her there's still hope.

Fuller says, "Unless they come up with some physical evidence, they won't be able to hold him."

"What physical evidence?" Nora asks. Her brain is dull. They've already been through the house; they have Ryan's car. They haven't found anything, as far as she knows.

"If they find her body," Fuller says delicately.

Nora shrinks back in her chair, numb. For the first time, she finds herself hoping they never find William's daughter.

"Who is the witness?" Al asks grimly. His face is drained of color.

"I don't know. They won't say," the attorney says.

They talk for a while longer. Then they have to discuss the question of payment for the attorney. Finally, Al gets her up on her feet and they head for their car to go home. It's almost dark. She can't bear to leave her son behind in the cells. What will happen to him there? They have to fight their way past the clutch of reporters waiting outside the station. She holds her hands up over her face as they swarm, and a police officer tries to clear them away. At last they make it inside Al's car and lock the doors. Al starts the car. It's such a hollow, empty sound.

Nora is mute on the way home, her mind catastrophizing. She tells herself that she does not believe that Ryan killed that little girl, but she's terribly frightened anyway. She has no control over what's happening. At last, she looks sidelong at Al, driving with his eyes fixed straight ahead, his hands tight on the steering wheel. His face takes on a ghastly hue whenever the streetlights play over it. She wonders what he's thinking. Does he think their son is guilty? Or does he know more than she does? This has been troubling her, lurking in the back of her mind. Is Al vengeful enough to have brought this on all of them by harming William's daughter?

She says quietly, "Al?"

Thirty-seven

He doesn't seem to hear her.

"Al?" she repeats, more firmly.

"What?" he says tersely.

And now she has to say it. It sticks in her throat like a glob of half-chewed food. She swallows nervously, clears her throat. "Do you think Ryan picked her up?"

He glances at her. "Fuck, how can you even ask that?"

"You must have asked yourself," she says.

"He didn't do it," Al says. He says it with conviction, as if he's certain. "He's not capable of something like that. You should know that—you're his mother."

She ignores the implied criticism. "I know," she says. "I just needed to hear you say it, I guess." She adds, and she knows she sounds frightened, "I just . . . I'm not sure Oliver believes him."

There's a long pause. Then Al says, "He's a lawyer. He doesn't care one way or another."

"I think he cares," Nora says.

"It doesn't matter what he thinks," Al says gruffly. "He'll do his best for him."

Does she dare say what's really on her mind? She begins with a tearful, "This is all my fault."

Al is silent. She knows he's not going to disagree with her. He believes in God's wrath.

She knows he's furious with her about the affair. *Just how angry is he? What might he have done?* She stares out the windshield into the deepening dark, into the oncoming traffic. "I'm sorry, Al. I'm sorry about the affair with William, about everything."

"Oh, you're sorry now, are you? You weren't sorry before," he says nastily. He drives in silence for a little, and then says, with heavy sarcasm, "Maybe Wooler called in the tip himself, to draw attention away from him."

She turns in the passenger seat and stares at him. "Don't be ridiculous," she snaps. "Besides, he would never hurt me like that."

Al flushes with anger. "You still think he's innocent?" he asks, sneering at her. "Well, I don't. I think he killed his daughter. He was probably molesting her himself, the pervert."

This makes her angry. "You've been awfully keen to think William did it from the beginning," she accuses him. "You'd love to see him go to prison, wouldn't you? So that we could never be together, is that it?" She's thrown away all caution now. She doesn't love this man, it's William she loves. She doesn't believe William killed his daughter—why would he? But in her escalating panic she can understand why Al might do it—to punish her and William for what they've done. Could he go that far? He'd sat in his car behind the dumpster while they were in the motel, every Tuesday afternoon, *for weeks.* And then come home and pretended he didn't know. What else might he have done, with her entirely oblivious?

He's on their street, and now he pulls into the driveway and turns off the car. She plucks up her courage. "Was it *you?*" she hisses.

"What?"

"Did you take Avery? To punish me and William? So that he would go to prison? And I would learn my lesson?" She's shouting now. "But you didn't anticipate someone lying and saying they saw her get into Ryan's car, did you? You didn't see that coming. You seem awfully sure she didn't get into Ryan's car! How does it feel, seeing our son in jail for something you did!" She's speaking quickly now, hysterically, the words tumbling over each other, and suddenly she feels a hard slap across her face. The blow stuns her, leaves her face turned to the passenger-side window. She stops talking abruptly.

"Shut your goddamn mouth," he says viciously. "You utter whore."

She turns back to him again, her face throbbing, her voice hard and cold. "Well, did you?"

He stares at her. "I can't believe you're actually asking me that." She waits. His voice, when he speaks, is low and menacing. "No. I didn't take her. But I guess now we know what you really think of me. You think I'm capable of *killing* your lover's child—a *child*— but you think he's innocent, and that he would never hurt you. Where does that leave me, Nora, eh?" He shouts at her now, sitting in the car in their driveway. "*Where the fuck does that leave me?*"

AL GLARES AT HIS WIFE in fury as she cowers against the passenger-seat door. He wants to strike her, but he restrains himself. He's already slapped her, and he's never done that before in his life. He's never been so angry, not even when he sat behind the dumpster at the motel. This woman, his wife, whom he once loved, hasn't just slept with another man. She hasn't just fallen in love with another man. She actually believes he is capable of harming a little girl, just to destroy her happiness.

How did they get to this point?

Abruptly he says, "Get out."

She opens the car door quickly and flees, slamming it behind her. She runs up the walk, already fishing her house keys out of her purse. She doesn't look back.

He puts the car in reverse and squeals out of the driveway and down the street, blind with rage. He shouldn't be driving. But he doesn't trust himself to be alone in the house with his wife, the house where they brought up their kids.

What will happen to the kids?

He drives out of the town, onto the highway, and realizes he's sobbing. He can hardly see the road for his tears. His son is in jail. He's not as sure of him as he pretended to be to Nora. He doesn't know if Avery got into Ryan's car. He doesn't want to believe it. If she did, he's sure that whatever happened was an accident. Maybe he was just giving her a ride as a favor. Maybe something happened, he doesn't know what, but Ryan could not have meant to hurt her. He could not have meant to kill her. And then he would be scared and deny everything. That's Ryan's way. He loves his son anyway. His son is not a monster.

But Al hates his wife. He realizes that now, realizes it's been building for a while. He hates his wife with a pure, white-hot zeal.

He could kill her. His son is not a monster, but Al realizes in that moment, driving too fast down that dark highway, that he himself might be capable of something unspeakable.

GULLY IS AT a drive-through, waiting for a burger and fries, before heading back to the station, when her cell phone buzzes. She sees that it's Erin Wooler calling. For a moment she feels guilty; she hasn't dropped in on her at all today, it's been so busy. Was it just this morning that she spoke to Alice Seton, thinking Avery might be somewhere in that house? And then identifying the witness, picking up Ryan. She'd meant to call Erin at various times throughout the day, but something always interfered. She takes the call.

"Detective Gully?"

"Hi, Erin," Gully says. "I'm sorry I haven't dropped by today yet. I was just about to call you."

"I was expecting to hear from you," Erin says, and Gully can tell she's not happy with her.

Erin asks bluntly, "Ryan Blanchard—did he take her?"

Gully sighs. "We don't know. So far he's denying it."

"Who is this witness?"

Gully's heart sinks. This is why she's been avoiding Erin Wooler, because Gully knew she would ask who the witness is, and she can't say, even though Gully thinks she has a right to know. "I'm afraid I can't tell you that."

"Why not?"

Gully sighs again and says, "That's just the way it is right now. There's good reason for it, that's all I can tell you."

"That's bullshit," Erin says. She waits a moment and then asks, "Do you believe them? That Avery got into that boy's car?"

"The witness is very credible," Gully says, avoiding a direct answer.

"Why did they wait so long?" Erin cries.

Gully hears the raw pain in the other woman's voice. "There's a reason for that, but I can't tell you what it is," Gully says, feeling awful.

Erin abruptly disconnects.

Thirty-eight

Avery is sulking in the basement bedroom. She's not happy that Ryan Blanchard is in jail. This was supposed to be about making her dad suffer.

She can hear Marion moving around upstairs. Marion wants her to leave. Avery will leave when she's good and ready. Has her father learned his lesson? Has he suffered enough? She's pretty sure he'll never hit her again after this. Maybe it's time to slip away and be found walking on the road in the middle of the night.

Her reappearance will create a sensation. Everyone will want to interview her. Maybe she'll be asked to go on some really big talk shows, like *Good Morning America*. Maybe there will be money in it. If there is, she'll make sure it goes to her, not her parents.

She will say she was grabbed by a man from behind, and something put over her head so she couldn't see, and forced into a vehicle and driven a long distance. Then she was taken from the car and into the basement of a house and locked in the dark for she doesn't know how long—she had no way to tell the time, no way to know what was going on in the outside world. She was terrified. The man never spoke. He wore a mask the whole time. He let her use the toilet in the basement, then he would lock her in the room again. She would never be able to identify him, would never know why he took her or why he released her. He didn't hurt her physically—they would be able to tell he hadn't touched her, so she can't lie about that. She wants them to believe her.

She'll say that he covered her head again, put her back in the car, drove a long time, and dropped her in the woods, took the hood off, and told her to lie down with her face to the ground and not get up till she counted to five hundred. Then she walked until she found a road.

Will they believe her? She thinks they will. The only one who might not believe her story is her father. He might guess the truth—that she ran away and hid somewhere and is making it all up. But he won't dare say so—how would it look? And he's the only one, besides her, who knows what happened in the kitchen that day. He'll be worried that she'll say something. He'll be careful around her. She finds she's actually starting to look forward to being home again.

Michael will be jealous of all the attention she'll get. He'll resent her, resent how crazy their lives will become. But she'll enjoy it.

Avery will watch the eleven o'clock news and then she'll decide. Maybe she'll tell Marion that she plans to leave tonight after all.

ERIN WOOLER IS so angry. She's angry at the world. She's angry at her husband, Detective Gully, and the mystery witness who failed to come forward in time. Her rage is the size of a mountain. It gives her purpose, it gives her strength. She wants to speak to this mystery witness herself. She wants to determine if this anonymous person is telling the truth about Ryan Blanchard. If so, then he took her daughter, and she saves her biggest rage for him.

She paces the living room, thinking about Detective Gully. She wouldn't tell her who the witness is—she's obviously afraid to, after what happened with Ryan Blanchard. It must be someone close by, to have seen what they claim to have seen. To know Ryan's car. To recognize Avery. It must be someone on this very street. She thinks of all the people on Connaught Street. She knows many of them by sight, and some to chat to, but she doesn't know all of them. She could go, now, to each house, and ask point-blank if they called the police about Ryan Blanchard. Surely whoever it is will tell *her* the truth, if she promises to say nothing about who it is? She is the mother of the missing girl. Most of the people on the street are parents themselves. She will shake the truth out of them if she has to.

Erin returns to the living-room window and looks out. She must know. She must know what happened to Avery. She can't stay trapped in this house, which has become like a tomb, waiting for something to happen. She goes upstairs once more to her son's room and knocks on the door.

When she opens it, she sees Michael back in his usual place on the bed, staring at his laptop. At least he's eaten something. She wonders what he's looking at but doesn't ask; she doesn't really want to know. It could be a game, or it could be something about Avery. He looks so lonely, so lost; she can't bear it. She realizes that at some point, they will have to talk about his father, about what's going to happen to them as a family. Maybe it will be just the two of them. But not now.

"I'm going out for a bit," she says.

"Where?" he asks, looking up from his screen.

She considers a white lie but remembers what happened last time, when she told him she was going to see his father at the hotel, and the journalists printed all those photos of her standing over Ryan Blanchard in his living room.

"I'm going to talk to the neighbors," she admits, "about Avery."

He doesn't try to dissuade her, as she expected. "Do you want me to come?" he asks.

That surprises her and nearly breaks her heart. He's worried about her. He wants to protect her. She realizes that she might be all he has left; she cannot go to pieces on him. "No. I think someone should be home, in case . . ."

He says, "Okay," and turns back to his screen. Everything about him seems hopeless.

She closes his door and makes her way back downstairs. In the vestibule she grabs her jacket and stands for a moment, staring at the empty spot where Avery's blue-jean jacket had been hung, before it was taken away by the crime-scene team. Then she steps outside. There is no one there. The press has gone. She stands alone in the silence for a moment, feeling as if everyone has abandoned her. It's dark and quiet. She locks the door behind her and decides to start across the street, at Alice Seton's house. Because it has occurred to her that if Derek Seton has been molesting Avery, she wouldn't put it past Alice Seton to call in a tip about someone else, true or otherwise.

Thirty-nine

Alice Seton hears the knock at the door and goes still. She has grown wary of knocks at her door. Her heart begins to pound. She doesn't want to answer it. She looks at her watch. It's almost nine at night. She's not expecting anyone. What if it's the police? The knock comes again. She gets up off the sofa, where she's been trying to read a book, and answers it with dread.

She's surprised, and discomfited, to see Erin Wooler standing on her doorstep. Erin looks how you might expect a woman whose daughter is missing to look. Unkempt, grieving, almost unhinged. "Erin," she says. She doesn't know what else to say.

"Can I come in?" Erin asks. She sounds reasonable enough. Alice remembers uneasily how this woman barged her way into the Blanchards' home the day before and physically attacked Ryan Blanchard. And then she remembers that it was Erin's son, Michael, who saw Derek in the tree house with Avery and accused Derek. Alice steps back, suddenly apprehensive. Why is she here? She doesn't know what Erin is going to do. She glances over her shoulder, as if hoping to find her husband right behind her, but he's upstairs.

"I'd like to talk to you—and your husband—if you don't mind," Erin says quietly.

And really, what can Alice do? She can't turn the poor woman away. Their daughters used to play together, and Erin seems mostly calm at the moment. She gestures her inside, closes the door quietly, and leads her into the living room. She knows Derek is in his room on his computer with his headphones on; he can't hear anything. Peter and Jenna are both upstairs. "Pete's on a work call upstairs right now," she says. But she knows that if she screams, her husband will come running.

She signals for Erin to sit on the sofa and sits across from her in an armchair, the solid coffee table between them. "I'm so sorry," Alice says, "about Avery. How are you holding up?" A stupid question, but she's uncomfortable, and it makes her stupid.

"As well as can be expected, I guess," Erin says, with a trace of bitterness. There's an awkward pause. Then Erin says, "I wanted to ask you—as one mother to another—if you are the one who saw Avery get into Ryan Blanchard's car?"

Alice is taken completely by surprise. "Me? No. Why would you think that?"

"Or perhaps it was your husband?"

"God, no. It wasn't us," Alice says.

Erin must believe her because her face seems to collapse in disappointment. "I don't know who this witness is," Erin says. "And the detectives won't tell me."

"Why not?"

Erin shakes her head. "I don't know. Detective Gully told me there's a good reason, but she wouldn't tell me what it was. I just need to know who it is and whether they're telling the truth."

Alice can see the tears starting in the other woman's eyes, and feels her own eyes begin to well up in response. It's terrible, what this woman must be going through. She begins to relax—relieved that Erin doesn't seem to be here about Derek after all. "Of course you do," she says sympathetically. "I mean—if it's true Avery got into Ryan's car . . ." She trails off awkwardly. She says, "The police must believe it, or they wouldn't have arrested him."

Erin makes a face that seems to indicate that she doesn't think much of the police. "I'm going to every house on this street to find out who called in that tip," Erin says. "And when I find them, I'll know if they're lying."

"How will you know?" Alice asks doubtfully.

But Erin doesn't answer. Instead, she says, "The police questioned Derek, didn't they?"

Alice bristles. "Yes, but it was just routine," she says defensively.

Erin looks her straight in the eyes. "They think he might have been inappropriate with my daughter."

"No. He wasn't," Alice says with heat.

"I can understand how that upsets you," Erin says, with heat of her own. "Imagine how I feel." She rises from the sofa. "We don't know our own children as well as we think we do. We don't know what they're doing every minute of the day." Her face is bleak. "We can't."

Alice stands up herself. "Derek never touched her," she insists, her voice low. She shows Erin to the door, and then watches as she goes down the sidewalk to her left, and up the driveway to the next house. She really means to find this witness, Alice thinks. She means to find the truth.

. . .

WILLIAM WOOLER PACES his small hotel room, weighed down with grief and guilt. He's trapped in an unimaginable situation. He wants to make things better, but it seems impossible.

His standing in the community is ruined. Even if Ryan is convicted, he will always be the infamous Dr. Wooler, who lied to the police when his daughter was missing. And if Ryan isn't convicted, what does that mean for William? There will be a permanent cloud over his head for the rest of his life. A significant number of people will always believe he killed his little girl.

His marriage is over. Even worse, his relationship with his son is probably damaged beyond repair. William collapses onto the bed and weeps for the loss of his daughter, his son—and his wife too.

Things will never be all right again with Erin. But he must try to mend things with Michael. He wishes he could go to the house, talk to him, but he doesn't want to face Erin, and he doesn't think she'll let him in. But he can call Michael's cell. He texts him first, to tell him he's going to call him from a new number.

He's nervous as his son's phone rings. It rings a few times. William is about to hang up in despair when Michael picks up. He doesn't say anything.

"Michael?" William says.

"Yeah."

William finds himself at a loss for words. "Are you okay?" he asks at last.

"Yeah."

He doesn't sound okay. He sounds lost, like he's hurting. And William knows he shoulders a lot of the blame for that.

"I'm sorry, Michael," William says. "I'm sorry for everything." His voice catches on a sob. "You know I love you, right? I love all of you." Michael is silent. "I've made mistakes. I know that. But I want—I hope—I can be there for you, Michael. I'm your dad."

The line goes dead. His son has hung up on him.

THE BURGER AND FRIES that Gully wolfed down sit in a lump in her stomach. That's the thing with cases like these, she thinks—it's all junk food and no sleep. No time for proper exercise either. It's hard to keep your mind sharp. She recalls her telephone conversation with Erin Wooler earlier that evening and sighs, exhausted. It's critical to know whether Marion Cooke is telling the truth. Is this just some wild-goose chase? Is the boy down in the cells innocent? Are they wasting precious time while the real culprit gets away?

She pulls up to the computer. She looks more closely into Marion Cooke. She's divorced. No children. She looks into her ex-husband. Greg Kleig. She runs a search on him. He still lives in Boston and has not remarried. He has a job in IT. And he has two assault convictions from charges against him brought by his ex-wife. She looks a little deeper and finds a record of the restraining order she got against him. It looks like Marion Cooke is telling the truth—about that, at least.

NORA SITS ALONE in the dark house, thinking about her son, alone in a cell. Faith is staying over at her friend Samantha's for the night—she'd again arranged for Samantha's mom to pick her up when they followed Ryan to the police station that afternoon. How dark the world has turned. She's frightened for Ryan. She's frightened for herself, afraid of her husband. Her face aches where he hit her.

Will he come back tonight?

And if he does, what will happen to her?

She wants to believe that everything is going to be all right, but she hasn't believed that for a while now. Not since Avery Wooler went missing. That's what started everything. If only she hadn't been sent home that day, none of this would have happened.

Nora could have decided to end her unhappy marriage, like millions of other women had before her. She could have divorced her husband, William could have divorced his wife, and they could have been together. They could have been happy. They could have made it work. Blended families are hardly unusual. But now . . .

She can't think of William without despair. Her guilt overwhelms her. She thinks that somehow their actions are at the core of all this horror. The last time she spoke to him, on the phone, he'd sounded like he was falling apart. He'd said he loved her. Now her son is in jail, suspected of murdering his child. What if William can't think of her now without revulsion? What if her husband is to blame?

She knows she should pack a bag and leave. But she has nowhere to go and children who need her. And she feels, somehow, that whatever is coming for her, she deserves. What she wants now is the truth. Whatever happens, she wants to know what happened to Avery Wooler.

She waits for her husband to come home.

Forty

Erin makes her steady way down the east side of the street, giving the Blanchards' house a wide berth. She knocks on doors, endures the looks of horror and pity she receives. Some people are genuinely kind and wish they could help; others don't want to talk to her, as if she's tainted somehow. But no one admits to being the anonymous witness, and none of them seems to be lying, as far as she can tell. She reaches the end of the street and curves around to the other side. She sees *The Winters* painted on the mailbox of the next house. Erin doesn't know the Winters or anything about them. She knocks.

When the door is opened, it's clear that the woman who opens it knows who she is though. How could she not? Erin's face has been splashed all over the news. She asks, "May I come in and talk to you for a minute? I'm Erin Wooler."

The woman hesitates and then says, "I know. And I'm so sorry. Come in. I'm Gwen."

She seems like one of the kind ones, Erin thinks. She's led into the living room, where a good-looking teenage boy is slouched in an armchair with an iPad.

"Adam, do you mind leaving us alone for a bit?" his mother asks.

He looks up, avoids Erin's eye, and quietly leaves the room.

"I know why you're here," Gwen says, once they're alone, seated in the living room.

Erin looks back at her, her heart beginning to pound. Has she found her witness?

"But I assure you, Adam had nothing to do with your daughter. That's just vicious gossip someone started because he's different. Adam has autism. The police were already here, and they know he had nothing to do with it."

Erin is taken aback. "Oh, I didn't know that." She pauses. "I imagine it's difficult," Erin says, "having a child on the spectrum."

"Yes, very difficult," Gwen concedes.

"Avery is very difficult too," Erin finds herself saying. She didn't intend to say it, it just came out. "She's got behavioral problems, she's very oppositional." She suppresses a sob. "I want her back more than anything."

"Of course you do," Gwen Winter says. "You're her mother. You love her, no matter what."

"There's an anonymous witness," Erin goes on, "who says they saw Avery getting into Ryan Blanchard's car."

"I saw that on the news," Gwen says.

"Was it you?"

"Me? No. I didn't see anything." She leans forward and says

gently, "You want to know who the witness is, to talk to them your-self. I'd be the same. I wish I could help you."

She seems to really mean it. Erin nods.

Gwen asks, "Can I get you something—a cup of tea?"

But Erin shakes her head and rises to go. "I have to find this witness. I have to know if what they're saying is true."

The other woman rises with her and says, "If you ever want to talk, I'm here." She adds, "It looks like you could use a friend."

AL BLANCHARD IS sitting in his car, parked, of all places, be-hind the dumpster in back of the Breezes Motel. He couldn't think of anywhere else to go. He'd sped down the highway out of town, his heart darker than the pitch-black night, and when he saw the motel, it seemed to call to him. There's a kind of strange comfort being where he's been so many times before, back where it all started. It feels familiar, almost safe. He feels a sort of nostalgia. Because back then, when he used to spend afternoons behind this dumpster, he knew only that his wife was cheating. His son wasn't suspected of kidnap-ping and murdering a little girl, and his wife didn't suspect him of the same heinous crime. He sits there for a long time, sometimes star-ing sightlessly into the night, sometimes weeping against his steer-ing wheel.

Stiff with cold, he thinks about what he should do. He feels like he's losing his mind. What he'd like to do is go home and put his large hands around Nora's long, lovely throat, and squeeze until she's gone. He imagines it, her eyes staring wildly back at him, pleading, as he snuffs the life out of her. And then he'll put her in the car and bring her here and throw her in that dumpster. After that, he doesn't know. His mind stutters—he can't see past the act of throwing her body in the dumpster, which has been witness to what she's done, and to his shame. It's where she belongs.

MARION IS IN the kitchen, making herself a cup of tea. She hears a knock at the door, and freezes. What if it's the police, back again? The lights are on; she can't pretend she's not home. She leaves her tea on the kitchen counter and makes her way to the front door. She opens it. It's not the police. It's worse than that.

"May I come in?" Erin Wooler asks, shivering on the doorstep, her wan face starkly illuminated by the porch light.

Marion feels the blood drain from her own face. She can't have Erin Wooler here. Her daughter is in the basement.

"Are you okay?" Erin asks, looking at her closely.

Marion calls on her training as a nurse and pulls herself together. *Treat it as an emergency. It's just an emergency. You can do this.* "I'm sorry," she says, bringing a hand up to her forehead. "I have low blood pressure and got up too quickly to answer the door. I thought I was going to faint there for a moment."

"Can I come in?" Erin repeats.

Marion tries to put her off. "Um—I was just going to run a bath." But Erin doesn't take the hint. She stands there on the front step, resolute, staring at her. "But sure, come in for a minute."

Marion turns away and leads her to the kitchen at the back of the house. If they keep their voices down, Avery might not even know her mother was ever here. And even if Avery does realize her mother's right upstairs, Marion tells herself, she won't reveal herself. She'll stick to the plan.

But what if she doesn't?

The kitchen is at the back of the house, rather than over the bedroom where Avery is hiding. There's less chance they'll be overheard here. Marion doesn't offer to make Erin a cup of tea. She finds herself looking at the door to the basement and quickly tears her eyes away. She pulls out a chair for Erin.

"I recognize you, of course," Marion says in a quiet voice. "You're Dr. Wooler's wife, the mother of the missing girl."

Forty-one

Marion keeps her eyes on Erin, and—she can't help it—on the door to the basement, over Erin's left shoulder. She is suddenly terrified that the doorknob will turn—but the door is locked. Avery might have heard her mother's voice on the doorstep; she'd heard the police officers. Marion watches it, irrationally fearful that it might rattle and thump as Avery tries to get into the kitchen, afraid that she might call out.

"Seriously, are you okay?" Erin asks, with concern in her voice. "You look like you've seen a ghost."

"Actually, I don't feel well," Marion says, dragging her eyes away from the door behind her, focusing on Erin's face. She tries to corral her fears. She must not let her nerves get to her. She just has to hold it together and get Erin out of here as quickly as possible. Even if Avery heard her mother's voice at the door, she'll stay quietly in her bedroom. She's not going to blow everything now. Though she'll want to know everything they talked about, afterward.

What flits through her mind next is whether Erin knows her husband has been sleeping with Nora Blanchard. She and Erin have that in common—they have both been callously rejected by the same man. He has chosen Nora Blanchard over both of them. She finds herself studying Erin's face, her hands, drawing the inevitable comparisons. Erin has not weathered this crisis well, Marion thinks, rather pleased. It's obviously taken a terrible toll on her.

"I won't stay long," Erin says. "I just want to ask you something."

Marion tries to focus on what the other woman is saying. What can she possibly want to ask *her*? "What?"

"Are you the one who called in the tip about Avery getting into Ryan Blanchard's car?"

Marion starts in surprise, feels her heart accelerate. She didn't expect this. Erin is staring at her.

"Are you?" Erin asks again. Her voice is louder now, suspicious.

"No," Marion says. "It wasn't me." She thinks she sounds convincing. She has always been a good liar, but she is off balance here, unprepared. She is too aware of Avery, hiding in the basement.

But Erin is staring at her now. "It *was* you, wasn't it? You called the police about Ryan."

Oh Christ. She watches Erin rise, the chair scraping loudly against the tile floor.

"You're lying," Erin accuses. "I can tell. Why are you lying?"

Erin's voice is louder now, and Marion gets up, too, and retreats, her lower back pressed against the counter as the other woman approaches her. Erin looks like a woman possessed. Marion remembers that she attacked Ryan in his own home, because of what she'd done.

"I'm not," Marion protests. She must handle this and get this woman out of here.

But Erin clearly doesn't believe her. "Why? Why are you deny-ing it?"

Marion looks back at her, trying to think. She's always meant to come out publicly as the witness—once Avery is gone. She'll enjoy it. She's even looking forward to it. She speaks very quietly, "Okay, yes, it was me."

"Why deny it?" Erin asks. "Is it true? Did you see her get into his car?" Her voice is wild now, too loud.

Marion pulls herself together. She must stick to her story. She deliberately keeps her voice low. "I didn't want my name made pub-lic because I'm hiding from an abusive ex-husband. He'll kill me if he finds me," Marion says. She's very convincing—it's as if she's convinced herself that her ex-husband wants to kill her. "And yes," she says quietly, "I did see Avery get into Ryan's car that day." She meets Erin's eyes. "That's the truth."

She expects that to calm the other woman, to diffuse the situa-tion. Once she knows, she'll go. But that isn't what happens.

"And you're absolutely sure it was Avery?"

"I'm sure."

"Then why the hell did you wait so long to call?" Erin cries. "You knew Avery was missing! Everybody knew! But you waited *more than a day!*"

Erin's face is livid with rage. Specks of spit fly out of her mouth. Marion thinks Erin is going to strike her. The situation is out of control. Marion tries to placate her. "I told you—I was afraid of my husband . . ."

Erin shakes her head, not accepting it. "No! You could have

called right away and not given your name. You didn't need to wait. She might have come home to me if you'd called right away!" She's weeping now. Weeping and shouting. "But you didn't. And if my daughter is . . . gone, it's on *your* hands!"

"Get out of my house," Marion says with cold fury. She needs this woman to leave, now.

Erin gives her one last, wrathful glare, and storms out of the house.

Marion locks the door behind her, heart thumping, and goes back to the kitchen, where she leans against the counter, her hands gripping its edges tightly. She stares at the door to the basement. Did Avery hear all that? She might have, even from the reaches of the basement bedroom.

Forty-two

Avery is standing behind the kitchen door, on the small landing at the top of the basement stairs. She knows Marion is in the kitchen, on the other side of the door, just steps away, because she's listened to everything. She'd heard the knock at the door and recognized her mother's voice. She'd heard the footsteps cross overhead and fade away as they approached the kitchen, and Avery concluded that Marion didn't want her to hear their conversation. Avery had wondered why not.

Marion would expect her to stay in her bedroom in the dark, not moving, not wanting to be found. But Avery wanted to know what was going on, so she crept quietly out of the bedroom and up the carpeted stairs, and listened at the door.

What she heard stunned her. *Marion* was the one who called in the tip about her getting into Ryan Blanchard's car, drawing suspicion away from her father. It was a lie. It enraged her. *Why did she do it?*

But Avery still wasn't about to make a surprise entrance and wreck all their plans.

Now her mother is gone, and Avery stands behind the door, seething with rage, thinking about what to do. She could open the door right now and tell Marion that she heard it all. See what she has to say for herself. That's what she wants to do. It takes a tremendous effort of will, but she returns to her basement bedroom without a sound.

WILLIAM WOOLER'S cell phone rings on the bedside table in his hotel room. He regards it nervously, then picks it up. "Yes?"

"William?"

It's his wife. And she sounds upset. "What is it? Have they found her?"

"No. But I know who the witness is."

Had the police told her? They'd refused to tell him. "Who?" he asks tersely.

"Marion Cooke. She lives on our street."

He sits back against the headboard of the bed. *Marion Cooke.* It's disconcerting—astonishing—to learn that she is the witness, that it's someone he knows. "How did you find that out?"

He listens while she tells him, impressed. It's more than he's done.

"She denied it at first," Erin says, "but then she admitted it. She says she's telling the truth about Avery getting into Ryan's car, and obviously the police believe her, because they've got him in custody. But, William," she's sobbing now, "how could she have waited so long to call? She saw him take her. If only she'd called right away—"

She's right, William thinks. If they'd known earlier, they might have found her in time. But now . . . he knows—they both know—that it might be too late.

He feels a rage well up in him to match his wife's. He can't find words.

"William?"

"I can't believe it," he says, his voice shaking. "She's a nurse at the hospital." He feels utterly betrayed by someone he sees regularly. She knew Avery had gotten into Ryan's car, and she said nothing for more than a day, even though it was all over the news that they were looking for her and that the police suspected William of harming his own daughter. She hadn't spoken up. Why? Marion has a lot to answer for. But if she's telling the truth, and Ryan took Avery—he feels the room spin.

"I didn't know you worked together," Erin says. "She didn't mention that." She sobs in despair. "If he doesn't talk, we'll never know what happened to her."

When she hangs up, William puts down the phone, his mind in turmoil. Erin thinks Marion's telling the truth about Avery getting into Ryan's car. Why would she make something like that up? But he doesn't want it to be true. Because if it is, Avery is probably dead.

William had thought, in the beginning, that Avery had run away. He's the only one, besides Avery, who knows that he hit her that day hard enough to knock her off her feet. He feels a deep shame thinking about it. He remembers going out to his car, hesitating, turning to go back in and beg once more for her forgiveness. But he hadn't. He's the only one who knows how furious she must have been. He knows she can be vengeful. He thought she'd run away, but as time went on and she wasn't found, that seemed less and less likely. He'd gone from fearing that she'd reappear and tell everyone how he'd struck her, to fearing she really had been taken by someone and that he would be wrongly arrested for murder. And now, worst of all—she was probably taken, and murdered, by the son of the woman he loves.

MARION LEANS AGAINST the kitchen counter, clutching its edges, for a long time. The situation had gotten out of control. They'd been shouting. She tries to recall exactly what was said, but now it's all a jumble in her head. Could Avery have heard it all?

She must go down and face the girl—her questions, her demands, her cold intelligence. She knows that the longer she waits to go downstairs, the angrier and more impatient Avery will get. But she must think. She opens the fridge and takes out an opened bottle of white wine. She pours herself a glass and drinks, finishing it quickly.

She has to face Avery. The more she delays, the harder it will be.

AVERY HEARS the kitchen door at the top of the stairs opening. She's left her bedroom door open, waiting. She's in a nasty mood. It's taken her long enough, Avery thinks. She was probably figuring out what to say. Avery's sitting on the bed. It's almost time for the eleven o'clock news.

Marion comes into the bedroom and faces her, her arms folded across her chest. "Your mother was here," she says.

She's trying to act normal, but she's not fooling Avery. "I know," Avery says carelessly. "What did she want?"

Marion seems to relax a little. She sits down on the bed. "She was going up and down the street, trying to find out who called in the tip about Ryan Blanchard. The police won't tell her who it is."

Avery stares at her. "I heard shouting."

Marion nods. "Your mother was very upset, ranting about the police not doing their jobs. She's out of her mind with worry."

Avery flicks her eyes to the television set. "The news will be on in a minute." She picks up the remote and turns on the TV but mutes it until the program starts. "I was thinking of leaving to-night," she says. But Avery wants to punish Marion. She says, "Un-til I heard you say that *you're* the one who called about Ryan Blanchard." She turns to face Marion now. "You think I didn't hear all that? You think I stayed in my room like a good little girl?" She sneers at her, feeling angry and superior. "I was right behind the kitchen door, and I heard *everything*." She leans in close to Marion's face and hisses it again. "*Everything*." She pulls back. "Why would you do that, Marion?" When Marion doesn't answer, she shouts, "*Why would you do that?*" And she turns and grabs the small lamp off the bedside table beside her and throws it against the wall, where it shatters violently, narrowly missing the television. But Mar-ion remains maddeningly calm.

She says, after a long pause, "I wanted to get back at his mother."

"Why?" Avery demands.

"I hate her," Marion says. "She's a volunteer at the hospital and acts like she's better than everyone else. She's not even a nurse. But she's got all the doctors wrapped around her little finger."

"Why?" Avery wants to know how this woman gets people to do whatever she wants.

"Because she's beautiful. That's the only reason."

"My father too?" she asks.

"Your father especially," Marion says bitterly.

She's jealous, Avery realizes. That's why she did it. Avery can understand that, but she doesn't like that Marion interfered with *her* plans. "Is she having sex with my father?" she asks. Marion looks at her as if surprised that a nine-year-old would say such a thing. She might be only nine, but she knows things. She knows what adults do.

"Yes."

"How do you know?" Avery demands.

"I saw them together, at the hospital. They didn't know I was there."

Avery digests this information. Finally, she says, "You're going to take it back."

"What?"

"You're going to go to the police and say you made it up, about seeing me get into Ryan's car."

"I can't do that."

"You can, and you will."

Forty-three

Marion stares back at the girl on the bed, the one who thinks she's pulling all the strings.

"I can't," Marion repeats.

"You have to," Avery says, "or I think we'll need a change of plan." Avery looks at her angrily. "You said you'd help me, Marion. But that isn't what you've done, is it? You've *used* me. So you tell the police that you lied about Ryan, or I'll tell them where I've *really* been all this time."

Marion looks at her, amazed that this nine-year-old thinks she's really that stupid. Stupid enough to put herself in the hands of a selfish, vindictive child.

Avery looks away, unmutes the television set. The news is starting. "Oh, and I'll be watching for it on the news, so I know you actually did it. Because I can't trust you anymore, can I?" She turns and gives her a cold look.

"Fine," Marion says at last. She gets up and says, "I just wanted to see her suffer, the way you wanted to see your father suffer." But Avery has turned her attention to the television and won't look at her. Marion doesn't stay to listen to the newscast. She leaves the room and goes back upstairs, locking the door silently behind her.

She's not going to recant her statement to the police. Not now. Not ever. Poor little Avery.

Little fool.

RYAN BLANCHARD HEARS a commotion coming his way. He stares catatonically at the painted concrete of the cell wall in front of him.

An officer is hauling a drunk, angry man down to the cells.

"Get your fuckin' hands off me," the drunk shouts.

"That's enough," the officer says.

Ryan is suddenly fearful that the officer will put the belligerent drunk in the cell with him. But he marches him past and puts him in the empty cell next door, where the man continues to curse in a loud, slurring voice. Ryan exhales in relief. But then he realizes that this is nothing. Real prison will be much worse.

They've taken everything away from him—including his shoelaces—so that he has nothing to kill himself with. But maybe there's a way.

They think he killed a child. He's afraid his lawyer thinks so, too, and he doesn't know what his mom and dad think. He's too frightened to cry anymore.

.   .   .

IT'S LATE. The night is clear and cold, and the crescent moon is crisp in the inky black sky. Al doesn't know how long he's been sitting in his freezing car behind the dumpster, thinking about killing his wife. He knows how he'll do it. With his bare hands. He knows what he'll do with her body. He knows she's at home, alone. She won't be able to fight him off. When it's done, he'll take her body through the kitchen and put her in the trunk of the car. The car will be in the garage with the garage door closed. Funny how so many of these houses have a garage attached to the house, he thinks— it makes it so easy to remove a body without anyone seeing. And then he'll bring her here. Someone might see him taking her out of the trunk and lifting her into the dumpster—that's a risk. He's not even going to wrap her in a blanket. He's not sure how he'll get away with it; he's not thinking that far ahead. And he doesn't really care. Everything's gone completely to hell anyway. He thinks about what his wife said, how she thinks he's a child killer. He could never harm an innocent child. But he could strangle his wife.

Maybe she saw something in him that he hadn't even realized was there.

He turns the key in the ignition with a shaking hand and starts the car. He pulls the car out from behind the dumpster and drives around to the front of the motel. He means to take the exit onto the highway, back to Stanhope and his adulterous wife, but instead he finds himself slamming on the brakes, suddenly unable to breathe. He pulls into an empty parking spot. His entire body is shaking.

He sits in the car, trembling like a leaf. *What was he thinking?*

He can't kill his wife. He's losing his mind. He got carried away with a fantasy.

He pushes open the car door, walks across the pavement to the flashing neon sign indicating the office of the motel, and requests a room. As he pays and gets the key—his hands still shaking—he realizes that the bored woman behind the counter has no idea what's been running through his disordered mind. He almost wants to warn her about people. People like him.

AVERY MOVES RESTLESSLY around the small basement bedroom, impatient and frustrated. It's been harder than she expected to stay hidden for all this time. Marion went out ages ago—how long does it take to tell the police you lied?

She nurses her feelings of rage and betrayal. Marion had gone behind her back and called about Ryan anonymously, never expecting Avery to find out.

Avery paces around the bedroom. She's so angry at Marion. Maybe she *will* change her story. Maybe she should say that she was held captive in this basement against her will, and that she escaped from Marion. After all, there's a reason Marion lied to the police— she had it out for Nora Blanchard all along. She could say Marion kidnapped her and kept her in the basement so that she could accuse Nora's son. She could tell them that she came over for cookies and sympathy that afternoon, like she'd done in the past, and that Marion lured her into the basement, knocked her out with something, and then kept her prisoner in the basement bedroom. It's so obvious that Marion is jealous of the beautiful Nora Blanchard. Marion is in love with her father. It all fits. She can make it work.

And no one is aware that she and Marion even know each other. Avery could even say that Marion was planning this all along, inviting her in for cookies throughout the summer and asking her questions about her father, just waiting for the right moment.

It's a much better story than the one she was going to use.

She paces the small bedroom, around the three sides of the bed, over and over.

But what if Marion tells the truth and says the "kidnapping" was all Avery's idea? She gives that careful thought. She doesn't think anyone would believe it. What nine-year-old child would do such a thing? And they'll know that Marion lied about Ryan because she never got into his stupid car. They'll believe Avery, not Marion—especially when Avery tells them that Marion is crazy about her dad and jealous of Nora. She'll say she was frightened for her life. She doesn't care what happens to Marion. Marion betrayed her.

She could leave right now, while Marion is out. Maybe she should.

She slips out of the bedroom into the main part of the basement. It's very dark, and she feels her way up the stairs. She knows Marion hasn't come home; she would have heard her. At the top of the landing, she tries to turn the knob of the door to the kitchen, but it won't turn. It's locked. She wasn't expecting that. She's furious, disbelieving. Marion has locked her in! How dare she! While she was hiding quietly in the basement, following the rules, and had no idea. She tries the knob again, rattling it. She kicks the door repeatedly in her fury. Why did Marion lock the door? She didn't have to do that. Maybe she doesn't trust her anymore since she threatened to tell the truth.

She turns around and stomps back down the stairs again.

As the night wears on, she starts to wonder what's keeping Marion. What if she lost her nerve? What if she never comes back? What if she took her car and her purse and her passport and never went to the police station at all? What if she's on a plane somewhere, Avery thinks frantically, and has left her to die here of thirst and starvation, all alone? She can't get out. She starts screaming for help, pounding at the barred windows, crying, until she is exhausted—but no one comes.

At last she hears a car turning into the driveway. A car door opens, then slams shut. Avery waits in the bedroom, her panicked breathing slowly returning to normal. She goes into the small bathroom and washes her face so that Marion won't see that she's been crying.

Of course Marion came back, Avery tells herself. Marion doesn't mean to harm her. She's a grown-up. She's been taking care of her. She's a nurse, her job is to help people. She just made a stupid, selfish mistake, that's all. She won't do it again.

Forty-four

Marion lets herself into the house. She'd treated herself to a rich dessert at her favorite all-night restaurant and stayed there for a long time, reading a book. It was nice to get away from the oppressive atmosphere of the house for a while.

She locks the front door behind her and makes her way to the kitchen. She drops her purse on the counter. It's very late, almost two in the morning. She'd like to go to her own room and go to bed, but Avery will be expecting her to report what happened. She stares at the door to the basement with loathing. Finally, she quietly unlocks it, peers down the stairs, and lets her eyes adjust to the darkness.

She walks slowly down the stairs, gripping the handrail, hoping that Avery is already asleep.

"Marion?" The child's voice reaches out from the darkness.

Shit. "Yes, I'm here." She feels her way into the bedroom—the door is open, waiting—as Avery flicks on the remaining lamp on the bedside table nearest the door. She's sitting up against the headboard. The small pool of light illuminates Avery from below, making her look creepy, like an evil child in a horror movie. She looks spoiled, angry, and menacing.

"So, did you tell them?" Avery demands.

Marion slumps onto the foot of the bed. "Yes."

Avery makes her recount every detail about her time at the police station. And Marion makes up every detail. She does a good job. She's always been an accomplished liar. At last, Avery seems satisfied.

"Good," Avery says. She looks at her with her cold blue eyes. "Don't *ever* try something like that again."

"I won't, I swear," Marion says earnestly. She must keep her sweet, until the time comes. She stands up.

"And, Marion," Avery says, "don't lock the door behind you anymore."

Shit, Marion thinks, *she tried to get out. She knows.* She nods. "Okay, I won't. Sorry, it's just habit. Good night, then."

Marion returns upstairs, gets into her pajamas, and climbs into bed. Of course she has locked the door to the basement. It's so well oiled it's completely silent. Avery knows now that she has been locking the door. But it doesn't matter anymore. Avery can't get upstairs. She can't get out. Avery had trusted her. She'd come into her house expecting to find a friend, but she'd walked into a trap.

Avery has made a terrible mistake.

Because Marion can't allow Avery to live. That Avery doesn't seem to realize this yet is almost laughable. Not when she might tell the truth someday about where she's been. Now that she knows she's been locked in. Kidnapping. She could go to prison for years and years. She can't be having that.

Once Avery is gone, Marion tells herself, everything will turn out the way she wants.

Everyone already thinks Avery is dead. The police have no idea where she is. They believe Marion saw her getting into Ryan Blanchard's car—she can tell they believed her. She will never recant her statement. She will go to her grave swearing that she saw Avery get into Ryan's car. All she has to do is get rid of Avery. And then she will come forward publicly with what she saw. She will seem brave, when people understand why she didn't come forward earlier, when they hear her story about her abusive ex-husband.

The truth is, her ex-husband had never laid a finger on her. Nevertheless, she'd had him charged with assault, twice—both times inflicting significant injuries on herself—and the authorities believed her, both times. When he'd told her the marriage was over, she'd wanted to destroy him, and that's what she'd done, without regret.

William won't be able to even look at Nora anymore. Nora's perfect life will be in ruins. And maybe William will fall in love with her now. Maybe this will bring them together. She plays a little fantasy in her head, of how William, finished with Nora, finished with his wife, sees her with new eyes . . .

But then her mind returns to practicalities. She will have to get rid of Avery, and any trace of her. She'll wrap her in garbage bags and put her in the trunk of her car late at night. No one is watching her. She's not a suspect. She'll drive to some deserted place and dispose of the body. She'll wear gloves, and clothes that she can get rid of after, someplace else.

The house is another problem. It will take days to clean the basement. She'll have to wash the bedding, scrub all the surfaces, vacuum the carpet over and over, and get rid of the vacuum bag somewhere. And she'll have to scrub the upstairs, too, because Avery used to come into her kitchen for cookies last summer when Marion was trying to pump her for information about her father. It's a lot to do. How can she be sure she got everything? But then, no one is going to search her house anyway. If Avery's body is eventually found, why would they ever search Marion's house? She didn't even know Avery. She's just someone who saw the girl get into a car.

Marion is malevolent, but she is not a violent person—maybe that's why she's been putting this off. Avery is violent, given to rages, and she will fight back. And so Marion's already decided that the best option is to drug her first. Put a dose of something into her food. Marion has enough sleeping pills in the medicine cabinet to knock her out. The girl eats like a pig; by the time she wolfs it down, it will be too late.

She will strangle her while she sleeps. And then she'll strip her naked and use the hand attachment on the vacuum to go over her body carefully, to remove any hairs or fibers. She'll do it tomorrow. And tomorrow night, after dark, she'll get rid of the body. It's time. She's been waiting for the police presence to die down. And she doesn't think she can stand having that little brat in her basement one more day.

AVERY LIES AWAKE in the darkness, wondering what Marion is thinking upstairs in bed above her. She's certain that Marion is as wide awake as she is. They don't trust each other. Marion betrayed her, Avery thinks; she deserves what's coming to her.

Avery is busy making new plans. When the time comes, she won't sneak out back into the woods and reappear with a story about a strange man like they agreed. She has a new story now. She will say that Marion kidnapped her and held her against her will, that she escaped, and they will believe her. And there's nothing Marion can do, Avery thinks, because Avery holds all the cards.

Forty-five

The next morning, Marion opens the sleeping capsules one by one and empties their contents into the glass of milk sitting on the counter. She will have to get rid of the packaging later. She worries briefly that Avery might taste the pills, but then decides she can probably count on her drinking the milk down with her toast and peanut butter. She's been bringing Avery that same breakfast every morning since she got here, and she always finishes it all. Marion looks forward to the day when she doesn't have to bring the little brat meals anymore. She wants to be alone in her house again. She wants things to go back to normal.

She stirs the last capsule's contents into the glass of milk. She unlocks the door to the basement and carries the plate of toast and the glass of milk carefully down the stairs. She gets to the room and pushes the door open wider with her foot.

She looks at Avery for a moment. She looks so normal, but Marion knows she isn't. But then, Marion knows that *she* isn't exactly normal either. They're both participating in some kind of hideous danse macabre together.

It's time to do something about it. She hands Avery the glass.

AVERY WATCHES the morning newscast alone, eating her breakfast. Marion had left quickly, saying she had things to do.

The morning news mentions nothing about the mystery witness changing her story. There is nothing about letting Ryan Blanchard go. According to the newscast, he's still in custody, suspected of abducting her. *Why?*

Avery's mind races. They would have let Ryan Blanchard go if Marion admitted to the police that she made it all up, like she said she did late last night. But maybe she didn't. Maybe Marion never went to the police station last night at all.

It becomes painfully clear to Avery, first as a possibility, and then as a certainty. *Marion didn't tell them.* She lied to her—again! She hadn't wanted to change her story, and she didn't. She's lied to her again, because she wants Ryan Blanchard to be blamed for her disappearance. But Marion must realize that once Avery reappears, they will know she never—

Oh. Avery's heart almost stops.

She puts down the half-drunk glass of milk. She's filled with suspicion and sudden fear. With a pounding heart, she thinks about the kitchen door. Is it locked? She creeps up the stairs and quietly tries the door. The knob won't turn. Marion has locked the door again. She's locked in. No one knows she's here. There's no way out of this basement unless Marion lets her out. And Marion's not going to do that. Not ever.

. . .

THERE'S SOMETHING BOTHERING Gully as she reaches for another cup of coffee at the police station. Something niggling at her, as if she's dropped a thread somewhere and she can't find it. What is it?

She returns to her desk, drops into her chair . . . and then she has it. She pulls it up on the computer. It's staring her in the face, something that she'd glanced over before. Marion, the credible witness, who is afraid of her husband. That she would be afraid of her husband is perfectly believable. He's had two assault convictions against him and a standing restraining order. But now Gully stares at the information on the screen that she hadn't paid enough attention to before. Marion had spent her entire married life living and working in Boston. But she grew up in Stanhope; her parents are here. If Marion didn't want to be found, why did she return to her hometown, to where her parents live? If her ex-husband wanted to find her, she hadn't made it difficult. She hadn't changed her name. So why did she hide behind an anonymous phone call? Is it all bullshit? They've been holding this kid overnight on the strength of her witness statement. But what if it's bogus? She gets up and finds Bledsoe, tells him her concerns. He nods, deep lines in his brow.

"Go see her," he agrees. "Get to the bottom of this."

UPSTAIRS, MARION BUSIES herself around the house, waiting for the sleeping pills to take effect. Then she sits at the kitchen table, her eyes alternating between the door to the basement and the clock on the stove. How long will it take for Avery to be completely out? Marion doesn't want to go down too soon. She has retrieved a rope from the garage, and it is sitting on the kitchen table, as if staring at her. She will have to get rid of the rope too.

When she thinks it's time to check on her, Marion summons her nerve and unlocks the door.

She opens it, and as she steps onto the landing and raises her arm to flick on the light switch, she feels a violent push to her hips, which completely upends her.

Marion crashes down the stairs. And as she goes, it's as if it's all happening in a slow-motion blur, and yet she's thinking clearly. She's thinking that Avery has bested her. She's shocked, furious, helpless as she tumbles down the stairs, her head and limbs smashing as she goes. The door behind her is open, Marion realizes. *How did she not see this coming?* She strikes the back of her head hard against the sharp post at the foot of the staircase and comes to rest on her back on the floor, stunned and in excruciating pain. She looks up at the ceiling, dazed, panicking that Avery is getting away.

But Avery hasn't fled, not yet. She's looming over her. She's smiling down at Marion, a horrible grimace of a smile. And now Marion knows for sure that Avery is truly bad, that she has no moral limits at all. Now Marion thinks Avery is capable of anything. She's got the cold, unfeeling selfishness of a psychopath. In that, they are alike. And in her final moment, as she feels blood trickling down her neck, Marion knows that Avery has won.

AVERY ENJOYS HER moment of triumph, reveling in the terror in Marion's fading eyes. She watches in fascination as the pool of blood expands beneath Marion's head. She's never seen anyone die before. Avery leans over her until she's sure. Marion's eyes are open, but she's gone. Marion is dead.

Avery sees the rope that has fallen from Marion's hand. So she was right. Marion *was* going to kill her. She can still hardly believe it.

But this is perfect. Marion died falling down the stairs while Avery was trying to escape. She can run out of the house now, run screaming down the street. It's not like they're going to charge her with murder. It was self-defense. She's nine years old, and she'd been kidnapped. Everyone will be on her side.

She takes one last look around, leaves everything as it is, and runs back up the stairs to the open door. She finds herself in the familiar kitchen. She spies an empty blister pack of sleeping pills on the kitchen counter.

Yes, it's perfect. They'll believe that she was held prisoner, that she was drugged, that Marion meant to kill her—because it's all true. She stops at the front door to study herself in the mirror over the hall table. She looks fine. That won't do.

She rearranges her face into a mask of fear and horror, pulls open the front door—and is startled to see a woman coming up the front walk. The woman stops dead, as if she's just seen a ghost.

Forty-six

Gully is stunned. She recognizes Avery Wooler, sees her sinking into a faint, and springs forward to break her fall. Her heart is pounding. She glances up at the open door behind Avery. What's happened here? Is Marion in there? Is anyone else in there with her? She grabs her radio and calls for backup, for an ambulance. She calls Bledsoe. Avery's eyes flutter open and stare up at her. "Avery," Gully says, her arms supporting the girl's small body. "Is there anyone in the house?"

Avery manages, "I pushed her down the stairs." Her eyes flutter then close again.

A police cruiser screeches up in front of the house, an ambulance right behind, while Gully's mind races. Avery must have been held here in this house, on her own street, all this time, and they missed it. Gully feels disbelief and a terrible sense of failure. They failed this girl. But she's alive, and safe now—no thanks to them.

The uniformed officers run up the steps, and Gully directs them to secure the house, while more cruisers arrive. The ambulance attendants bend over Avery as Gully steps back. The officers return to the front porch and report to Gully that the house is secured; there's the body of a woman in the basement.

Bledsoe arrives and directs one of the officers to fetch Erin Wooler from down the street. He arranges for someone to bring William Wooler to the scene. Everything is happening so fast, but for Gully, it feels as if everything has slowed down. She feels as if she's been in an explosion—she's stunned, disoriented, everything is muffled and muted.

Erin arrives, with Michael, while the ambulance attendants are checking Avery over, and pushes her way forward. She falls on her daughter, sobbing.

"Avery, Avery," she cries, hugging her daughter tightly. She hugs her as if she will never let her go.

Michael watches from the sidelines, tears running down his pale face.

Gully feels her own eyes welling up, and she can sense the emotion in Bledsoe and the others standing nearby. This girl was missing for four days, probably given up for dead by many. God only knows what she's endured. But they have a happy ending. She has come back to them.

At last William arrives and crouches down beside his wife, crying and studying his daughter closely. It seems neither parent can quite believe that their daughter is alive.

Bledsoe finally steps up and gently asks Erin and William if he can speak with their daughter. They pull away, nodding. Avery seems reluctant to release her mother from her grasp.

"Avery," Bledsoe says, squatting down beside her. "Can you tell us what happened?"

Gully moves in closer to hear.

Avery nods. They help her sit up. She seems to struggle to speak at first, but when she gets the words out she sounds hysterical. "She locked me in the basement. She was going to kill me but I pushed her down the stairs!" The girl is hyperventilating now.

"It's all right, Avery. She can't hurt you now," Gully says. "She's dead."

Gully glances up at the parents. They both appear to be in shock. She says, "It was Marion Cooke."

WILLIAM MUST FIGHT a wave of nausea. *Marion Cooke did this. Marion Cooke had his daughter all along.* He can't believe it. How could she be such a monster?

He stares at his traumatized daughter. Marion is dead. It sounds like she died in the fall down the stairs. It takes a moment for that to sink in. His little girl has killed someone. He doesn't want to imagine it. He tells himself that her life was at risk, and that excuses anything.

ERIN WATCHES HER DAUGHTER, her happiness at finding her again marred not at all by the revelation that Marion is dead. Avery pushed her down the stairs, and it killed her. Erin recalls her visit to this house the evening before. Avery must have been in the basement the whole time she was here. She feels like she might be sick.

Avery did what she had to do. Her daughter is a survivor. She didn't give up. She's like her mother that way. But what she doesn't understand is, why did Marion Cooke take her daughter?

GULLY WATCHES THEM load Avery into the ambulance. There is now a crowd gathering on the street, press and bystanders, all agog. She and Bledsoe will speak to Avery officially after she has been thoroughly examined at the hospital, but now they have work to do. Gully glances at Bledsoe as he reaches for his phone and calls in the crime-scene team.

She turns and walks heavily into the house. She'd missed this. They had all missed this. It will go down as the biggest gaffe of her career. Why had they not looked more closely at Marion Cooke earlier? She'd seemed a credible witness, saying she'd seen Avery get into Ryan Blanchard's car. And the whole time Avery had been held captive in her basement. It might all have turned out quite differently if Gully had arrived just minutes earlier.

They'd been assuming a sexual motive, because the vast majority of these cases are sexual in nature—young girl is taken by a man, assaulted, and murdered. It had not occurred to her—to anyone—that Marion Cooke might have taken the girl.

Bledsoe is pulling on latex gloves and she does the same.

Gully considers what all this might do to Avery—the ordeal of being kidnapped, of killing another human being in order to survive. Maybe they will have to add PTSD to her other diagnoses.

The living room looks undisturbed, and they head for the kitchen. Bledsoe immediately spies the empty package of sleeping pills on the kitchen counter. "Look at this."

Gully says, "She was drugging her."

Bledsoe nods, glances around the kitchen. They both see the open door leading down to the basement. They see the body lying at the bottom of the stairs. Slowly they make their way down and stand over Marion Cooke in silence, not getting too close, not wanting to disturb anything.

"Jesus," Bledsoe says.

Gully takes it all in, sees the rope on the floor. "Looks like Marion drugged her, maybe meant to strangle her."

Just then they hear a sound from upstairs. The crime-scene team has arrived.

Forty-seven

Erin Wooler is at the hospital. It's the hospital where her husband works, where Marion Cooke worked. She waits for the doctor and nurse to finish examining her daughter.

She is so grateful to have her daughter back, alive and apparently unharmed—at least, not harmed in the way she most feared. But she will be damaged by this, terribly damaged, and Erin will have to be there for Avery and work diligently to help her through it. She wonders if William will be around to help their daughter too. Their marriage is finished, but he is still Avery's father. He must do his part, although she has always done the lion's share of raising the kids, especially their difficult daughter. She has her arm around Michael as they sit on the plastic chairs in the waiting room. Michael seems to have had an enormous weight lifted from his shoulders.

She lifts her eyes to look at her husband, who is sitting across from her in an identical row of plastic chairs; he's got his elbows on his knees, and is leaning down, staring numbly at the floor. The big-shot doctor, reduced to sitting in a waiting room while his colleagues do their jobs. She stares at him as she tries to make sense of it all, tries to figure out why Marion Cooke would take their daughter.

WILLIAM CAN FEEL his wife's eyes on him, but he doesn't look at her. He doesn't understand what's happened. Marion is dead. She can't tell them what she was thinking.

At last, the doctor comes out to the waiting room and beckons to them. William stands up briskly and he and Erin follow the doctor into another room farther down the hall. Michael remains behind in the waiting room.

The doctor sits down and directs them to sit in the chairs in front of him. William swallows nervously, afraid of what he's about to hear.

The doctor says, "She's perfectly well physically. She appears to be well hydrated and well fed. She has not been harmed or violated physically in any way. She has, however, obviously experienced severe trauma, and you must get her help with that. I can give you some names."

"Thank you," William says.

Erin nods beside him. "Yes, thank you. Can she come home?"

"Oh yes, I think that's the best place for her."

WORD HAS GOTTEN OUT, and now everyone knows that Avery Wooler has escaped from her abductor. There's a crowd waiting outside the hospital for them, and Avery has to stifle the impulse to appear triumphant. She feels like a hero, and she would like to be hailed as one. But Marion is dead, and she can't walk out of the hospital, head up, pleased with herself, after what she's been through. That's not what people will be expecting. They will be expecting a traumatized child, bewildered and still frightened, and that's what she will give them.

They have a police car take them to their house, and that's exciting. She is ushered into the back of the cruiser with her mother, while her father follows behind with Michael in another police car. As they leave the hospital they are chased by reporters, and Avery turns around and watches them out the back window for as long as she can, because being alone with her mother makes her uncomfortable. She doesn't want her mother to see through her. But her mother loves her and thinks the best of her even when she really shouldn't. Her father's not like that. It's her father she should be nervous about. But he's already afraid of her, and she'd like to keep it that way.

Her mother doesn't speak the whole way home but clasps her hand tightly and looks at her constantly, as if she can't believe she's real. Avery is quiet and tearful and lets her mother hold her hand, even though it's not something she would usually tolerate.

When they arrive at the house, they are shepherded inside quickly by the uniformed officers, who surround her as if she's something precious. There are reporters here, too, waiting for her return. Avery enters the house first, after her mother unlocks the door. It's been only four days since she walked out the back door of this house and appeared at Marion's back door. It feels like a long time ago. Her mother comes in behind her. Her father and brother arrive, and they all go into the kitchen. The two uniformed officers remain inside the house with them.

Her father is pretending to be happy, she thinks, but he eyes her uneasily. Avery knows he's remembering the last time they were in this kitchen, when he hit her so hard she ended up on the floor. He's wondering if she's going to tell. She might. She tries to convey that to him with her eyes, and he looks away.

"Why are you still here?" Avery asks the police officers.

"We're to remain with you until Detectives Bledsoe and Gully arrive," one of them explains.

She doesn't like that. She'd like a bit of privacy, some downtime, but there's nothing she can do about it. The detectives are coming here, and she must be ready.

MICHAEL HAD RIDDEN home from the hospital in the back of a cruiser with his dad, who was unusually quiet. Michael is relieved beyond measure that Avery has been found. Now his mother will go back to normal. He's been incredibly worried about her. But he is still a little uneasy. The woman who took Avery is dead. He's unsure about what's going to happen next.

Once they get inside the house, the atmosphere is charged, strange. They all wanted Avery back and now she's here. But it's like they're all walking on eggshells. It doesn't help that the two police officers are in the house with them. They find themselves in the kitchen.

"Do you want something to eat, Avery?" their mother asks, as if to break the tension.

Avery sits down in a chair at the kitchen table, as if she's suddenly too weak to stand. "Sure," she says.

It all seems quite awkward, Michael thinks. No one knows what to say, how to act, after something like this.

"I can make you some eggs on toast, would you like that?"

"Okay."

Michael catches their father looking at Avery with something like fear. He's never seen his dad look at her quite that way. He wonders what it's about.

As their mother starts frying the eggs, Avery asks, "Can I have some cookies?"

"Don't you think you should have your eggs first?" their mother says.

"I want the cookies now," Avery insists.

Her mother gets them from the cupboard and hands the package to her. Michael is staring at Avery, and she stares back at him as she noisily eats the cookies, straight from the bag. She doesn't offer him any.

"I'm glad you're back," Michael says truthfully.

Avery looks back at him as if she doesn't believe it.

It occurs to him that maybe she can't really recognize love.

Forty-eight

Alice Seton is dismayed. She's standing in her living room, peering out the window at the Wooler residence across the street. There's a crowd of media there, and other people too. She sees a handmade sign on poster board and makes it out: WELCOME HOME AVERY.

She must be the only one who's not completely happy that Avery is alive and well and back home.

When she heard the news that Avery had reappeared, she couldn't believe it. She wasn't home when Avery had been discovered outside Marion Cooke's house, so she didn't see any of it with her own eyes. But she heard all about it afterward, from various neighbors, when she arrived home with Jenna from her ballet class. She saw the commotion in the street and got the whole unbelievable story.

Marion Cooke, she thinks, staring out the window. She can't believe that either. Like probably everyone else, she'd assumed Avery had been taken and murdered by some man. She'd worried for the safety of her own daughter.

She hadn't known Marion Cooke, except by sight. And now she's dead. Why would she have taken Avery?

She's not proud of it, but her first thought when she heard Avery was alive was not relief or happiness. She'd thought that Avery was dead. She'd taken a certain unholy comfort in that. Because if Derek *had* ever done anything to Avery, no matter how mild or innocent, she wouldn't be around to tell. She never trusted Avery. There's something about her. Jenna says she tells lies.

Now, she watches nervously from across the street. She tries to be happy for Erin, but her mind frets. Will the police follow up on her story about an older boy? Or will they let it go? Erin is not likely to let it go. Maybe Avery will admit she made it up. Maybe it wasn't Derek at all. But maybe she'll tell them something else, something nasty and untrue. Peter comes up quietly behind her, puts his hands on her shoulders.

"Don't worry," he says, as if reading her mind. "There's no way Derek ever did anything to Avery. Let's just be happy that she's okay."

THE ATMOSPHERE is one of celebration in the Blanchard house. Ryan has been released and has come home. They almost can't believe this sudden reversal of their fortunes. But there's an undercurrent of distress.

Al had come back this morning. Nora hasn't spoken a word directly to her husband since he got home. He doesn't seem at all remorseful for striking her. She catches him looking at her occasionally with an expression of revulsion, or perhaps alarm—she isn't sure; she can't read him anymore. She can hardly bear to be around her husband. She's afraid of him.

She, Al, and Faith were home when it happened. They were in the kitchen. Faith had come back from her sleepover at Samantha's. They noticed the commotion—a police cruiser sped down their street, siren blaring, then an ambulance—they watched it all happen from a distance.

Not long after that, Ryan was released and brought home. Nora had almost collapsed with relief, giving silent, fervent thanks to God.

Now it's been hours since Nora found out that it was Marion who'd had Avery all along. Her husband hadn't done anything to that poor girl. Now that she knows the truth, it seems impossible that she ever suspected him. She must have been out of her mind with fear for her son, and with her own guilt. She couldn't have been thinking straight. Al wasn't capable of such a thing. He'd hit her, but she'd just accused him of murdering a child! It wasn't Al who was a wolf in sheep's clothing—it was Marion, a nurse at the hospital, someone she regularly worked with. And she'd had no idea. No one had.

So far, there's nothing in the news about why Marion might have done it; all they know are the barest facts—Avery was held captive in Marion Cooke's basement, Avery escaped, and Marion is dead.

But Nora knows why.

Marion was in love with William. Nora had always known it, had seen it in how Marion acted around him, how she looked at him when she didn't think she was being observed. And Marion must have known, somehow, that William was in love with Nora. So Marion took his child and blamed Nora's. Marion is the monster, not Al. But it's Nora who's to blame. If it weren't for her, her adultery, her sin, none of this would have ever happened.

And every time she glances at her husband, she wonders if he's thinking the same thing, that she's at the center of this somehow. But he doesn't come near her, doesn't quietly throw it in her face that she was so wrong about him. Instead, he avoids her.

It stuns her, all of it. What if Marion had succeeded? What if she'd killed Avery? Avery might never have been found. Ryan would never have been cleared of suspicion, and neither would William. Their lives would have been destroyed. Erin would never have recovered. Marion's plan was perfectly designed to sabotage any possibility of happiness for her and William together. How evil Marion was. How she must have hated them both.

Forty-nine

G ully switches on the video recorder, and they begin. She and Bledsoe are in their usual armchairs, while Avery sits on the sofa, flanked on either side by her two parents. In view of her tender age, they've decided to do this at her home rather than in the police station. Michael has been asked to retire upstairs, and he went willingly enough. Gully wonders if he'll be listening around the corner, out of sight. That's what she would do if she were him.

"Avery," Bledsoe begins, "I know this is difficult, but it's important that you tell us everything that happened, from the beginning, on Tuesday afternoon. Can you do that?"

She nods bravely and takes a deep breath. "Okay. Ms. Burke sent me home from choir." She stops.

"Did you come straight home?" Bledsoe prods. She nods. "Can you speak for the tape, please, Avery?"

"Yes. I was supposed to wait for Michael, but I didn't want to.

Mom and Dad haven't given me my own key yet, but there's a key under the front mat. Michael told me." She continues. "I went into the kitchen." She pauses again.

It's almost like she's dragging things out slowly for effect, Gully thinks. She tries to dismiss the uncharitable thought, but now that Avery is in front of her, rather than an idea of a girl she's trying to find, she realizes she's not warming to the real girl. There's something about her. From what she's briefly observed, Avery seems to have her mother, father, and older brother wrapped around her little finger. They seem to be completely in her thrall. It's an odd family. She didn't think so until Avery returned, just that they had problems, like everybody else.

Bledsoe prompts her, "You went into the kitchen, and what happened then?"

"My dad came home." She glances at her father.

Gully notes that William seems to go still and can't look at his daughter. They all know he slapped her. She senses that Avery is being deliberately dramatic.

"He was upset to find me home," she says. "He asked me what I was doing there." She stops again.

"And then?" Bledsoe prompts.

She asks, "Do I have to tell the truth, even if I don't want to?"

"Yes, of course, you must tell the truth," Bledsoe says.

Avery says, "He hit me so hard he knocked me to the floor."

Gully hears Erin gasp, and she watches William stare at the floor, denying nothing.

"And then he begged me not to tell my mom," Avery says. There's an awful silence at this. "And then he left."

"And then what?" Bledsoe asks.

"I was crying. I went out the back door and through the gate to the woods behind our house, and along the fence line to Marion Cooke's house. I knew her. We were friends."

"You were friends?" Bledsoe interjects in surprise.

She nods. "Yes. She saw me in the woods one day last summer and invited me in for cookies." She hesitates. "After that, I would go over there sometimes. She asked a lot of questions about my dad."

Bledsoe says, "Go on."

"So that day I went over to her house and knocked on her back door. She was in the kitchen, and she saw me and let me in. I told her what happened. She gave me a snack. I woke up in the basement in the bedroom. I felt really out of it." She pauses for a moment, looks at them watching her.

"And then?"

"I tried to get out of the basement, but the windows were barred, and the only way out was through the door at the top of the stairs into the kitchen, but it was locked. I banged and banged on the door, but she wouldn't come." She stops.

"That must have been very frightening," Bledsoe says.

"It was," Avery agrees gravely. "I was terrified. I couldn't understand why she was keeping me prisoner. Until she told me that she was in love with my dad, and that he'd been having an affair with Nora Blanchard and she was going to make them pay."

She stops—almost as if to gauge everyone's reaction, Gully thinks.

Avery continues. "She saw them making out at the hospital." The words are coming faster now. "Marion hated her. She said she acted so superior, and she was just a volunteer. She said she got everything she wanted because she was so beautiful, including my dad."

So Marion was carrying a torch for the handsome doctor, Gully

Focus.

thinks, glancing at Erin, who has been rigid throughout, but has now gone a pale, sickly color. It's all starting to make a hellish kind of sense. She can't believe what goes on in this town.

Avery continues. "There was a TV in the room, and she would sit with me on the bed and let me watch the news sometimes, so I knew what was going on. She told the police that she saw me getting into Ryan Blanchard's car so that he would be arrested. I begged her to let me go. I promised I wouldn't tell." Now tears begin to form in Avery's eyes. "I realized that she was going to kill me so that he would be blamed." Avery takes a deep breath. "She was bigger and stronger than me. I figured the only way I could escape was to surprise her at the top of the stairs when she opened the door. So I waited there today for her to open the door. And when she did, I pushed her as hard as I could down the stairs, and then I ran out of the house." She adds, into the silence, "It all happened so fast."

Now Avery seems like a tragic heroine, pale and trembling, overwhelmed by what she has suffered and what she has done.

Gully and Bledsoe observe the girl. Her parents are also watching her closely, her mother with a terrible pity, her father with— Gully's not sure, but it might be dismay.

Avery's face darkens. "I never meant to kill her. I just wanted to get away."

Fifty

rin stares speechlessly at her daughter; she can't yet bring herself to look at her husband. This all began with him, with his lover, Nora, and Marion, the scorned woman. None of it had anything to do with her, Erin thinks numbly, or her innocent daughter. Then she turns to regard William with hostility, as he begins to understand what he has brought upon them all. He won't meet her eyes.

Erin blames her husband for all of it—his good looks, charm, and philandering ways are to blame for everything. Marion Cooke fell in love with her husband, while he was in love with another, and that nasty little love triangle led to this. She can never forgive him. She fears Avery will be scarred by this trauma forever.

WILLIAM FEELS the hatred coming off his wife in waves. He knows that he deserves it, some of it at least. But he's not to blame for what Marion did. No reasonable person would think so.

At least Avery's back safe and the nightmare is over. No one thinks he's a murderer anymore. But the truth sickens him. He'd never done anything to encourage Marion. He'd had no idea. Who could imagine Marion—a competent, professional nurse—was capable of something like this? She was going to kill his daughter! She essentially accused an innocent boy of murder, out of malice. This is a woman who tried to destroy lives, out of jealousy. It's truly frightening. It was a diabolical plan, perfectly calibrated to make each of them suffer and to keep him and Nora apart in mutual suspicion. She didn't care that his daughter would have to die to make it all work.

It troubles him to learn that she and Avery were friends. That Avery went over there that day, of her own volition. He tries to ignore his doubts, shake them away.

But Marion failed. Avery is fine, she's safe. They know the truth. Nora's son had nothing to do with Avery's disappearance. And now they know that William didn't either. He feels like he can start to breathe again.

Bledsoe says, as they pack up to leave, "There will be an autopsy on Marion Cooke. All pretty straightforward."

AVERY HAS GONE UP to her room to rest, exhausted after everything that's happened, especially the interview with the detectives. It went fine. The main thing is, Marion's dead; she can't contradict her.

She listens intently and hears the detectives leave the house. Her father hasn't left with them. Her parents are still in the living room, talking in low voices. Michael is in his room, the door closed. She creeps quietly out onto the landing, where they can't see her, and tries to overhear what they're saying.

At first she can't make it out, but then, as always, they forget to keep their voices down.

Her father says, "Aren't you worried about her?"

"Of course I'm worried about her!" her mother replies.

"I—I don't mean that," her father says.

"What do you mean, then?"

She hears her dad walking toward the foot of the stairs and ducks out of sight. He's probably checking to see if she's there. She hears him go back into the living room, and creeps back out.

"I mean"—her father lowers his voice, but Avery can still hear it—"do you believe her, that it happened the way she said it did?"

"Why wouldn't I?" her mother asks, aghast.

"Oh, you always believe everything she says," her father says, sounding irritable. "You always have."

"I believe you knocked her to the floor!"

"Yes, I did," he admits heatedly. "I don't know what came over me, Erin. It was like she was goading me, on purpose—but I know that's no excuse. I was instantly sorry. I've never felt so much shame and remorse in my life. I hated myself for it; I still do. I begged her to forgive me. I told her I loved her, that I didn't mean to hurt her. That I should behave better. For Christ's sake!" His voice sounds frustrated. "She left that bit out of her account." Now he sounds bitter. "But she didn't forget about how I asked her not to tell you." There's a silence, and then he says, sounding uneasy, "Don't you think she's—manipulative?"

"Children are always manipulative," her mother says dismissively. "They try to get their own way."

"Not like her though," he says. "Michael's not like that."

Avery feels a familiar spurt of anger at her father.

Her mother speaks. "I know Avery is difficult, I'm not denying that. God knows. She's willful, and oppositional, and not very good with people, but I don't like what you seem to be implying." She pauses. "You seem to be suggesting that—that things didn't happen the way she says."

"What if they didn't?"

Avery has to strain to hear him now.

"How can you say that?" her mother replies angrily. "After everything she's been through! Talk about blaming the victim! She's only nine years old!" There's a moment where neither of them speaks. Then her mother says, "I think you should leave."

"I'm going."

Avery can hear him moving downstairs; she'll have to retreat, so that he doesn't see her from the door.

"Erin," her father says, "I love Avery, she's my daughter—but I'm afraid of her. I'm not sure what she's capable of. Just . . . keep your eyes open."

"Get out."

Avery sneaks back to her bedroom.

Fifty-one

Erin remains on the sofa, unmoving, after her husband leaves. She's thinking about how they used to be, as a family, and what they'll be like now.

It's repugnant to her, what William was suggesting. She thinks he's trying to whitewash what he did—to shift the blame for his shameful behavior onto his daughter somehow. He struck her and he feels embarrassed and ashamed and sorry for himself now that she and the detectives know the real extent of it. He doesn't like it that Avery is still angry at him for it—angry enough to tell the truth. Perhaps he's worried that he might be charged. Maybe he should be.

Manipulative—because she left out that he begged for her forgiveness? Why shouldn't she leave that out? Why do men always think they should be forgiven? That they only have to ask? Maybe what *he* thinks is relevant is not what her daughter and she and millions of other girls and women think is relevant. So he begged

for forgiveness—*so what?* That makes it all right? And now he's trying to discredit their daughter—*don't believe everything she says*—
because that's how he sees the world, through his male bias. As if
Avery had a hand in it somehow. Well, it's not how she sees it.
Avery is a victim, anyone can see that. And Erin has been a victim,
too—of her husband's infidelity, of all his filthy lies.

How did she not see this in him before? She sees it clearly
enough now. Erin is still angry at the world—at her husband, his
lover, and the crazy, dead woman who was obsessed with him.
They have caused all of this. And now she's left with an even more
damaged daughter, with nothing but a list of doctors' names to
help her. William clearly isn't going to be much help.

She gets up slowly. She finally has a chance to be alone with
Avery, to talk to her privately, with no one else listening. She doesn't
know if she can get her daughter to open up to her; she knows
what she's like. It's going to take time. She wonders what's ahead:
Will there be nightmares? Withdrawal? Will she act out—be angry,
volatile? How will she manage the return to school? Oh God—she
must, at some point, go back to school, and everyone will know
what's happened to her, what she's done. Maybe they will have to
move away, to protect Avery from the publicity. Must she uproot
poor Michael, who's happy here, with his friends, and his teams,
and who may still want to maintain some kind of relationship with
his father?

For a moment, it all overwhelms her, and she sits down suddenly
on the bottom stair, overcome with exhaustion. But then she remembers that her daughter is alive and has come back to her, which
is what she prayed so desperately for, so she can't feel sorry for herself now. It's just—when she imagined getting Avery back, she never

thought beyond that joyful moment, to what would happen after. To what's ahead.

She rises and makes her way upstairs and to Avery's room. She taps lightly at the door and opens it.

"Hey," Erin says. Avery looks at her. She seems wary. "It's just us now," Erin says soothingly, "you, me, and Michael. Everyone else has gone." She comes over and sits on the bed.

Avery nods and says, "Good."

Erin can't help it—she reaches for Avery and pulls her body close, kissing the top of her head, trying to soothe her as she knows she must need to be soothed, and knowing that this is nowhere near enough, but it's all she has. And Avery lets herself be held, which is unlike her, so she must recognize the need for it, too, Erin thinks. They have both been through so much. She holds her and whispers into her hair, "It's going to be all right, Avery. Everything's going to be all right." She holds her and waits for her little girl to cry, to let it all out. But she doesn't. She's quiet, unemotional. It's Erin who's crying.

Finally, Erin pulls back and looks at her dry-eyed daughter. She must still be in shock, Erin thinks. It's going to take time. The doctors will help—if she'll let them. Avery has never cooperated with any of the specialists they've taken her to. But surely this is different? Something terrible has happened to her. Erin says, "Avery, I'm here for you, you know that, right? Any time of the day or night, I'll listen. Or if you just want a hug . . . If there's anything you want to tell me . . . it might help to share it."

"Okay," Avery says, but stops there.

"Okay," Erin agrees. Avery's obviously not ready to open up yet. It's going to take time. But Erin has time, she has all the time in the world for her daughter. Still, there's one thing she wants to ask. "I was there, at Marion's house last night, while you were in the basement . . . Did you know I was there? And you couldn't call out?"

Avery shakes her head. "She kept me drugged. I must have been sleeping."

Erin nods. "Of course." She says, "I love you, Avery. Never forget that. When you were gone, I—" She bursts into tears, unable to articulate any of it.

Her daughter pats her awkwardly on the shoulder. "It's okay. I'm back now. Everything's going to be all right."

And it's so odd to hear that coming from Avery that Erin stops crying and stares at her. She nods. "Yes. It is. We're going to be fine. All of us." And for the first time, she believes it. But there's still something bothering her. "Avery, I need you to tell me the truth. Did anyone else ever bother you? An older boy?"

Avery turns away. "I don't want to talk anymore. I'm really tired."

Erin doesn't want to push her. She rises from the bed, far from reassured. "Okay, you get some rest."

She exits the bedroom. She walks down the hall and taps on Michael's door. He needs to know what Avery has told them; it will be in the news soon enough. As usual, he's sitting on his bed with his laptop. He takes off his headphones.

She sits down beside him on his bed. "Are you okay?" she asks.

He bursts into tears. She pulls him into a hug, whispers into his hair, much like she had with her daughter. "It's okay, Michael. Everything is going to be all right." Her son is the more sensitive one; she knows he needs to let it out. This has all been so awful for him.

Finally, he pulls away from her, wiping his eyes with his hands, and says, a worried look on his face, "What's going to happen to her?"

"Nothing is going to happen to her. Marion's death was an accident. Avery was trying to escape—it was self-defense. She's nine years old. No one is going to blame her or hold her accountable. She'll be here, with us. We'll both have to help her, Michael. She'll need a lot of support."

He looks away and, after a pause, asks, "What about Dad?"

She chooses her words carefully. "Your father won't be living with us anymore. But you can still see him all you want, okay?"

He has no response to that. Instead, he says, "I heard . . . what Avery told the detectives. I was listening. It's all his fault."

Erin swallows. She wants to agree with him, but she says, "Your father has done some awful things, but he's not to blame for what Marion did. He had no idea Marion took Avery." She doesn't know if Michael will want to have a relationship with his father after everything that's happened, with what he knows about his father. She won't try to influence him one way or another.

Michael and Avery have always been closer to her. Which makes sense; she's spent more time with them. She's their mother. She's the more nurturing parent. She knows them better than William does.

Fifty-two

What?" Avery doesn't like what she just heard her mother say.

They're sitting at the breakfast table the next morning, Sunday. Avery had slept well, back in her own bed. Michael is a late riser and hasn't come down yet. Outside, the crowd of media and curious onlookers has dissipated somewhat from the day before. Avery has already snuck a few peeks out the curtained living-room window, despite her mother calling her away, telling her to ignore them, not to worry about them. *Ignore them and they'll go away*, she'd said, sounding anxious. But Avery doesn't want them to go away, and some of them already have. The ones welcoming her home with banners and signs have gone, but the media people are still there, desperate for an interview, a photograph, a story. And she wants to give it to them. She wants to be the center of attention, she wants to be famous, and she wants a lot of money for it.

She wants to be in control of her own life. And now her mother is suggesting they *hide*?

"I just think it might be better," her mom says, "if we move away from here. You don't want to go back to the same school, do you, after this?"

Avery thinks quickly. "What about your job?" she asks.

"I can get another job."

"What about Michael?"

Her mother nods. "I know. I've been thinking about that. But I think he might agree. He won't want to live in the middle of all this craziness either." She adds, "It might be the best thing for all of us."

"For you, you mean," Avery says.

Her mother is taken aback. "No, Avery, this isn't about me. It's about what's best for you. For all of us." She urges, "We could make a fresh start, where no one knows us."

Avery shakes her head. "I don't want to move."

"Oh."

"I mean, the news will just follow us everywhere anyway," Avery says.

"Not if we don't let it," her mom counters. "If we don't talk to them, it will all die down and we can go on with our lives. You don't want to live under a microscope."

There she goes again, Avery thinks, *telling me what I want. She doesn't know what I want.* "It doesn't bother me," she says, and reaches for another piece of toast. Her mother looks speculatively at her. Avery knows what she's thinking. She's thinking that she's just a child and doesn't know what she's doing. But Avery knows exactly what she's doing.

"I think I *should* talk to them," Avery says.

"What? No, Avery," her mother says nervously, "I don't think that's a good idea."

"Why not?"

"Because—because you're just a child. They'll exploit you. They'll take over your life and never leave you alone. They'll twist everything you say, take things out of context. The press is very powerful—you have no idea what they might do." She adds in distress, "Whatever they print will follow you forever. You don't want this to define you."

"I'm not afraid of them," Avery says. "I know what to say."

"Just—no," her mother insists. "Let's think about this. Let's not be rash. You may feel differently in a day or two."

Avery considers. She can wait a day or two. That might even be better.

NORA LEAVES THE HOUSE, taking the car, saying she's going to pick up some groceries. She doesn't normally get groceries on a Sunday morning, but nobody says anything. Al studiously ignores her.

She has to get out of the house, with its claustrophobic atmosphere. It makes her want to scream. The kids have picked up on the fact that there's something seriously wrong between her and their father—they've seen the bruise on her face—but they're afraid to ask. It's put something of a damper on the celebration of having Ryan home, and Avery being found alive. She will have to tell them about her and William, before they see it in the news. She knows the police are going to hold a press conference at noon today. It will all come out then, why Marion did what she did. Everyone will know. It makes her feel ill.

She's thinking about William. Where is he? Is he at home? She drives past the Wooler house and sees that there is still a crowd of media milling around outside, waiting for something to happen. She can't tell if he's there or not. His car isn't there, but it might still be with the police or in the garage.

She drives to the Excelsior Hotel, where she knows he's been staying. Is he there now? There are no reporters here anymore. She parks and sits inside her car. Does she dare go inside? She might as well wear a scarlet letter on her breast. This is a conservative town. People go to church. They have opinions, they judge. She should know, because she's one of them.

She must decide what she's going to do, who she's going to be. She can't remain married to Al, not after everything that's happened. Whenever she thinks of him sitting in his car behind the dumpster at the motel, she feels a tide of revulsion. And every time she thinks of how he came home afterward and pretended nothing was wrong, was his usual, detached self, she's afraid. She doesn't know who he is at all. She doesn't know what's going on beneath that familiar surface.

They hate each other; the poison between them will leach out to their kids. They will all be better off if they separate. If they stay together, they'll become more twisted versions of themselves. She will have to leave him, or perhaps he will offer to go. It would be better if she stayed in the house with the kids. What if he won't go? What if he blames her, the scarlet woman, and throws her out? If he does, she will take the children with her. That gives her pause. What if he wants custody of the children? Would he get it? She's not faultless. Does a woman have to be faultless to keep her children? She doesn't know. She feels fear in her heart.

William knows now that Ryan had nothing to do with his daughter. She knows that William is blameless—except for falling in love with her. The only thing keeping them apart is their own guilt and shame—and public opinion. Can Nora live with the public condemnation if she chooses William, after the truth about Marion gets out? What about her children?

She sits for a long time, then starts the car and drives home. She can't do it. She won't see William again. She has to put her children first now.

Fifty-three

It fills Erin with joy to have her daughter back. She finds herself looking at Avery frequently, just to reassure herself that she's real. But it's not as if things have returned to the way they were before. Everything has changed.

Even though she has so far been shielded from the press, Avery is a front-page story, not just locally, but nationally. Over the last twenty-four hours, since the police gave their press conference, reporters have converged outside the house, there have been requests coming in for exclusive interviews, and even an offer for a book, something to be ghostwritten with Avery, for an astonishing amount of money. It all makes Erin's head spin. She doesn't like any of it, and neither does William, with whom she has been in frequent contact by phone. It makes her queasy.

Erin's afraid of what all this publicity might do to her daughter, to all of them. It's bad enough already, but Avery *wants* to do the interviews and the book. She and William are dead set against it.

It will be hugely invasive. Hugely embarrassing for all of them. What if Avery regrets it? It sickens her more than a little. If they let her do it, it will make them look like parents capitalizing on their daughter's tragedy. But the more she says no, the more her daughter insists, becoming an all-too-familiar power struggle, until Erin calls an attorney at the firm where she works for advice.

GULLY FOLLOWS BLEDSOE into the medical examiner's office early on Monday afternoon. They are here for the autopsy results on Marion Cooke. They make their way to the autopsy room. Gully isn't bothered by autopsies, she has a strong stomach, but she imagines Bledsoe hasn't been to as many of these as she has. In Chicago, she came across dead bodies all the time. She's curious to see how Bledsoe reacts.

The room is similar to others she's been in—tile floor, stainless-steel counters and gurneys, all very clean and medicinal. It looks like an operating room, and that is exactly what it is, except that the patient is always dead already. They aren't here to observe the autopsy; the ME has called them in to discuss the results.

"What have you got for us?" Bledsoe asks after the preliminary greetings. He looks comfortable enough, Gully observes, not the queasy sort at all.

"Come, have a look," the ME says, gesturing for them to come closer.

Gully looks down at Marion Cooke, so pale and cold and waxy. The sheet is drawn up over her chest, only the shoulders and head showing. Gully remembers questioning this woman at the police station, oblivious to the fact that Avery was being held prisoner in her basement. How convincing she was in her insistence that Avery got into Ryan Blanchard's car. And now she's dead.

"This is what killed her," the ME explains, as she tilts the head and points to the wound. "The corner of the stair post penetrated the back of her head." She pauses. "It probably happened in the fall." Gully and Bledsoe look at her, waiting. "Although not necessarily."

"What are you saying?" Bledsoe asks.

"I'm saying I can't be completely sure. Falls are tricky. She might have struck her head hard enough at just that angle. And if she'd been alone, I would rule the manner of death as accidental as a matter of course. But she wasn't alone at the time of death, and the circumstances were unusual." She adds, "People do die from falls down stairs, but certainly not always. For every hundred falls down a flight of stairs resulting in injury, very few are fatal—only about one percent." Into the silence she adds, "I'm going to rule the manner of death as undetermined, because I simply can't be sure."

"I see," Bledsoe says. "Thank you."

Gully follows Bledsoe out. She and Bledsoe walk back to the car in silence. They don't speak until they are inside and the doors are closed. "What do you think?" Gully asks.

Bledsoe sighs and leans back in his seat. "I don't know."

"That girl troubles me," she says. "Something about her."

"I know what you mean," Bledsoe agrees. "She's a bit—*off* somehow." He sits silently, considering. Then he says, "Is it possible that Avery went to the bottom of the stairs and struck Marion's head against the post while she was lying there?"

Gully is silent.

"She's nine years old, for Christ's sake," Bledsoe says, as if dismissing the idea.

After a while, Gully shakes her head, staring out the windshield. "It's such a bizarre case. There was never any actual physical evidence against Ryan Blanchard—he would never have been convicted. What was Marion thinking?"

"She was nuts," Bledsoe says. "Don't you watch *Dateline*? *Forensic Files*? I do. People do strange—unbelievable—things. It might have been enough for her to ruin his life, to have that cloud hanging over him. And over Wooler too. Keeping him and Nora apart."

"She must have seen Ryan drive his car down the street just before Avery appeared at her back door. How could she have done it otherwise? What if Ryan had been at work? She saw him drive down the street that day, at that time, which we know he did. Then Avery appears at her back door, without her jacket, her hair in a braid—and she sees an opportunity."

"Yes," Bledsoe agrees.

Gully starts the car.

Fifty-four

Erin is anxious as she arrives at the police station late on Monday afternoon, having been called in by Detective Gully. William is already there when she's brought into an interview room. What can they possibly want now?

She doesn't have to wait long to find out. Bledsoe tells them rather delicately about the autopsy findings, that the ME is going to rule the manner of death as "undetermined" rather than accidental.

"What are you saying?" Erin protests. "It was self-defense!"

"Self-defense is a legal defense, not a manner of death," Bledsoe explains. "For a death that is not from natural causes, the ME can only make a ruling of accident, homicide, suicide, or undetermined."

Erin stares back at him, wondering what he's getting at, exactly. Bledsoe continues. "In this case, the ME can't be completely certain the fatal injury was sustained in the fall, or whether it happened immediately afterward."

Erin gets it now. "I don't believe this," she says staunchly, although she is shaken. "Are you implying that Avery might have deliberately hurt Marion *after* she pushed her down the stairs to get away?" She glances at William; he is quiet but looks startled—and concerned. He doesn't leap in to defend their daughter like he should. She's furious at him.

"Please," Bledsoe says. "Don't alarm yourself. There will be no charges against your daughter. No one thinks Avery did anything but push Marion down the stairs to escape."

There's a silence filled with tension; no one seems to want to speak. Finally, Gully asks, "How is she doing?"

The thing is, Erin thinks, Avery has been fine. Just the same as she was before the abduction. Moody, demanding, uncooperative, controlling. But no different than before. Except—if anything—she might be more cheerful. She isn't withdrawn or having nightmares or wetting the bed. Erin will try to make an appointment with a doctor—one from the list—soon, but she worries that Avery will refuse to go.

Erin answers, "I don't know. She seems okay, but maybe she's still in shock." The mutual liking and respect that had existed between Erin and Gully at the beginning of the investigation has evaporated. The successful conclusion, after all, had nothing to do with good police work, and they both know it. And now there's this. Erin can't help thinking that if they had done their jobs better, they might have found Avery *before* she'd been forced to push Marion down the stairs. But she's too well behaved to say this out loud. Erin wonders if Gully can read her thoughts—her regretful expression indicates that she might.

"And Michael?" Gully asks. "How's he doing?"

"It's been hard for him," Erin admits. "It's been hard for all of us," she says as she gets up to go.

Gully warns as they leave, "Just keep her away from the press. They can be savage."

William follows her to her car and asks if he can get a lift back to the hotel. They both get in the car. This latest revelation sits between them in the front seat like an unexploded bomb. Erin can sense William wanting to say something, but he doesn't. Erin begins to drive him back to the hotel, and they soon begin to argue. He doesn't want Avery talking to the press—*especially now*, he emphasizes—and tells her not to allow it.

It infuriates her. "And how am I supposed to do that?" she says. "Lock her in her room? The press are camped right outside."

His silence tells her that he has no idea how to stop her either. They have never been able to control Avery, that's the problem. She does what she wants, and they are helpless to stop her. If she wants to talk to the press, all she has to do is walk out the front door and open her mouth. It's not like Erin can keep her in restraints.

She drops William at the hotel and drives home, her mind reeling. The detectives seem to be hinting that Avery may have deliberately hurt Marion after she pushed her down the stairs. But if that's what really happened, Erin can understand it; she can even forgive it. That hideous woman had held her daughter prisoner for days, had planned to *kill* her. Avery would have been frightened for her life, traumatized, not responsible for her actions. She's only a child! Why don't they see that? It worries her, what the police think. What William thinks.

Somehow, she finds herself at Gwen Winter's door.

Gwen will understand, Erin tells herself. Gwen knows how hard it is. Although she can't have any idea what it's like to be in Erin's shoes right now.

Gwen greets her at the door, and they go into the kitchen, where Gwen begins to make a pot of coffee. Erin's not really sure why she's here except that she needs someone to talk to, someone who will understand, a little bit, about how hard it is. Gwen Winter knows what it's like to have a difficult child, and to have everyone judging you, blaming you.

"How are you doing?" Gwen asks, but she must be able to tell that Erin isn't doing well at all.

Her kindness provokes a sudden sob, and Erin, seated at the kitchen table, covers her face with her hands and tries to stop, but she can't. All the tears she can't release at home in front of the children pour out of her in front of this other woman, who is almost a stranger.

"That good, huh?" Gwen says, when Erin finally looks up. Gwen hands her a box of tissues.

"I'm so sorry," Erin says, embarrassed.

"No need to be sorry. You've been through a lot. You're going through a lot."

Erin nods numbly. "I had no idea it would be so difficult . . . I was so focused on getting Avery back, I wasn't prepared for what it would be like after."

"You can't prepare for something like this," Gwen says. She adds thoughtfully, "And when there's good and bad mixed together, it can be confusing."

Erin nods. "That's just it. I'm overjoyed to have Avery back. But—it's not easy. All this. Living in a fishbowl."

She has been judged for years—by teachers, other parents, strangers in restaurants—for Avery's behavior. It wasn't her fault, she tried to tell herself. Michael was fine. Erin did her best, but Avery has always been a challenge. Avery is Avery.

"You love your daughter," Gwen says. "But that doesn't mean it can't be really, really hard sometimes." Erin nods. "Are the press still pestering you?"

Erin nods again. It's on the tip of her tongue to tell her—what the police said, what William thinks. But the moment passes.

"They'll leave you alone eventually," Gwen says, trying to comfort her. "It can't last forever."

Fifty-five

Michael isn't going to school today. He's not ready to face it. The stares. The whispers. The questions. And it's about to get worse. Because today is the day that his sister is going to talk one-on-one to a well-known journalist and tell her story. On TV. They're going to tape it right here, in their living room, this afternoon. She and their mom argued about it, lawyers were consulted, but Avery has her mind made up. Avery does whatever she wants. She always has.

It makes him sick, all of it. He hates the press being outside their door, surrounding their house, trying to look in the windows to get photographs. The police have been here a couple of times to clear them back to the sidewalk, but they just creep up again. It's been worse since Avery came home. He feels trapped in the house, unable to go outside. Avery has always thrived on attention, but this is taking it to a whole new level. She knows he hates it. She's even been rubbing his nose in it.

"Oh, does it bother you?" she said the night before at supper, meaning the milling crowd outside. He looked back at her, speechless.

"Of course it bothers him, Avery," their mother snapped. "It bothers me too. It would bother anyone but you." His mother sounded as if she were at her breaking point, drained of energy. She'd already lost the argument with Avery about the television interview. She'd finally agreed to let her do just one, in a controlled environment.

Michael has a lot of confused feelings. He was genuinely glad to see Avery again, relieved that she was unharmed. He'd been so worried about her, and so concerned about his mother—he feared that his mom might break down and never recover, and with his dad gone, she was all he had left. But now Avery's back, and it's like she never left, only worse. Now she's acting like she's famous, and the thing is, she really *is* famous. He feels like he's living in some awful reality TV show, only none of it feels real.

He gets dressed and makes his way to Avery's bedroom. He taps on her door.

"What do you want?" she asks.

He opens her door. Alone with his little sister, he finds he's a bit tongue-tied, not sure how to say what he's come to say. He knows that his mother and father each see Avery differently. His mother thinks much better of Avery than she really should. But that's because Avery plays differently to each of them. She is one Avery to her mother and a different Avery to her father. Their dad quite frequently sees through her, and so does Michael. She doesn't pretend so much with them. But she's still his little sister. "I wanted to ask you something."

"What?" Now she's giving him her full attention.

He plucks up his courage to ask the question he needs to have answered. "Did Derek ever do anything to you, in the tree house?" He feels his face flushing.

She looks at him in surprise. "Derek? No. Why?"

"Jenna told the police you told her you had a boyfriend. The police thought it might be Derek."

She laughs dismissively. "I made that up."

He stares at her for a moment. "So it was a lie."

She shrugs as if to say *so what*, and he turns away in anger.

Fifty-six

A very is ready. She's wearing a light-blue dress and her hair is braided neatly down her back. She's been secretly practicing her facial expressions in the bathroom mirror upstairs, telling her story silently to her reflection, mouthing the words.

The technicians have been in the house for a while now, buzzing around like bees, disrupting things and making lots of noise. They've rearranged the furniture in the living room and in doing so seem to have taken over the entire house. Her mother is clearly distressed by all of it, while Michael hides in his bedroom. Avery knows he wishes this would all go away. She hopes he comes out of his room to watch her interview. Her father is supposed to arrive soon, before they begin. Avery wants him there too. She wants to be seen and heard. Large floor lamps with hot, bright lights are set up in the living room, where chairs have been placed for Avery and the interviewer—the prominent television journalist Casey Wong—to sit.

"Five minutes," a man says, as Avery watches Casey, who is sitting in a chair in the kitchen, having her makeup touched up. Avery has had makeup done, too, which makes her feel like a movie star. She wonders if someday she might be an actress. The idea thrills her. Will she be pretty enough? she wonders. She doesn't know yet. She would have to be thinner. Her mother was pretty—Avery has seen photographs—but she isn't anymore.

They move her into the living room, into her assigned chair. Now that she's sitting here, under the lights, with everyone looking at her, she begins to feel nervous. She can feel her heart racing. She tells herself that it's just excitement—finally, her moment in the spotlight! She and Casey have already had a little chat earlier, when they were setting up, so they could get to know each other, and so Casey could set her at ease. Casey's big brown eyes are kind and empathetic. Her mother chose Casey Wong because she is always so kind and sympathetic to her guests. She's not aggressive, like some of them, her mother had said. When she talked to Avery, all the bustle in the background faded away, and Avery felt like it was only the two of them in the room. That's what Casey said, "just two friends, having a private conversation."

Now Avery lifts her eyes to the side of the living room. Her father has arrived and stands near her mother, looking grim. She resents him for it. Why can't he be happy for her? He's just worried about himself, she thinks, about how bad all this makes him look. But everyone already knows why Marion did what she did. The police have released the facts, as they understand them. Now she's going to give her side of it, her personal story, of what it was like for her. Her mother looks as if she's going to be sick, as if *she's* the one about to be interviewed. Michael has come down from his bedroom now, but he won't catch her eye. None of them even gives her a thumbs-up, she thinks grudgingly, and she's about to go on *national television.* Sometimes she hates her family.

Casey comes up beside Avery and takes her seat, flashing a warm smile at her. "You're going to be great," she whispers. The crew fusses over the mics, the light meters. Everything must be perfect.

The man on the periphery of the living room counts down. "Three, two, one . . ."

Avery watches him do the countdown and feels a spike of adrenaline. She swallows. And then she has no time to think because Casey is introducing them, and Avery's throat has gone dry.

"Avery," Casey begins warmly, "you are so brave to agree to tell us your story—a story that has transfixed the nation. And I'm so honored that I'm the first journalist you're going to tell it to. Thank you." Avery nods, smiles uncertainly. "I know this will be difficult, so take your time, and just relax," Casey says gently. Avery nods again.

"Avery, we all know the basic outlines of what happened to you— you disappeared on Tuesday, October 12—just over a week ago. At first it was thought that you disappeared on your way home from school. Your parents declared you missing, and a massive manhunt was underway. Can you tell us what happened that day?"

Avery finds her voice. She starts slowly, but gains confidence as Casey nods encouragingly at her. She tells how her father found her in the kitchen.

"What happened when your father came home?" Casey asks gently.

"We had an argument, and he left," Avery says. She glances briefly at her father, and she sees the relief on his face. *He owes her one*, she thinks. No one outside their family—except the police—knows he hits her. She tells how she went to a neighbor's house, Marion Cooke's, how she had considered Marion a friend, and how she woke up in the basement, locked in, unable to escape.

Casey looks at her sympathetically, shaking her head, her eyes like warm pools. "I can't even imagine. What were you feeling when you found yourself a prisoner?"

"I was scared."

Casey nods again. "Of course you were! It must have been so frightening." Her voice is soothing, her expression one of concern. "Did she restrain you?"

Avery shakes her head. "No. But I was locked in, and I couldn't get out."

"Did she hurt you, physically?"

"Not really."

Casey asks gently, "Did you know why she'd done this?"

"She told me."

"What did she tell you?"

Avery feels quite comfortable now. "Marion was a nurse at the same hospital where my dad worked. He's a doctor. She told me she was in love with him, but he was having an affair with Nora Blanchard. She was a volunteer at the hospital, and she's Ryan's mom. Marion wanted to hurt them both. So she locked me in her basement and told the police that she'd seen me get into Ryan Blanchard's car."

Casey looks back at her, shaking her head. "How awful. And you're just an innocent victim in all this, an innocent child."

Avery nods. "She was going to *kill* me."

"What did you think about, for those four days, when you were trapped in that basement, alone, afraid for your life?"

"All I thought about was how to escape. But I couldn't. She kept the door to the upstairs locked. The windows were barred. There was no way out."

"And at what point did you realize—I'm sorry, Avery, this must be difficult—at what point did you realize that she meant to kill you?"

Avery pauses. It was when she realized that Marion had been locking the door, had gone behind her back about Ryan, and hadn't admitted to the police she'd lied like she said she would. But she can't say that. She thinks, unsure of what to say for a moment. "I knew all along," Avery says. "Her plan wouldn't work unless I was dead. She couldn't let me go. I knew what she'd done, and why. She was afraid I would talk." Avery's voice has dropped almost to a whisper, and she puts on the pained expression that she'd practiced in front of the mirror.

Casey shakes her head as if in horror. "All I can say is, you are a very brave and resilient young lady, and I'm glad you're sitting here with me today." Her eyes seem to fill for a moment, as if she might spill a tear or two. She composes herself and asks, "Did she bring you food and water?"

"There was a bathroom downstairs with running water. And she brought me food."

"You were trapped in that basement, with no idea what was

going on outside those four walls, the massive search going on for you. What did you imagine was happening?"

"Oh, I knew. We watched the news together every night, so I knew what was going on."

"You watched the news together? So you weren't in the basement the whole time?" Casey looks back at her in obvious surprise.

Avery has made a mistake. She must fix it. "There was a television in the basement," she explains. "Marion would come down and make me watch it. She wanted me to know what was going on—she wanted me to see how clever she was. I think she wanted someone to talk to about it, and she didn't have anyone else she could tell."

"I see," Casey says slowly. "It must have been odd, since you were friends before, and then watching television together, knowing that she meant to kill you. It must have been confusing."

"It *was* confusing. And terrifying."

"Can you tell us about the day you escaped? What happened?"

Avery clears her throat. "She was bigger and stronger than me. I realized that the only way to escape was to take her by surprise. So I hid behind the door at the top of the stairs and waited for her to open it. And when she did, I pushed her down the stairs as hard as I could and ran."

"That was good thinking," Casey says.

Avery allows herself a small smile.

"Marion Cooke was, unfortunately, killed in that fall," Casey says, "but thankfully you escaped, and you're able to talk to us today."

Avery watches Casey wrinkle her forehead, as if she's confused about something.

"I'm just wondering about something. If you knew from the beginning that she meant to kill you, was there a reason you waited four days before pushing her down the stairs?"

"Pardon?"

"I mean, if she was bringing you food every day—presumably her hands were full—I'm wondering why you weren't able to push her down the stairs sooner?"

"I—I didn't think of it."

Casey's eyes are still kind, but now more curious too. Her voice is gentle as she says, "Really?"

Casey is looking right at her, and Avery feels a surge of panic. She can't think. Her eyes dart away, searching for her parents on the edge of the living room. But then she recovers and turns back to Casey and says, "She gave me sleeping pills. I was out of it a lot of the time."

Casey nods. "I see. So you pushed her down the stairs and ran out of the house, ran for your life. You must have been so frightened, so angry."

"I *was* angry. She double-cross—" She stops herself. Avery can hear her own heart thudding in the abrupt silence.

Casey misses nothing. "She double-crossed you, is that what you were going to say, Avery?"

Avery looks back at her, speechless and afraid. Casey's eyes are still warm, still coaxing, and more curious than ever.

"How did she double-cross you, Avery? . . . What do you mean?"

Avery has messed up. Panicking, she again seeks out her mother, latches on to her mother's horrified face. They stare at each other for an awful moment. Her mother will know now, she'll know what Avery's really like. She wants her mother to step in, put a stop to this, but she appears to be frozen. Now Casey is speaking again in her gentle voice, and Avery turns back to her, frightened, paralyzed. She doesn't know what to do.

"There's more to this story, isn't there, Avery? Why don't you tell us what really happened, from the beginning."